Valley of Reckoning
Post-Apocalyptic Thriller

Apocalypse Trail
– Book 2-

N.A. Broadley

Angry Eagle Publishing

Dedication:

To Christine, my side-kick sista, who has always believed in me. I love you.

To my husband, Michael. Your endless patience as I worked on this novel.

Acknowledgments:

Wow. So many people have helped me with this book, and my list of thanks is long. It is amazing to me how many jumped in and helped me create this dream and turn it into a reality.

Dorene Stalter and D.J. Cooper, I love you ladies. For your help, your patience with my endless questions, and for your inspiration. You are both great mentors and authors, and I can only strive to one day be as wonderful a writer as both of you. Thank you for not allowing me to give up on this book. I couldn't have done this without you.

Truth Seekers, and you know who you are, thank you. For the endless questions, you've answered and the many times you've read through the slush words as I bounced ideas off of all of you. The inspiration you've all given me to continue with this story...you are my peeps, my brotha's and sista's of the soul. Every one of you has taken a very special place in my heart, and I will forever love all of you.

To Roger Boyenga, thank you, my dearest friend. Thank you for the endless hours of reading as you slogged through the first of many rough drafts. For the words: "Keep going," even as I doubted my own storytelling ability. I am so honored that you were the first to read this evolving story and hung in with me as it went through the many changes it had. Hugs, my friend.

Printed in the United States of America
First Printing, 2019
ISBN 978-1-7326212-3-7

This is a work of fiction. Names, characters, places, and incidents are the product of the author's imagination or used fictionally. Any resemblance to actual events, organizations or persons, living or dead, is entirely coincidental.

This is a work of fiction. No techniques are recommended without proper instruction or safety measures and training. The author nor publisher assumes no liability for any action presumed from this book.

Editorial, cover, and formatting provided through Angry Eagle Publishing.

Angry Eagle Publishing

https://angryeaglepublishing.com

Valley of Reckoning

The Valley

of

Reckoning

By N.A. Broadley

TABLE OF CONTENTS

Sarah

Sarah closed her eyes and grimaced. She took a deep breath and repugnant odors filled her senses. Bobby's breath stank of stale booze, cigarettes, and rot as he leaned into her face and grinned; she turned away in disgust. His arm tightened around her waist, pulling her closer. She arched away from his hot breath on her neck.

"Oh, you are gonna be so much fun to break, little one" he threatened.

The horse moved slowly, and the longer she spent in the saddle with him, the more her imagination wandered into terror. She ran her tongue across her lower lip and tasted dried blood. Bobby had only beat her once so far, but it hurt enough to terrorize her as she imagined her future with this group.

Images flitted through her mind, ghosts of sadness. Pictures flashed: Spike, dancing as bullets hit his body; Jessie, yelping as the knife sank into her side; Beth, lying in a pool of blood; and Brian, cradling Beth's body. She recalled the tortured expression on his face. Her ears still echoed with the screams of those around her.

Surely, Brian would come after her. This thought nagged at her as the horse and rider brought her further away from those she loved.

She'd been their captive for three days

now. And each hour brought her fear level higher. Why hadn't Brian come for her yet? Tears stung the back of her eyes and her heart skipped a beat with the thought of being abandoned. Would he have done that to her? Bobby's hand slid under her shirt and brought her back to the present. Angrily, she slapped it away and winced when he grabbed her stomach roughly.

"You better get used to the feel of me touching you. Or we're gonna be in for a rough ride, girlie," he hissed.

Bobby hadn't hurt her much yet, but she knew more pain would come. He looked a lot like his brother. The same cruel twist to his mouth, the same insane glee in his eyes when he looked at her. The thought of what he could do frightened her. Something about him sent a wave of terror through her heart. The way he looked at her, the greasy grin, and the hungry glances reminded her of a predator sizing up its prey. He had a trace of madness in his eyes.

This single terrifying thought sent chills down her spine.

The Compound

Beth clawed her way through the fog and darkness. Nightmares flashed in her mind, scattered like the petals of a windblown flower. Terror clutched her heart, making her gasp as she fought against the tangle of blankets. The last thing she'd remembered was Brian's face and his arms around her, the murderous glint in his eyes. Him promising he would right this wrong. Sarah's terrified, beautiful blue eyes screaming silently, while the man jerked her onto the horse. The stranger's smile enjoying her struggle against him.

She felt strong hands pressing down on her and screamed. She struggled weakly against them and opened her eyes, lifting herself from the nightmare. She found herself gazing into a stranger's face, as the soft voice reached across the nightmare, crooning and soothing. Gentle hands...attached to a woman standing over her.

"It's okay, you're safe, Beth."

"Where am I?" she croaked, her throat burned.

"You are at the compound. In the infirmary. You've been shot."

She struggled to focus, trying to get a look around the room. White walls, a bedside table with a pink plastic water pitcher on it, and a basin. Hospital? She glanced back at the woman by her bedside; confusion clouded her mind making her thoughts jumbled and disjointed.

"I'm Jill, one of your nurses."

"Hi, Jill. How long have I been here?" Beth murmured as she moved ever so slightly.

Pain ripped through her hip and back, and she sucked in a deep breath. She shivered slightly, the air chilled her bare arms, and she rubbed at the goosebumps.

"Mmmmm...about three days. You've had surgery on your hip so no sudden movement, okay?"

Three days? What about the others? She shifted her weight and the pain hit her again. What did she remember? Bits and pieces floated in her mind, and she grabbed onto them. Bobby and his gang had ambushed them. Her stomach lurched with anxiety.

"Where are the people I came with? Are they okay?"

Jill nodded and smiled. "Later. We'll talk later. Let me get you something for the pain then we can sit you up for a bit."

Beth swallowed hard against the anger as it rose up in her throat, raw and biting, and she grimaced. "No! We'll talk now!"

"Okay, easy. We'll talk now," Jill replied, then turning on her heel, she walked out of the room only to return a few seconds later with

Brian following behind her.

He sat on the chair beside the bed and pressed his face into hers, his breath warm against her skin. His gentle touch calmed her.

"I'm here. I'm here, Beth," he murmured. She choked on a sob and fought the burning of tears behind her eyes as she sighed.

"Brian."

She struggled to sit up and felt Brian's warm hands on her back as he helped. Jill adjusted the pillows behind her back, pain sang through her hip, and she sucked in a hissing breath to keep from screaming. Weakness flowed through her body as she looked at Brian.

"Sarah? Did you get her back?" she asked.

"I'm going to get her back. I promise you that." Her heart sank, and she brushed away a tear as Brian shook his head.

"Leave today. Go get our girl."

His lips pressed into a tight line, and she saw a glint of cold creep into his eyes. "I'll go. Soon."

"Spike? Is he okay?" She remembered seeing the bullets slam into his body; how he danced like a puppet as he fell.

Brian smirked.

"Yeah, that jerk is just fine. But Roger, his grandfather, lost a few of his men in the fight, though. Jessie got hurt too, but she's up and around just fine now."

Yawning, barely able to hold her eyes

open, Beth sank against the pillows as fatigue and despair seemed to swallow her.

It came back to her. They were headed to the compound to get help from Spike's grandfather. Bobby and his gang were chasing them. Then in a flash, all hell broke loose around them. One minute, Spike was smiling and riding toward a group of men led by his grandfather. The next minute, the attack.

"Okay, enough for today, girl," Jill said as she moved beside the bed. Beth felt the sting of a needle as sweet pain medicine flowed into her veins. Weakly, she struggled to keep her eyes open as the drug took hold and sleep drifted her into darkness once again.

Part 1 — Into the Valley

Chapter One

Brian turned in the saddle and glanced at Spike. The real summer heat hadn't even started yet and, the sun was already hot on his shoulders. He felt the muscles in his lower back relax, and sighed. Giving a nod, he nudged his horse and took the lead. Three long days at the compound had been spent worrying about Sarah, whether or not Beth would make it, and what his next move would be, had nearly driven him to the brink of insanity.

Beth argued that he should have left sooner to rescue Sarah, and it made him second guess his decision. Should he have left earlier, rather than wait? Gut instinct told him no. If he set off after Bobby too soon, he would have been walking into that vipers' nest unprepared. And that would have just ended up getting Sarah, Spike, and himself killed.

Roger, Spike's grandfather who was the founder of the compound, was right. Plan carefully, prepare, and then rescue Sarah. Let Bobby and his men think they'd won. It would make them careless. Lifting his hand, he wiped the beads of sweat from his brow and squinted at the sun. A sudden sneeze made his eyes water and his head hurt. Goldenrod, grass, and pine pollens, floated invisibly through the air, causing his seasonal allergies to kick in. He swore softly. What he wouldn't give for a dose of antihistamine right now.

Dust burned his mouth and throat. He guzzled warm water from the canteen, hoping to wash it away. They'd been riding hard, and his back whined at him with a dull aching pain. A brook off to the left bubbled noisily, and he grinned, watching Jessie splash and play in the clear water.

Whereas it took two days by road to Lee, Massachusetts; by trail, it would only take them eight to ten hours. Traveling all night left his eyes heavy with grit and fatigue.

"Only another hour or so and we'll be on the outskirts of town. I know a place where we can camp and do some recon," Spike said.

Brian nodded. He hated the thought of Sarah being with Bobby and his men for even another second. He knew they had to get in, get her out, and not get them all killed in the process; recon was the logical thing to do. He lifted his hand and rubbed it across his face and groaned when he thought of another hour sitting in the saddle.

∞

He and Spike camped on a craggy rock-strewn hill hidden by a tall cluster of pine trees. Shadows played in and out of the trees, keeping them hidden from view. Below, they had a good view of Main Street. From his vantage point, Brian could tell this was the gang's home base.

On one side of the street stood a large brick building, Lee Bank and Trust. Next to the bank looked to be a small convenience store and a couple more run-down businesses. On the other side of the street stood the police department, town office, and a library. Behind the library ran an alley that butted against a wide overgrown field. It was the perfect place to enter the town. From what he'd observed over the past few days, there were no guards patrolling the area near the field. Anyone could just stroll on in.

"Oh, aren't you a cocky little dude," he murmured as he lay on the ground and watched the town below. Lifting his hand, he swatted a fly from his face.

Curiously, the only guards Brian could see were posted outside of the library and police station. Were they that arrogant? Careless? Or perhaps just stupid? Shaking his head, he climbed up off the ground, dusted the pine needles from his pants, and walked back to camp. They would breach the town that evening. It's high time they got Sarah back.

Just before dark, Spike made his way through the tangled brush and into the field. He quickly crossed through the tall, damp grass, sticking to the shadows as he darted through the alleyway that led to the corner of Pearl and Main. He could smell a mixture of the rancid horse manure that littered the tar road, and fish that someone must've been cooking for dinner. The disgusting combination made his stomach lurch queasily.

The man standing guard in front of the police station had his back to him, and Spike quietly moved in. He hoped Brian was in position; otherwise, he just might find himself in deep trouble.

Spike smiled, lifting one hand to his mouth and coughing lightly to get the man's attention. A soft laugh bubbled from his lips. He watched the man spin around, bring up his rifle, and level it at him. He noticed a shake in the man's hands. Inexperience? Fear? Surprise? Shaking his head, he grinned.

"Who the fuck are you?" the man squeaked, caught off guard. His eyes were wide with fear. Spike looked at him and winked.

"Just your average bitch," Spike drawled.

The man scowled and took a step toward him. Spike felt his shoulders tense and whistled lightly through pursed lips.

"Well, bitch! You just made a big mistake."

Spike felt a menacing smile touch his lips. The man shook his head in confusion. What was this? Was he some idiot? From behind him, he felt the sharp prick as a knife settled and dug lightly into the area just above his kidney. With an expression of surprise on his face, he froze as he felt hot breath against his ear.

"No, bitch. The mistake is yours," Brian whispered into the cup of his ear. The man turned his head and the gaze that met his sent ice water running through his veins.

∞

Brian turned to Spike and smiled grimly. He brushed his dirty hands across the leg of his jeans. His hand hovered over the sheath that held his knife. He could feel the pull of the blade. It wanted, like a living being, to be held and used. A familiar feeling that tugged at his gut.

"You may want to take a walk, buddy."

Spike nodded. He didn't have the stomach for what he knew was about to happen. Pictures of Brian's past victims flitted through his mind, and he cast a pitiful glance down at the man tied to the tree and issued a soft warning.

"You might want to man- up and simply tell him what he wants to know," he warned.

The man laughed, showing a mouthful of rotted and broken teeth. Spike shook his head. "Don't say I didn't warn you, man."

He turned on his heels with a sense of pity roiling in his gut. Whistling to Jessie, he strode toward the overlook that sat high up on a hill above the town, where he wouldn't be able to hear the man's screams.

For two days, they'd watched the activity. They had studied the routines of Bobby's men; careless and haphazard at best, arrogant in their sloppiness, almost like they believed they were untouchable.

Settling himself on the ground, he pulled out the binoculars and leaned his arms on his knees. He peered down on Main Street. He saw guards lazily sprawled out in front of the police station, the library, and the town hall. No guards were posted on either end of town blocking the two main roads coming in. Perhaps they believed no one would dare make a run at them? Laughing, he shook his head. The joke's on them. He'd already been in their little town, and they'd been none the wiser. The fools were wide open and vulnerable.

∞

Brian looked down at the man with a mixture of pity and hatred. His hands shook, and he clenched his fists so that his nails bit into his palms. A fevered glaze settled in his eyes while bloodlust sang to him. Dirty work, bloody work, just the kind of work he'd sworn to leave behind.

The man's face bore the scars of acne, a light scruff of dark facial hair covered his pointed chin, and his smile sarcastic and filled with rotted teeth. Brian had stripped him of his clothes, and although the night was downright cold, the man's face was reddened with the flush of pain, and shiny with sweat.

His green eyes were wild with terror. Brian moved the knife one more time lightly across his stomach, slicing a thin line of red. A soft groan escaped his lips.

Brian grinned. He could keep this up for hours and would until he got the information he wanted. He didn't mind the knife at all. In fact, as his hand gripped the handle and his fingers tightened for the next cut, he let himself sink into the familiar feel of it. The tiny, shallow cuts were the worst. They inflicted the most pain. He chuckled while he looked deep into the man's eyes.

"I wish I could say this is gonna hurt me more than you, but then, I'd be lying. It is gonna hurt you a whole lot."

He would get what he wanted from this man. "So, tell me. Where are they keeping the women?"

Glaring, he raised his eyes and spat at him. "Go to hell! You're gonna kill me either way, so why should I tell you a thing?"

Brian nodded. It was true. He would kill him. And Hell would be where he'd end up for sure. With a flick of his wrist, he once again let the blade inflict another long, shallow pass along his stomach; this time lower, along the beltline, and he heard a tortured moan.

His mind flashed with memories, distant, yet still painful, as they gnawed at his gut. The same knife blade that, a long time ago, had left scars burning on his own back. The dank, musty cell with no windows; his home for over a month before rescue. The hiss of pain, something he couldn't hide behind clenched teeth.

Shoving these memories away, he concentrated on the task before him. With each pass of his knife, he went lower and lower, leaving Ernie no doubt where the final cut would end up. Yes, he'd learned from the best. And that best had nearly driven him to insanity.

"Ahhh, you are so right. But what you don't know is that I can either do it quickly or very, very, very slowly. That just depends on you, my friend. The question is, how much do you want to suffer? Because ya know... I am damn good at making people suffer."

A defiant grin met him. He looked down into the man's eyes.

"Okay then," he murmured. Skillfully he set to work with his knife. "I guess we'll be doing this the hard way."

Sweat rolled down Brian's back, and he sighed heavily. It hadn't taken long before he had the man spilling his guts, telling him everything he needed to know. With a steady hand, he wiped the bloody blade of his knife on the man's pant leg and took a step that brought them together, nose to nose. He stared deep into the man's eyes; his face so close he could smell the foulness of his breath. He whispered one last question.

"So, the new girl? Where did you say Bobby is keeping her?"

He just grinned and spat out a wad of blood. It mixed with the dirt and pine needles on the ground. Panting, he lifted his eyes to Brian's and looked at him with malicious glee.

"At Gregory's house, on School Street. But you're too late. Your girl is about as good as dead. Gregory likes to hear em' scream, ya know."

Brian shook his head and sighed, not showing the man how much what he'd just said, rattled him.

He calmly placed the tip of his knife gently between the man's eyes. Fear flashed in those eyes, just before his open palm worked like a hammer, driving the knife in deep. Giving it a hard twist, he watched the life drain from the man's face. Removing the knife, the body sagged against the ropes holding him.

A bird chirped loudly, and Brian smiled as he glanced up into the trees looking for it. He paid little heed to the flies that lightly landed on the bloodied face.

Chapter Two

Sarah walked along Main Street with her head down and shoulders slumped. Hatred and rage tore at her heart. She scuffed her boots against the pebbles and dirt that covered the dark tar beneath. Gregory followed behind her, strutting as proud as a peacock, puffed up and in his glory. He had a reputation for being cruel and sadistic; the man had been assigned, by Bobby, to train her. She belonged to him now, along with Rose, a young woman of what Sarah guessed to be in her mid-twenties.

It boggled her mind thinking about how society had become this; how the event had turned normal citizens into these monsters. Was it the event that had unleashed all the twisted, cruel, and perverse in mankind? Why were people turning on each other, like rabid and vicious animals? Or had mankind always been this savage, this cold-hearted, and the event had only brought it out in them?

A shove to her back caused her to stumble, she snapped her head up and anger blazed in her eyes. Gregory pushed her roughly and she clenched her small hands into fists. Hatred burned in her eyes. She whipped her head around and stared at him. The sun cast long shadows, bouncing off his greasy dark hair.

"Stop dawdling."

Rose, beside her, shook her head and whispered, "Don't fight him, he'll only make it worse."

They were both bound together with a long, bright red dog leash, which had silver, tinkling bells attached to it. The sound of the bells when they moved, as abhorrent as the man who held the leash.

Sarah cut a glance toward Rose and pressed her lips together in anger. Fight him? She'd kill him the first chance she got.

In the past several days she'd learned what life would be like with these monsters. Scraps of food, thrown to her like a dog. Given tepid, dirty water from a rusted can. Tolerating leers and grins, while Bobby paraded her in front of his men like some prize heifer at a fair. She'd rather die than suffer day in and day out being their prisoner, than to be sent to the library where Bobby held the women and children he'd taken prisoner. A place where the air reeked with the stench of human misery; dark and filthy.

Every night, while bound and huddled to Rose with ropes so they wouldn't escape, Rose talked and told her about the library and how those girls and women suffered much worse. Sarah found it hard to believe it could be worse than this.

The door opened and Gregory shoved her roughly inside. She stumbled, waving her arms for balance. The odor of stale cigarettes wafted in the air. She longingly glanced over her shoulder at the sunshine out the door just before Gregory slammed the door behind her.

The first punch took her by surprise when it landed on the side of her face. Pain rocked her jaw and she crashed to the floor. She spat out a wad of blood and crawled away in shock, trying to catch her breath. She turned her head and looked through a veil of hair to see Rose crouched in the corner, tears spilling from her eyes. Her teeth clamped around her closed fist to keep from screaming.

Sarah lifted her eyes to her and shook her head. Blood ran freely from her nose, spattering the floor. She silently screamed in agony as hatred saturated her heart. Fat, bright red droplets stained the black and white mosaic tiles—her blood. A kick to her back pushed her deep toward the edge of passing out, and she collapsed when sharp pain fired through her body, leaving her gasping for just a teaspoon of breath.

She panicked, struggling to breathe. She looked up to see Gregory standing over her. His beefy hands planted on his hips, breathing hard and laughing. She stared at his fingernails, her mind grasping to focus on anything other than the pain that zig-zagged like lightning through her body.

He looked down at her with a grin. "I'm

just getting started, my little blue-eyed girl."

By the time he finished with her, she would be subservient and docile. Just the way the customers liked the girls to be.

In two steps, he towered over her. She back crawled, steeling herself for more pain. She heard him laugh and a shiver ran down her spine when she heard the hiss of his leather belt sliding from the loops of his jeans. The smell of sweaty leather wafted to her nose, and a chill crawled down her spine and tightened the muscles in her stomach. Tears stung at the back of her eyes, and her mind screamed with pain, when the first biting lash landed against the bare skin of her back, then another and another.

"Let the training begin."

Curling herself into a ball, she choked, fighting for breath. She focused on the hatred that burned in her chest, while her mind spun with agony and fear. Biting down on her bottom lip, she winced when another blow landed on her back.

She dug her fingernails into the linoleum and struggled to crawl away, blinded by the pain that flayed her back with each blistering sting of the belt. A gasp tore at her chest. Silent screams and bitter bile erupted from her throat to spatter the floor in front of her.

She turned her head and sank to the floor, her cheek lying in the hot vomit. Through the haze of pain, her gaze met Rose's. The look of helplessness and despair tortured the other woman's face.

Blow after blow racked her body until she sank flat to her stomach, gasping for air. She felt him move beside her and kneel. She listened numbly, her breath hitching in and out in little gasps, tears flowing down her cheeks. He whispered in her ear.

"This is just a taste of what you will get if you step out of line. Now, get up!" Gregory growled.

Struggling to her feet, she turned and pulled herself up, using the stove for stability. There sat a cast iron frying pan. She grabbed it and with a grunt of fury, swung it hard against his face. Blood splattered as his nose crushed. Her arm sang with pain when the blow connected. She heard him grunt in surprise.

Tripping, she fell backward over her own feet, weakness tangling her legs together. Gregory lunged for her. He hit her again with his fist, and the blow felt like it shattered her cheekbone.

She fell to the floor, gasping and writhing in pain, while her body danced with the fire of agony consuming her. She couldn't seem to find enough air to fill her lungs as one blow after another slammed into her. She heard screams, from Rose, as Gregory pummeled her into a bloody mess. Darkness danced at the edge of her vision.

She felt his hand wrap in her hair, jerking her to her feet. She stood swaying, her chest heaving, and her legs barely strong enough to hold her up. Her eyes felt swollen into little slits; she could barely see. She let her head fall forward, limply, as she watched the dance of shadows and sunlight tease the edge of her vision. He spun her roughly to face him.

"You are now the property of the Alliance. All the men of the Alliance will be your masters. You are no more than an object to us, one that we will use at will. You have no rights here. None, whatsoever! We are in a new world, baby, and in it, you are nothing! Do you understand?"

Raising her eyes, she nodded. She let herself fall into him. He grabbed her roughly, but she wrapped her arms around him. She grabbed the gun in the waistband of his jeans, all while staring into his surprised eyes. She pressed the barrel against his back, flicked the safety off, and pulled the trigger.

The bullet tore through him and she felt it slam into her shoulder, sending burning pain, ripping into her. He fell backward, and she felt his arms tighten, dragging her with him. She landed hard on top of him.

She smiled with blood-stained teeth, and kissed him deeply, then screamed into his face "I would rather die!"

Finally, she'd found her voice.

Rolling off him and onto her back, she stared up in shock at the ceiling. Her lungs burned as she fought for air. The ceiling was dotted with specks of dead flies, dust, cobwebs, and yellowed from cigarette smoke. She felt Rose kneel beside her and heard her sobbing. With a tug, the woman helped her to her feet.

Sarah staggered and leaned heavily against her. She gazed down at the blood staining the floor, then to her hands, which were bright red with both his blood and her own. Shifting her gaze, she stared down at Gregory. Hatred burned in her heart, dark and consuming. He was no more than an animal carcass to her, staring at her through dead, wide eyes. She brought her booted foot up high and smashed it down on his face, smiling in victory as she felt his bones crush beneath it and watched as an arc of blood spurted upward.

She screamed, bending over with her hands on her knees, pouring all her pain and rage into empty air. Taking a deep breath, she straightened up and turned to Rose. They needed to move quickly. Once someone discovered that Gregory was dead, their lives wouldn't be worth a plug nickel.

Choking back a sob, she reached for her shirt on the living room chair and felt Rose's rough, calloused hands against her skin as she helped slide it on. She winced when the material brushed lightly across the welts on her back. Her left arm hung uselessly by her side; blood dripped from her fingertips to the floor.

Glancing around the kitchen through swollen eyes, she spied a blue and white terry cloth towel hanging by the sink and grabbed it. Bunching it into a wad with a shaking hand, she pressed it hard against her shoulder to stem the flow of blood. Her head spun with dizziness, and she grabbed Rose for support.

"Shit, we gotta get you some help!" Rose hissed between sniffles as she steadied Sarah.

Sarah shook her head, violently. Getting help would get them killed. She pointed to the back door and made a motion for Rose to follow her. Her legs shook as she opened it and stuck her head out. Seeing no one, she took Rose's hand and led her out into the weak afternoon light.

The sky above threatened rain with storm clouds billowing dark and ominous. Holding Rose's hand for support, she limped her way toward the woods at the other end of a long field. Wet grass pulled at her legs and she wondered if she would ever be able to run far enough to rid herself of the terror that sang through her veins.

∞

Kevin heard the thud and then the sharp muffled sound of a gunshot. Turning, he looked at the door and hesitated. No one entered Gregory's home without permission. His job? To wait until Gregory finished with the women then he would take them to the library; or the pit, as everyone called it.

They would stay there until he received instructions to get them again. He hated this place. He hated Bobby. But, with nowhere else to go, he stayed. He stayed and he watched, in silent misery, the brutal treatment of the women and children. He participated in the raids on other towns although everything in him wanted to turn his gun on those who were so willing to commit these violent acts against the innocent. He'd lost weight since he arrived. He hitched up his pants, that sank low on his hips, and tightened his belt another notch while he cast nervous glances toward the front door of Gregory's house. He didn't want to go in there. He'd rather do anything else than have to knock on that door.

He'd wandered into this town a month ago, on a cold and wet day. He'd been hungry, sick, and weak, and had lost everyone who meant anything to him to the virus. Alone, he left New Hampshire and went in search of people. He couldn't be alone. He wouldn't survive and he knew it. He'd been an accountant, for God's sake! His life had consisted of sitting behind a desk, shuffling papers and crunching numbers. Then the virus came. No more job, no more family, no more life as he'd known it.

When he stumbled into town, Bobby took him in. What he didn't know back then was the price he would have to pay for being part of Bobby's gang. If he'd known then what he knew now, he would've avoided the town and made a full circle around it. He would've gladly accepted death on the road rather than live this life. He was not a killer. He was not like these men. His old life was one of normalcy, and this was anything but normal.

Sucking in a deep breath, he knocked on the door and waited. After a few minutes, he tested the doorknob and opened it with a shaking hand.

"Shit!" he muttered when he gazed down at Gregory lying on the floor in a pool of blood. Drawing his weapon, he glanced around nervously while he walked from room to room. The kitchen floor looked like a horror scene out of a movie; blood smeared across the tiled floor, chairs knocked over, a frying pan lying on the floor with a hunk of what looked to be hair and flesh clinging to the side of it. Did one of the women bash Gregory's head with the frying pan? This thought almost made him laugh.

Looking up from the disgusting mess he noticed that the back door was cracked open and he walked toward it, his eyes darting nervously around the room. Nudging it with his foot, he stuck his head out and saw the two women running across the wide-open field. His heart thudded in his chest, and he swore softly.

"Damn!"

He gauged the distance and knew he could easily take them down with a single shot each. That would make him a hero in Bobby's eyes. He raised his gun and aimed, steadying his shaking hand and holding his breath while the seconds passed.

He couldn't bring himself to pull the trigger. To shoot two innocent women in the back like some sniveling coward, he just didn't have it in him to do that. Sighing, he pulled the door closed and walked back through the house, giving Gregory a passing glance as he stepped over his body. Nervously he ran a hand through his dirty hair. He struggled to come up with a plan. Bobby would be pissed. But the bastard Gregory, he got what he deserved. Somehow, he would figure out a way to provide the women with a good head start, a fighting chance, before he'd report what happened to Bobby.

He walked the short distance to Bobby's house. He hated going there about as much as he hated standing guard outside Gregory's. Knocking on the door, he waited nervously for Bobby's shout to come in. Hearing it, he sucked in a deep breath and entered. The foyer was cast in shadows, dark and gloomy, and smelled of stale booze, cigarettes, and piss.

"Dude, what's up?" Bobby asked. Laughing, he came down the stairs buttoning his shirt. Kevin looked at him, taking in the blood that dotted his knuckles and the snide grin on his face. Behind him at the top of the stairway stood a young girl of what he guessed to be, fifteen or so. Her face appeared swollen, her eyes teary. Averting his eyes, he looked back at Bobby.

"We got a problem, boss. Gregory's dead and the two girls escaped."

He watched Bobby's face grow dark with anger.

"The girls escaped?"

Kevin nodded.

"And they killed Gregory?"

"Yup."

Bobby shook his head in disbelief. How could a ninety-pound mute girl take down one of his best men? Gregory was a towering, massive dude. He stood six foot two inches tall; with legs as thick as tree trunks and arms that could crush those girls easily. Glaring into Kevin's eyes, he snarled, his lips curling in disgust.

"Get Tim, Bailor, Junior, and Tyson. Saddle up the horses and find those bitches!"

Kevin nodded.

"Oh, and tell them, I don't care what they do to Rose, but the other girl comes back here alive! I will take care of that one myself!"

This message sent chills down Kevin's spine, and he felt his stomach curl with nausea.

His mind grasped the implications of what Bobby said. No, he would not pass the message along to the men. It would be like tossing a piece of raw meat into a cage full of rabid dogs. They would tear Rose apart, and by the time they finished with her, there would be nothing left but a bloody, ravaged body.

"I'll tell them, boss."

Turning on his heel, he made his way to find the others. But first, he wanted to take care of a few things. He would be party to most anything Bobby demanded of him, but not this. He would not be party to the slaughter of these women.

Kevin stepped around the back of the barn, just as the skies opened, sending chilling rain down over him. Ignoring the goosebumps on his arms, he cut three long blackberry switches. Sharp thorns pierced his skin as he carried them into the barn. Grabbing four-saddle blankets, he pinched the thorns off of the vines and placed several of them on the underside of each. Satisfied, he nodded. It would do the trick. Once those four saddled up the horses and climbed on top, all hell would break loose. Laughing, he moved on to his next idea.

The walk to his house took only minutes, a short distance, and in that time he gave thought to his next move. No more would he condone the cruelty, the violence caused by Bobby and his gang of thugs. He was done. He was a simple man. And before the event, he had led a quiet life. He thought he'd seen the evilness of man before the event. It was nothing compared to what he now experienced with this gang — the sheer terrorist tactics of pillaging, and destruction. The pure unadulterated evil of their twisted minds on their rampage of rape, murder and torture of innocent citizens as they violently took over one town after another. He hated this life, and he hated himself for being part of it.

By the end of this day, he would either be free of this nightmare or dead. Either way it would end his pain. Entering through the back door so no-one would see him, he dug deep into a box in the closet and pulled out a reel of deep-sea fishing line with a test weight of 130 lbs., meant for marlin and tuna. It would be perfect for what he had in mind. Quickly, he stuffed the spool into his jacket pocket and let himself out the way he'd come in. He had work to do.

Chapter Three

Spike swore when he heard Jessie growl. He watched her jump up and bolt down the hill, plowing through brush and brambles. He was soaked to the bone and chilled from the quick burst of rain that pelted him. Clenching his teeth to keep them from chattering, he stood and wrapped his jacket tighter around himself and shouted to the dog.

"Jessie! Come!"

Jessie paid no attention to him. Lifting his rifle, he peered through the scope and his heart dropped. He watched two women running through the field below. Adjusting the sight, he zeroed in on one of the women, bringing her into view. He swore under his breath and clenched his jaw as he recognized Sarah. About a thousand yards behind her, and coming fast, were five men on horses.

"Shit!" He dropped his rifle, placed two fingers to his lips, and blew out a short, then a more prolonged whistle; a distress call for Brian. He swallowed hard past the lump of panic in his throat. Lifting his rifle to his shoulder, he watched the horror unfold in the meadow below. Drops of rain trickled down his face, and he swiped a hand across his eyes to clear his vision. His heart began to beat hard, and his hands shook. With a deep breath, he steadied the gun.

He muttered softly, pleading. "Lead him in Sarah, just a bit more, my girl," he said while he sighted in on the lead rider.

Brian heard the whistle burst and then the echo of a gunshot. He climbed onto his horse, wiped the cold droplets of rain from his face, and gave one last look to the man tied to the tree, the blood pooling on the ground around his feet. He'd deal with that mess later.

A swift kick set the horse into a run, climbing the steep hill toward Spike. He pulled his rifle from the leather, even before his horse skidded to a halt. His feet hit the dirt with a jarring thud, and he scanned the shadowed woods looking for danger.

Spike turned his face to him and snapped, lining up for another shot.

"It's Sarah!"

His first shot missed the lead rider. He was too far out of range. He shook his head. Brian shoved him out of the way.

"Move!"

Brian laid on the ground and, using a fallen log for a brace, zeroed his scope in on the man. Wet pine needles clung to his legs soaking through his jeans. Fat droplets of moisture plopped from the tree branches onto his back, yet his focus never wavered.

The man and horse were barely twenty yards from mowing Sarah down. Through his scope, he could see the terror and panic on her face as she ran alongside another woman, and his heart exploded with rage. They were too far away for him to be of any help. Swearing, he jumped up and back onto his horse, and down the embankment, shouting back at Spike.

"We gotta get down there!"

He'd never forgive himself if those men killed Sarah. Beth would never forgive him.

∞

Tim was forty or so yards from the women, and he hooted with laughter. His horse stormed forward and the wet wind whipped across his face. His hands itched with the temptation to draw his gun and shoot them both in the back, but he stayed the itch. Bobby would kill him if these girls were not brought back alive. He kicked his horse harder, ignoring the foam spilling from its mouth and the deep panting, as its lungs pushed for even more speed.

Bailor was two horse lengths behind him and gaining fast. Tim got within ten yards and yanked hard on the reigns, bringing the horse to a halt. With a shout of triumph, he jumped from the saddle.

He tackled the mute girl and drove her into the ground with his body. He grinned when he felt her weak struggles beneath him as the wet grass soaked them both. He laughed at the fun of it. Hell, he might even decide to have a little go with this one before he dragged her sorry ass back to Bobby. Her struggling beneath him only served to entice him further, and he grabbed a fistful of her hair yanking back on her head. He hissed into her ear.

"Keep struggling, baby, it feels good,"

Flipping her over, he started yanking at her jeans roughly. Yes, this one was gonna be worth Bobby's wrath, he thought. He grinned hungrily into her terrified eyes.

He was so intent on the woman beneath him, he failed to see the black and white shadow coming at him. Growls filled his ears as teeth sank into his throat. He screamed in pain and punched at the dog with both fists to get it off of him.

Before his eyes, Bailor barely got out a scream as a thin line of invisible wire cut into his throat, decapitating him in one quick motion.

Kevin watched the whole scene unfold with a grin while he held his mare at a slow canter. He'd strung that wire days ago it stretched just the right height from one tree on the left side of the field to another tree on the right. He'd been planning his own escape, but it satisfied him to witness the death of these evil men. How Tim missed the wire was a miracle, or so he thought, until he saw the huge German shepherd. The wire would have been a quicker death.

Behind him, still on the edge of the field,

horses screamed and bucked furiously as the thorns dug into their backs beneath the saddles. He turned, snickering, while he watched the last two riders, Junior and Tyson, fall from their saddles. He pulled his gun and took aim, grinning widely as he pressed the trigger and watched Tyson's head explode into a wet, bloody mess.

Jumping from the saddle, he saw Junior roll up onto his knees and take aim at him. He felt the first bullet slam deep into his gut, then turned his head and puked. Junior watched Kevin crumple into a heap on the wet grass. Another bullet rocked him as it exploded into his chest. He sank to his knees, and stared at Junior, stunned. He waited for death and thought of the two women. At least he tried to save them. Coughing, he stared up into the sky as the last breath left his body.

Junior picked himself up and lunged for his horse, his legs slipping on the damp grass. They'd been set up, ambushed. He ripped the saddle off the screaming beast, jumped onto her bareback, and raced back toward town to alert Bobby.

∞

Brian rode through the light rain, watching the mess spread out before him. In confusion, he watched as one man fired upon the others. Shaking his head, he drew his rifle up; the only survivor was mounting in retreat.

He couldn't let him escape to warn the others. His jaw tensed as he tapped the trigger and brought the man down.

Confusion was written across his face when he glanced over at Spike, who shook his head and shrugged his shoulders.

"What just happened?" Brian laughed.

This wasn't how he'd planned Sarah's rescue, but he would take it. With a smile, he gently nudged his horse into a trot and spoke over his shoulder to Spike.

"Let's go get Sarah."

∞

Sarah stumbled and her hands slipped on the wet grass. She picked herself up with a cry, limping, and struggling to run. She could hear the horse's hooves pounding behind her, and her throat constricted painfully with fear and defeat.

Blood soaked through the dirty dish towel under her shirt, and she felt its sticky drops running down her arm. Weakness; terrible and dizzying weakness, screamed inside of her as her heart threatened to burst from her chest.

They'd kill her. They'd kill Rose too. Bile rose in her throat. Defeat tugged at her frenzied mind. She screamed at Rose, she pushed harder, fighting waves of dizziness and nausea. Her breath hitched in and out of her lungs. When the body hit her and drove her to the ground, she let out a howl of anguish. Grass and dirt ground into her face; the smell, pungent and earthy. She struggled to breathe against the man's weight.

With her last ounce of energy, she turned and fought: clawing, punching, and kicking. She felt her pants being tugged and she brought her knee up, smashing the man in the groin. She heard Rose's screams beside her. Her breath rasped in and out and her hungry lungs gasped for air. The man's cry of pain erupted in her ears as she felt him knocked from her, and she rolled away. Growls filled her ears and turning; she saw Jessie. Her heart leaped with joy. They didn't abandon her; they didn't forget her. Tears of relief ran hotly down her cheeks.

She crawled to Rose and through hitching sobs she whimpered, "We're saved!"

Chapter Four

Brian leaped from his horse and ran toward Sarah. She stood, wavering on shaky legs. He reached for her and felt pain rock his jaw as her hand swung out with the fury of a hellcat and struck him.

"You! You left me here! Why didn't you come sooner? Why did you let them take me?" she screamed, then threw herself into his waiting arms.

She stank of smoky campfires and sweat. Brian breathed it in pulling her closer. Her sobs, her tears soaked the front of his shirt. Her small body trembled against his and he tightened his arms around her. Stroking her hair softly and gently, he felt the sting of tears behind his own eyes.

He shot a look of sheer agony over her head toward Spike. Would she ever understand? Would Beth ever understand why he hadn't rescued her right away? If he'd gone sooner, Bobby would surely have killed Sarah. He couldn't have gone into this fight blindly, with nothing but rage to drive him. That would have been the worst thing he could've done. How could he explain that his delay was to prepare— to plan, and not walk or run blindly into this nest of vipers, not knowing how many he would be up against, or even where they were holding her.

"Baby girl," he purred, his voice a whisper. He tightened his arms even more around her. Looking down at her face, he saw the bruises, ugly and purple, the busted lips from the beatings. A rage, dark and poisonous, filled him with hatred, and his whole body shook. He wanted to kill everyone in that town for what they'd done to her. Skin them alive for their part in her pain. Sucking in a deep breath, he stepped away from her and clenched his fists by his side.

"Spike, let's saddle up. We gotta get these girls as far away as we can right now!" he snapped.

Lifting Sarah, he gently sat her atop his saddle. There would be time later for talking. The moment finally hit him, snapping his head toward Sarah.

"My God! You're talking!"

"No shit, Brian!" She smiled weakly.

"Now, will you please take me home?"

He felt a smile tug at the corner of his lips, and he shook his head. A teasing light sparkled in his eyes. "Oh boy, we seem to have a smart ass on our hands now."

He climbed up in the saddle behind her and heard Spike's husky laughter behind him. "Yeah, buddy...the girl's got spunk!" Spike said then kicked his horse into a trot, he and Rose leading them toward the wood line.

They rode hard and fast for hours before Brian finally called a halt. His bones felt jarred and saddle weary. Through clenched teeth he climbed down from the saddle; pain rocketed through his knees. He lifted Sarah down and set her gently on her feet. Blood soaked the front of her shirt, and she swayed dizzily. Reaching out, he steadied her and helped her to a fallen log, insisting she sit down.

He sighed and stretched his back while he gazed up into the clear sky. The rain stopped some time ago, and the air smelled of fragrant fresh pine. The temperature chilled his skin, raising goosebumps on his bare arms.

He looked back at her and shook his head. "Shit, we gotta get you patched up Sarah."

Digging through the saddlebags, he found the medical kit Roger had insisted he pack. Spike and Rose moved up beside him with worried expressions.

"I didn't have time to tend to her." Rose murmured, and Brian turned to her.

"What happened?"

"Gregory beat her, badly. She shot him, but the bullet went through him and into her," Rose whispered hoarsely.

"And Gregory?"

"He's dead. That bastard is dead!" Sarah growled. She bent forward and leaned her head into her hands. There wasn't a spot on her body that didn't feel battered. Pure hatred flashed in her eyes, "And I'd kill him again if I could."

Spike laughed softly, and his eyes sparkled with pride. "That's my girl!"

Brian slid the shirt from her arm and gasped when he saw the bloody welts across her shoulder and back. What in the hell had they done to her? Biting back his rage, he examined the wound in her shoulder. She could use stitches for sure, but the bullet just grazed her, leaving a deep, long gash. He picked up his canteen of water and gently washed the wound, then applied an antibiotic salve. He added five butterfly Band-Aids and pulled the flesh tightly together taping gauze over it. It was the best he could do for the time being.

He felt Sarah's eyes on him, and he looked over at her and smiled. "That must've hurt like hell, Sarah. You've been so brave through this."

Sarah nodded weakly. Brave? That's what he thought? She wasn't courageous; she'd just been fighting for her life. That was sheer instinct, not bravery.

Glancing at him, she felt her face flush with shame. "I'm sorry I hit you. I thought you abandoned me. I waited so long for you Bri."

Brian swallowed hard against the lump in his throat and with a touch as light as a feather, he stroked her swollen cheek. "I would never abandon you, child," he whispered. "Never."

He turned when he heard Spike cough

from behind him.

"Okay, we've got to plan. You know it ain't gonna be long before Bobby finds those men in the field. Then he's gonna be riding hard and gunning for us. I suggest we ride straight through the night. We can make the compound by morning."

Then looking at Rose and Sarah, he shook his head. "I know you ladies have been through hell and back today, but are you up for it?"

Sarah nodded. He had no idea of how much hell she'd been through these past few days. If riding through the night meant safety, then she'd guide that damn horse herself.

Rose frowned. "I can't. I have to go back," Rose whispered and started sobbing.

They all looked at her with expressions of shock.

"Why? Why on earth would you even think to go back?" Brian asked. Rose's eyes widening, she stepped back from him and splayed her hands wide.

"Because…" she stuttered between sobbing hitches, "my baby sister is back there. She's only seven years old! I can't leave her. I'm the only thing between her and Bobby. Without me protecting her, you have no idea of what they will do to her!"

Sarah felt her heart fill with a sick dread. She looked desperately at Brian, her eyes pleading with him.

"Sarah, I don't…" he muttered helplessly. He saw anger spark in her blue eyes.

Standing up, she shouted at him. "No! No! I know what those animals are capable of doing! We are not leaving that child behind! What they do is bad enough for a grown woman but a child? A child?"

Spike moved up beside her and laid a hand on her shoulder, turning her toward him. He had to make her understand. It would be too dangerous to try and go back. With just the four of them, they didn't stand a chance in hell against Bobby and his men.

"Sarah! Listen! We can't save her!"

He cast a glance at Brian, looking for support, "Think about it! There are only four of us against how many? It would be suicide!"

Brian nodded. It chewed at his gut thinking of the little girl: defenseless, scared, and probably crying for her sister. His stomach turned, thinking of what his imagination told him would happen to her. With a shaking hand, he roughly wiped at his face. There had to be something they could do to save her. But God, as hard as he tried, he could think of no solution. Frustrated, he stormed off into the woods, away from the group. He needed time to think; he needed quiet.

His gut roiled queasily with worry and memories of Talia, his younger sister. The past rammed at his brain. For the first time in his life, he felt helpless, inadequate, and defeated. How could he save a young girl—risking both Sarah's and Rose's life, never mind Spike's and his own? For what?

There were hundreds of girls in the same situation. He couldn't save them all. And why should he? In this new world, there was no saving anyone. Just existing and surviving. And honestly, it wasn't up to him to save everyone.

The thought of the little girl weighed heavily on his shoulders, and he rolled them to ease the pain. He was one man. One man! Anger clawed at him. Anger at the world, the situation, and mostly at himself for getting caught up in this mess. He was torn inside because at the same time, he knew he couldn't and wouldn't walk away. Sarah, Beth? Somehow, they became his responsibility. From the first time he set eyes on the two of them he knew his fate was sealed and he'd die to protect them.

"See? I told ya…you are a chump, boy!" his father whispered deep in his mind.

"No, Dad, I'm just human," he replied, rubbing his hand over his burning, tired eyes. "Just human."

He walked back to the group. Spike met his eyes and nodded.

"I think we've come up with a solution, Brian."

Brian nodded, listening.

"We can't possibly go back. As much as I

want to bring down the hounds of hell on those bastards, it would be a suicide mission. You do know we just took Bobby's toys, and he ain't one to share. I ain't keen on getting my ass handed to me on a platter," Spike said then smiled crookedly, "But, I think if we ride hard tonight, we can reach the compound by dawn. We can gather up all the men that Roger can spare, take the road back and plant ourselves in the woods."

Brian tilted his head slightly. "Go on."

"Bobby is lazy; we saw that from the haphazard way his men guarded the town. I'm betting he'll ride the road looking for us. This time we'll be ready! We ambush them the same way they did us. And this time, we will leave no survivors! We take the whole group down, then once we're done; we free that friggin town for good!"

Brian looked at Sarah and Rose. Did they agree? He saw by the nods of their heads they did. Breathing a sigh of relief, he nodded. "Okay, let's ride then."

Chapter Five

Beth sat at the table. Her body hurt, but the warm spring sunshine eased the pain a little. She turned her face up to the sun, closing her eyes, to enjoy its warmth. The smell of coffee wafted on a slight breeze, enticing her. The compound that Roger had built loomed large before her. It was just this simple; life would go on place.

With the sun's warming rays came hope, but also, thoughts about how stupid she'd been. She was an Emergency Responder; she should have been better prepared. But then again, how do you prepare for something like this? Her mind was foggy, and her head spun from the pain medication. Her thoughts were scattered, like leaves in the wind, making it hard for her to capture one and keep it.

She'd attended all the classes; emergency response, critical response, and such. She believed the CDC and the government talking heads when they broadcasted over the airwaves that they would get a handle on this unknown virus. She purchased all the personal protection equipment, PPE for short; planning for herself and her family. They relied on the information the media gave out; it was wrong, and they failed to use it in time. It was too late. A tear, warm and wet, slid from behind her closed eyes and made a damp track down her cheek.

It made sense the way the cards fell. First, the power went down. She assumed it happened because there was no one left to run the power plants. Then services went down. No hospitals, no road crews to plow the roads, no ambulance service, no long-distance truckers to bring in the food. One cascade of failures after another.

Could it have been bioterrorism? Or perhaps some unknown person came through the loose borders of the United States and unknowingly brought it with them? Or maybe, even worse, the terrifying thought that their own government; a government that they trusted, unleashed this hell on its citizens. She would probably never know.

Her hip burned, the pain at times was almost unbearable. Even still, she was glad to be up and out of the infirmary, even if just for a few hours. She would be on crutches for the next three weeks, and she looked at the wooden things with a hateful glare. From what Doc said, the bullet had lodged itself deep into her hip, shattering the bone. Brian had carried her to the compound where Doc, Marcus Linsler, performed the surgery to remove the bullet and tied her back together with nuts and bolts. Jill, her nurse, also told her Brian spent days planning for the rescue and nights sitting at her bedside; waiting for her to wake up.

Jill looked at her with a wistful expression

and a grin. "You're lucky to have a man like that."

Beth didn't know much of Jill's story other than she was divorced. The marriage ended just before the virus hit, leaving Jill single and longing for someone to share her life.

Beth gazed out toward the horizon and wrinkled her brow. Roger followed her gaze and shook his head. "He'll be back. Soon."

"I hope so. I am so damn mad at him!" she hissed.

Roger grimaced and glanced at her. "Why?"

"Because he should have gone right away to get Sarah! Why didn't he? Why did he wait four days before rescuing her?" She agonized as her eyes implored Roger for an answer. She saw him shake his head and mutter under his breath.

"Woman, have you always been this hard-headed? Good, God! That man is risking his life to get Sarah back! Spike, my grandson, is risking his life!"

Beth felt a flush of shame spread over her cheeks, and she bowed her head.

"I know, but they should have left sooner."

Roger turned on her angrily.

"He wanted to! He was insane with rage and grief! I talked him out of it! And you wanna know why? Because if he left half-cocked, then he and Sarah both would have been killed! We needed time to let Bobby's gang feel like they pulled the ambush off, to think that we were not going to retaliate. To let them think they hurt us enough that we were hiding, scared of them!

We needed time for them to get careless. And we needed time to plan and prepare; to watch and see whether or not that gang of thugs would attack here! So yes, Brian could have turned right around and chased them down trying to get Sarah back, but I guarantee you, they both would be dead right now."

Although she hated to admit it, Roger was right. She would have made the mistake of rushing headlong into the lion's den to save Sarah, and it would have cost her both of their lives. She'd always had a bad temper, hot and quick, and this often led her into doing things she would later regret.

Sighing tiredly, she looked at Roger and nodded. "You are right. I hate it, but it's true."

It had been days since Brian left—days of worry and waiting. What was Sarah going through? Was she dead? Did they hurt her? Did Brian find her yet? The not knowing chewed at her gut like a hungry rat. She absently fiddled with a stray lock of her hair that had slipped from the elastic band, winding it around her fingers.

Roger slid his arm from the sling and wincing, picked up her dirty gun from the table. He saw flecks of dried mud on the barrel.

"Looks like this gun could use a little cleaning."

Beth laughed softly and turned her face to his.

"Cleaning? I've only fired it twice, and on one shot I missed. I barely know how to shoot it, never mind clean it."

Roger grinned and shook his head. "Woman! I guess I'd better be teaching you how to clean your gun."

Beth nodded. There was so much she needed to learn, and cleaning the gun was only the tip of it. She grimaced. The air smelled strongly of warm soil and sunshine, and Beth breathed in deeply, filling her lungs. May, the month of flowers blooming and green growth. With an expression of confusion, she looked at Roger.

"Have we missed Memorial Day?" Roger shook his head, and she sighed. Sadness floated across her heart. Memories of past Memorial Holiday weekends crowded her mind, and a single tear slid down her face. With a swipe of her hand, she brushed it away.

A sigh of sadness escaped her lips. Would there be a Memorial Day in the future of America now?

Tears filled her eyes, and she sniffled. With another quick brush of her hand, she wiped them away angrily. Why did she suddenly feel so emotional? What was going on? She hardly ever cried. Not much rattled her emotions. Stubbornly she bit her bottom lip and willed away the nostalgia. She averted her gaze when Roger looked deeply into her eyes.

"Talk to me."

Hiccoughing, she shrugged her shoulders and turned to face him. She waved her arm around. It angered her that he saw her tears. In her mind, tears meant weakness.

"This!" she motioned to the gun. "I don't know what I'm doing. I don't know anything about surviving this! I have no experience to draw from. I can't preserve foods; I don't know the first thing about defenses or digging a well or hunting or any of the things that will help me survive. Will there ever be any more holidays? Or is that a thing of the past? How about birthdays, and Christmases, and picnics in the park? All gone, and I hate this new world! It's a wonder I've lasted this long," she spat out in a single breath. She pushed her backpack away with an angry shove and crossed her arms in defiance of their new world.

Roger smiled empathetically and gave her a one-armed hug. "Oh, girl. Do you think we were born with this knowledge? Do you think Mary Anne knew how to preserve food and run a homestead? No. These are all things that we learned, and they are teachable to those who want to learn. You've done the best you could, and now that you know better, you can do better. We'll teach you." And with that, he began to show her how to clean her gun.

She watched him take apart her gun while he explained to her the process of cleaning it.

"First, this gun is a Smith and Wesson 642, so it'll be a simple and straightforward process."

Beth nodded and watched as he spun the barrel to check for shells.

"Once you've determined it is not loaded, you can then take a bit of solvent on a clean cloth and swab the barrel like this," he said, using a thin rod to push up through the barrel, "and then do the same to each cylinder. Lastly, use light oil and swab again," he said as he finished cleaning the gun for her. Grinning, he handed her back her gun with a satisfied expression.

Beth grinned. It looked easy enough to do.

"Now, every once in a while, you will need to remove the grip and the plate to deep clean the guts of this thing, but that doesn't need doing every time."

"Beth, your gun is a tool. And to keep your tools in operating condition, you need to be sure to do this every once in a while. You don't want to have to use the gun only to find out it is misfiring because of neglect."

She thought about the only time she fired it, and this thought sent shivers down her spine.

Thinking of this made her wonder what

Brian and Spike were facing. Bobby's gang had caught them with their guard down. Hit them hard out on the road and from what she remembered of the fight; he brought at least twenty men with him. What odds were facing Brian and Spike?

"Roger? Why didn't you send men along to help Brian and Spike?"

Roger grimaced and turned his face into the sun. The day grew long, and he sighed. He was tired, plain and simply exhausted. He rubbed his thumb lightly across the wood of the picnic table while he pondered her question.

"Brian wanted one week to get in and get Sarah. I promised I'd give him that. He feared if we rode in there, this Bobby guy would kill Sarah before we even got the chance to get close. But I will tell you this. If Spike and Brian are not back soon? I'm gonna break my promise and head out first thing in the morning. Come hell or high water; we are going to wipe that miserable scourge from the face of this earth. We need to get Sarah clear first though. And once she's back here and safe? Then, let's just say, Bobby and his gang will not be terrorizing anyone anymore."

Beth nodded. A feeling of dread overcame her. They were facing war. Never could she have dreamed that the citizens of the United States; her friends, her neighbors, would be fighting against each other. Hell, in her wildest imaginings she would never have thought that life would come to this.

Turning her eyes to Roger, she shook her head. "Do you think it will ever get back to normal?"

Roger nodded, and he shifted his gaze to four-year-old Kayla, who played with a sand bucket and a shovel in the dirt of the yard. Her brown hair shone in the sunlight, her happy chatter reaching his ears. Her parents were victims of the virus. She came to them by way of a neighbor—dirty, hungry, and sick from a rat bite. The neighbors had heard her cries and found her in the barn at her parents' house and had rescued her. She became everyone's child, but truly, she belonged to Mary Anne. His wife took her under her wing like a mother dove would a baby bird.

"I do. Maybe not in our time, but perhaps with her generation," he said nodding his head toward the child. "I think for us, you and me and all the others who've survived this? Well, this will be our fight. And hopefully, we can win. Ya know, the good guys. For her sake...." he finished as he pointed to Kayla.

Beth smiled weakly. She hoped so too. Turning, she glanced at Mary Anne walking toward them from the house with a tray of tea. Weariness coursed through her body, and she leaned heavily on the table.

"Can you ask Jill to help me back in?"

Roger nodded.

"I may be an old man, but I still can help a lady to her bed," he replied. He smiled and helped her up. Gritting her teeth, she stood on her good leg, wobbling unsteadily. Pain shot through her hip, and she stumbled only to be caught by Roger's strong arms. She shot him a grateful glance.

"I think you've done enough for this morning, girl," he murmured. With a strong grip he helped her back to her room in the infirmary. Jill stepped quickly to her side and helped her onto the bed. Beth sank wearily down onto it. Weak light filtered through the shades and Jill pulled them closed.

"Thank you both," she whispered closing her eyes. Sleep, merciful and sweet, closed over her.

∞

Roger sat at the table next to Mary Anne after helping Beth back to the infirmary and handing her over to Jill. Sipping a cup of coffee, he glanced at his wife. Her expression told him her thoughts were a million miles away. He rubbed his thumb against the handle of his cup while his eyes gazed out over the green grass and mountains in the distance. Spring growth had started to peek its head up out of the cold ground, and he breathed deeply of the fresh air.

"Garden should go in soon."

Mary Anne smiled, teasing him. Already one step ahead of him.

"Yup, got it covered, old man."

The stress of the past few months, of running the compound, of the one hundred and one things he worried about daily showed in the deep creases around his eyes.

"We tilled the ground yesterday. The seeds and starters from the greenhouse will go in today. I've got Connie, Alisa, Travis, and Cain all working on it."

Roger nodded. He should have known. Turning his face into the sun, he closed his eyes. A troubled frown creased between his eyes and he rubbed at it lightly with a calloused fingertip. The compound grew daily now that spring had arrived, and people were moving from their houses and traveling away from the death winter left behind. Just this morning, seven more refugees showed up asking for help.

"We've got a woman that came in this morning with a two-month-old baby. A cute little bugger. We'll have to dig into the infant supplies. The poor woman came with nothing but the clothes on her back."

Mary Anne nodded and sighed. She pinched the bridge of her nose with two fingers and willed the beginning of another headache to go away. Roger glanced at her, concern shadowing his brown eyes. She'd been pushing herself too hard lately; up at dawn every morning, organizing the kitchen for the buffet type breakfast the women of the compound took turns cooking. Adding that to all her other tasks kept her busy until well into every evening.

"You okay?"

Smiling, she nodded, and Roger reached out and brushed a tendril of her graying hair from her face. She leaned her cheek into the palm of his hand for a second and sighed softly before winking at him.

"Old man," she teased, her blue eyes sparkling with mischief. He loved that about her. She never failed, in all the forty-plus years they'd been married, to lose that mischievous sparkle in her eyes. Even now, with things so hard for so many, she kept her sense of playfulness, of humor and good faith.

"I'll gather up a box of supplies from the storeroom. Where did you put the woman and her baby up?"

"I put her in with Tillie and her young-un. I figured they were about the same age. Tillie will be able to help her get settled."

"That's good. I'll go over there later and welcome her to the community. God bless that she and the baby made it here. Do you know where she came from?"

Roger shook his head.

"No. I haven't found the time to sit and talk with her."

Mary Anne would fix that, he knew. She always welcomed the new people and jotted pertinent information down in the little notebook she carried. She used it as a census of sorts. It helped them keep track of how many mouths they were feeding, what supplies they would need to add to the daily kitchen where the meals were served, and when the newcomers were settled, the list helped to assign them the tasks that would keep the compound running. It was work-as-you-go type situation. If you wanted to eat, then you helped with the work. It was just that plain and simple.

Smiling softly, Mary Anne pecked Roger on his grizzled cheek.

"You need a shave, old man," she teased. He grinned at her and playfully slapped her butt.

Sighing heavily, she groaned and slid her shoes back onto her bare feet. She loved the feel of the grass on her toes, and whenever she had a chance, she would slide her shoes off and walk barefoot.

"Well, I guess I can't sit in this glorious sunshine all day. Got work to do and so do you, old man," she teased. She pushed herself up from the table, grabbed both their cups and carried them with her to wash.

Roger watched her walk away and sighed deeply. He let the worries that nagged at him flit across his mind. He solved problems best when alone. When he could mull them over quietly; once done, he would then bring it to the group for discussion. There were seven of them in the group that made decisions for the whole compound. Together, Roger, Mary Anne and Julie, Doc, Rusty, Thomas, and Calvin, all gave equal say in matters concerning the welfare of the community.

He'd heard a lot of chatter on the HAM radio from all over the country about the virus. What they thought had run its course and died out, was now reported to be cropping up again in New York, Wisconsin, Florida, Washington State, and California. Joe Nagler out of Wisconsin said he implemented a quarantine of his compound, no more refugees in and no one leaving. The virus was running rampant, all around his area, and he wasn't taking any chances.

Shaking his head, he groaned. How could this be? Several of his contacts reported hearing of heavy spraying of what was supposed to be a new antiviral, grown in a medical lab somewhere down south. Spraying by whom? The group doing it didn't identify themselves as any part of the fractured United States government. And stranger yet, in every area they purportedly sprayed, new cases of the virus cropped up.

The second area of worry for him were the reports of a large group of unfriendlies, moving out of New York and Boston, heading straight for the North East. The large group of two hundred plus were clearing the significant highways for several tanker trucks that were slowly making their way from town to town. His contact also told him that many in the group were wearing gang signs on their jackets. Everything about this set off warning flags for Roger. He'd heard of the gangs in New York and Boston, and what he'd heard had him scared shitless.

Lastly, and the most immediate of concerns, were his grandson Spike and the newcomer Brian, who'd taken off after Bobby and his gang to rescue the girl, Sarah. Should he have sent some of his men with them? Eventually, Bobby and his group would need to be dealt with. The safety of his community depended on it.

Chapter Six

Bobby shook with fury. He exploded with dark rage and slammed his fist into the wall, punching a hole in the plaster. Pain slammed up his arm. His knuckles busted open and blood flowed down over his fingers. Five of his men had died because of those two bitches! Five! Glaring, he stepped toward fifteen-year-old Amy with his hands curled into fists. She cried out and attempted to cover her face as he threw punches into her in a fit of temper.

"What is with you women? When will you all learn your place?" Each word uttered he drove home with a punishing fist—until she lay on the floor, sobbing. Jacob stood by silently wincing and watching each blow land on the defenseless girl. He shifted his eyes and stared at a speck on the wall rather than witness it.

Spent and breathing hard, Bobby turned to him and sneered.

"Go tell everyone; we meet here in an hour! Now!" He knew exactly where those bitches were going, and he intended to take care of that problem for once and for all. Jacob nodded and turned quickly on his heels. Anything to get the hell away from Bobby.

How could this have happened? Two women besting five of his men... what was wrong with this picture? He knew he should have just taken his pleasure with the mute girl then killed her. A soft mewling whimper brought his eyes back to Amy. Sunlight poured through the window and surrounded her in a soft glow. Dust particles floated and danced in the yellowed rays. He looked at her with disgust.

"Get up, go wash your ugly face!" A smile of satisfaction touched his mouth. He watched her scurry away. He hated her. He loathed everything about her. But he needed to train her for his brothel. And she was a good student. That much he'd give her. Not as good as Tamara. He regretted how that turned out. He'd lost his temper, and well...?

Pushing it out of his mind, he focused on more important things. The Alliance and their fuel trucks would be here in less than two weeks, and he still needed to find ten women to add to the eighteen he had for trade. His mind spun with the possibilities, and he smiled coldly. He knew where he would get the additional women, and if his plan worked out the way he thought it would, he would be getting so much more than just women. Throwing a light jacket over his shoulders, he slammed out through the front door and into the sunshine. He had a man to see.

He walked along Main Street, whistling a light tune and turned left onto Mary Rowe Drive. Dust kicked up under his boots. He spied

Ray riding toward him, leading a man and woman, both bound with rope. Stopping, he waited.

"What's this?" he snapped. Ray brought his horse to a halt a few feet away from him.

"I caught these two sneaking out of town."

Bobby glanced at the man, Tom? Tim? He couldn't remember his name. Then he glanced at the young girl, and he swore softly.

"April? What the hell, woman! You know better than trying to escape!" he purred. With a grin he reached out and stroked a dirty hand across her cheek. He chuckled when he saw her flinch. He watched her eyes widen in fear. Looking up at Ray, he nodded.

"You know what to do." Ray nodded in reply and laughed. Yes, he knew what to do. There would be a show in town tonight.

Bobby stepped around the two and continued on his way. What was going on here today? His men…trying to escape? The women he could understand. But his men?

"You're losing it, Bobby. Losing control and the men know it." His mother's voice whispered deep in his mind.

"No! You shut up!" he muttered.

"You're a loser boy, a bastard loser. You couldn't even take care of your brother, now look, he's dead because of you!" His father's voice shouted.

Bobby screamed and covered his ears with his hands, spinning in circles. A frantic terror filled his heart.

"You're dead! Stay dead!" he yelled to the empty air.

Was it true? Was he losing it? Perhaps he'd pushed the crazy too far; now his men were sneaking out to get away from him. Grinding his teeth so that they hurt, he shook his head. No! No way! His men respected him! They feared him! He was king in this little town!

Sweat dappled his forehead and ran into his eyes. The sun suddenly felt too hot and shone too bright. Sucking in a deep breath, he gagged on the stink of horse manure that littered the street. He walked cautiously, avoiding the big piles left behind by the horses. He made a mental note to have Ray gather up some of the women and make them clean up the nasty shit.

Stopping in front of a large, white Victorian house he knocked on the door. A slender woman of about fifty opened it and smiled widely. She held her arms out for a hug before she'd move to let him in, and Bobby welcomed it.

"Cathy," Bobby murmured. He gave her a quick peck on her sunken cheek. The aroma of fresh baked bread met his nose and teased his senses.

"Bobby? It is so nice to see you again."

"Is Henry around?"

"Yup, working in the cellar. Come in my brother. "

Bobby stepped into the cold, shadowed hallway. Henry and Cathy, the only two people on this earth that he feared and respected. He let Cathy usher him into the living room where he sat down on a blue paisley sofa.

"I'll go get Henry."

She hurried away and he let his eyes roam around the room. Statues of baby Jesus and Mary crowded every available tabletop. Bibles littered the coffee stand. Not a particle of dust shone on any of the surfaces. On the wall hung crosses of the crucifixion and in the corner, near the fireplace, a table sat as an altar. The room reeked of radical religion.

A shuffle of feet drew his attention to the far side of the room, where a young woman of about seventeen stood shackled to a bar on the wall. He smiled; his eyes taking in her terrified eyes, the curve of her hips and the fullness of her lips. Such a shame that this girl's talents were wasted with these two. No, Henry nor Cathy would have none of that. She was their slave, pure and simple. She did the cooking, cleaning, heavy lifting, so Cathy didn't have to. He sighed and winked at the girl, teasing her and chuckled as she cast her eyes downward.

"So? What brings you to my humble home?" Henry asked with a booming voice then smiled as he wrapped Bobby into a tight hug.

The man was a beast—six-foot-plus, with arms that could easily crush a man.

"The project? How's it coming along?"

Laughing, Henry winked and motioned for him to follow.

"Come see for yourself, my son."

The pipe bombs, about twenty of them, lay in a neat row on the wooden workbench. Bobby grinned nodding his head. Henry was a genius!

"Are they ready? Hot?"

Henry nodded and grinned.

"God willing, they are, my son."

"Good, I think I'll be needing them very soon."

Henry wrinkled his brow and gave Bobby a questioning look.

"I've got some trouble. Two women escaped this morning, and then I found out another one of my men had tried escaping," he muttered as he kicked the toe of his boot into the dirt cellar floor. "The compound, I need to hit it soon."

Henry shook his head. "You stay the course, Bobby. It is God's plan. The sinners will fall. You and I both know that."

Cathy, who stood at the bottom of the stairs, moved over to Bobby and placed a firm hand on his shoulder while she made the sign of the cross with her other hand. She bowed her head.

"Amen. Henry is right. The Lord has sent his wrath upon these sinners, cleansing the world through plague," she murmured. Bobby nodded. The woman, in his opinion, was bat shit crazy, worse than her husband by far.

Henry nodded and looked deeply into Bobby's eyes.

"Stay strong, soldier. The Lord will guide you. Look at all you've done since the plague hit. You've gathered up the sinners, the whores and the weak. Your work is cleansing this town, building a new God-fearing society. Yes, there will be a few who turn against you, but you are strong and in the great hands of our glorious Savior. You are traveling the Godly way. Those whores, they're nothing, nothing anymore.

Before the plague they were harlots, gluttons, parading themselves around with no consequences! Going against the way of our God! Now, look at them, slaves! It is God's punishment. Men and women of no morals shall perish." Henry ranted, his voice rising to a fevered pitch.

Bobby smiled. He didn't believe in this God stuff. Never had and never would, but these two didn't have to know that. They thought they were doing God's work in helping him and he wouldn't tell them any differently?

"Amen," he replied, then grinned. Yes, religion... ahhhh, what a beautiful thing.

They made their way back upstairs. Cathy

veered off to the kitchen to make them some tea. Bobby looked at Henry and coughed lightly.

"I have two prisoners that we'll need to deal with tonight. Will you do the honor of speaking?"

Henry's eyes lit with insane delight and he rubbed his hands together in excitement.

"Of course, I surely will, my son."

Bobby smiled. He needed to feed those closest to him, no matter how perverse their appetites.

Chapter Seven

Darkness crept in around them as they made their way through the woods. A weak glow from a half-moon cast shadows among the trees. Jessie's sleek body silently moved in and out, among the shadows. The air felt saturated from the earlier rain, and smelled of freshly turned earth. Spike led them through narrow deer trails and over rough terrain. Brian looked ahead and could barely make out the silhouettes of Spike and Rose a few yards ahead. His bones felt like shattered glass as the horse jolted and stumbled over a rock on the trail. He instinctively tightened his arms around Sarah to keep her from falling, feeling her warmth against his chilled body. She rode in front of him, leaning heavily against his chest. Night riding wasn't the ideal situation, but nothing about today had worked out the way he'd planned.

Whistling softly, he caught Spike's attention and motioned for him to stop. They needed a few minutes to let the horses rest and to be out of the saddles to stretch the kinks out. He grimaced and climbed down from the horse then helped Sarah down. She stumbled with fatigue as he set her on her feet. Her wound, bandaged, still bled heavily. Swearing under his breath, he dug in the saddlebags for the medical kit. Jessie moved up beside him and sat. He gave her a light pat on the head.

Sarah needed to be stitched up, but he didn't have the proper equipment to do this. So, he would re-bandage and hope it would slow the bleeding enough to get her back to the compound where the doctor could take care of it.

Spike sat on a boulder on the side of the trail with Rose leaning tiredly against him. He curled an arm around her shoulder, giving her some of his warmth. Brian cast her a pitying glance. He knew it must be agonizing for her, knowing she'd left her little sister behind.

"We're making good time. We should be at the compound by first light."

His heart slammed guiltily in his chest. He thought of the child left behind. He wished he could save her. But he couldn't. Not without exposing Sarah and Rose to more danger. And with just the four of them, it would be an impossible mission. They needed the help of Roger and his men.

Brian nodded and muttered. He doubted things would go off that smoothly, but he could always hope.

"Good. Hopefully, Bobby and his men won't start hunting for us until daylight. We'll have time to drop these girls off, gather up reinforcements and set up the ambush."

The more he thought of Rose's younger

sister, the more rage pulsed in his gut. Bobby was a psychopath. A man that needed killing. If it weren't for Sarah and Rose, he would have turned his horse around and gone back to that town. His hands itched with the desire to hunt Bobby down and make him pay for the misery he caused to so many. Every time he looked at Sarah's battered face, he burned with fury. What kind of man could be so twisted and perverse? He was an animal who took pleasure in hurting others.

The night folded in around them. Brian breathed deeply, inhaling the chilly air, tasting the scent of pine. Sarah leaned heavily against him, her breathing soft and even, sleeping peacefully. He tightened his arms around her, ignoring the ache in his shoulders. Night sounds, the creatures stirring behind the wall of darkness, lulled him into a soft place where memories floated.

The virus. It had raced through the prison like a roaring wildfire. At first the guards quarantined the sick, but then the sick outnumbered the areas they could put them. Having run out of sickbeds, they left them in their cells to die on their own dirty, stained mattresses. Wingman, his cellmate, died early on. Wingman had been a young man, barely twenty-one, goofy and obnoxious, but Brian liked him. And he always looked out for the boy. His heart gave a sad tug as he remembered his sandy hair, green eyes, and goofy smile.

He thought about his parents; the last time he'd talked to his mother. How she'd wept openly when visiting hours were over and how her face collapsed in agony when his father, roughly grabbed her arm as she leaned in for one more hug. And how this had brought him to the brink of rage, leaving him feeling helpless. Anguish ripped through him. They hadn't understood why he did what he did. They hadn't realized the burning hunger that clawed at him, driving him to right the wrongs that happened to Talia. Those men, the ones who took her, they destroyed the little girl through their savagery and cruelty. The chill of the night air matched the coldness in his heart.

His father had accused him of becoming the man he so hated. Just a killer, on the same level as Bobby. The blood that stained his soul screamed yes. The deaths of the men, from his hands, screamed yes. Did it matter, the reason for killing? If the law couldn't or wouldn't serve up the justice, then he would. And he didn't regret one moment of the misery he'd inflicted upon his enemies.

He remembered his father's eyes condemning him. Even while his mother wept, his father stood, stone-cold and distant. They didn't understand. And he would never regret his actions. Talia deserved his vengeance upon those that hurt her. Pushing this thought away, he pulled a tin of chew from his pocket and stuffed a pinch between his cheek and gum. Acrid saliva filled his mouth and turning his head; he spat onto the ground. The nicotine gave him a temporary fusion of energy and the long night demanded all the strength he could get. Darkness floated around him and he gazed into the trees. Weak moonlight penetrated the heavy leafy cover of the forest.

Spike pulled his horse to a halt and climbed out of the saddle. Rose climbed down and stood beside him tiredly. Motioning to Brian, he grinned.

"I gotta pee, man." he sauntered off into the darkness on stiff legs. Brian took time to stretch his legs. Sarah walked up beside him, yawned and stretched.

"I'm so sore and tired."

Brian smiled. They were all sore and tired. His back felt as though someone had beat him with a sledgehammer, his joints popping as he twisted and stretched. He pulled the canteen from the saddlebag and took a long drink. Wiping the rim, he handed it to Sarah.

"Not much further. You need to hydrate. You've lost a lot of blood."

Sarah tilted the canteen to her mouth and drank deeply. She saw Rose do the same with Spikes canteen of water.

"I can't wait to see Beth. I've missed her so much."

Brian smiled.

"She's gonna be one happy lady to see you too."

"Are you sure she's gonna be okay? The doctor fixed her?"

"Yes. Beth is strong. She's gonna heal up from the hip surgery just fine," he assured her.

They'd talked on and off through the night; about Beth, about what had happened, about why he'd waited a few days before he set out to rescue her. They talked about Bobby's plans to take the compound and his ties with the Tri-State Alliance. They talked about the shipment of gasoline that the Alliance would be bringing into Massachusetts and how, having been their captive, Sarah had overheard many conversations surrounding Bobby and his plans. All things Roger would need to know. What they didn't talk about was what she'd gone through with Bobby or Gregory. Whenever he tried to broach the subject with her, she shut down.

"I know you've gone through some rough stuff, Sarah. Sometimes it helps to talk about it."

He saw a shadow of pain cross her eyes.

"It is done and over. It makes no sense to talk about it. Leave it alone, okay?"

Nodding, he glanced up when he heard Spike come stumbling through the darkness, zipping the fly on his jeans.

"Feel better?"

"Hell yeah. I'm ready to ride," Spike said then laughed.

Chapter Eight

The meeting took place at the town's library, in the conference room. The brothel in the basement of the building would serve its purpose tonight and Bobby specifically planned it this way. Tonight, they would lay plans to attack the compound; then after the meeting, he would allow his men to visit the basement and have a little fun.

The library was the largest area in town and able to comfortably hold a large gathering. Every single man in Bobby's gang, all hundred and twenty-five of them, showed up. They sat on brown folding chairs, on the carpeted floor, and on top of the hard oak tabletops. He looked out at the crowd of faces and grinned. His force had grown significantly over the past few months. He'd started with just a handful of friends and had built it to this. Clearing his throat, he motioned for Terrence to call the meeting to order. Bobby stood up and moved to the podium. With a roar of confidence, he greeted the crowd.

"Good evening, Alliance members!"

Nods and greetings met him.

"You're probably wondering why the last-minute meeting, so I'll get right to the point," he said, shuffling papers on the podium in front of him.

His hands shook with excitement. His stomach turned queasily. He hated public speaking. Smaller groups were more to his liking. And this group was far beyond small. Clearing his throat and taking a sip of water from the glass in front of him, he looked out at his men.

"Our timeline for taking the compound has been moved up. I don't know how many of you have heard, but that woman we brought in? The blue-eyed mute woman? Well, she managed to kill six of our men today." Grumbles and roars erupted from the crowd, and he held up a hand to silence them.

"I know. I don't know how the bitch managed it. I am assuming she found help and when we find out who? Well, let's just say that person or persons will pay dearly; but back to the topic at hand. I know this woman is heading back to the compound. Now, who knows what she's overhead about the Alliance and our plans, but we must assume she will be warning the compound of the Alliance's coming this way with our fuel. So, we are pushing up our timetable. We cannot let them interfere with our delivery in any way!"

"Damn straight!" a man shouted from the crowd. Bobby looked to see who shouted and smiled when he saw Ray's snarling grin. Bobby gave him a nod and then continued.

"So, be ready to leave early tomorrow

morning. Max will assign twenty-five men to stay behind and guard our interests here. The rest of you, plan to go to battle!"

Grumblings, hoots, and hollers met his ears, and he raised his arm, pumping his fist in the air. His men were more than ready.

"Two last things before I let you hoodlums loose," he snickered and leered, "first, we have a thief among us, and so, at nine o'clock, we will be taking care of him at the town common. Bring your families, instruct your neighbors they are to all attend. We will be having a hanging, boys!"

The crowd erupted with cheers.

"Lastly, after our meeting finishes up here, you boys are more than welcome to visit the ladies downstairs — my treat. But remember, no rough stuff!" he said then laughed loudly. Chuckles and off-colored comments met his ears and smiling he nodded at his men.

"Meeting over."

Bobby let himself out the front door amidst the laughter of his men. There were things to do; otherwise, he would join them in the basement for a little late afternoon fun. It was tempting. He pushed himself toward home. The streets were quiet as he walked the short distance; his mind lost in frenzied thoughts. His boots echoed on the tar. The sun hung low on the horizon, setting the mountains in the distance aglow. The hanging, he hadn't had one in quite some time. It sounded like severe punishment for the man and woman who tried to escape this town, but he needed to set an example. To make the townspeople watch, so they would know what happens when someone crosses him. The man, Jim... Tim... he couldn't remember his name. He didn't give a rat's ass about him, but he hated to lose the girl. Perhaps he needed a different punishment for her?

Smiling, he thought a public whipping would suffice. He could see it in his mind's eye, stripping her from the waist up, tying her to a post and letting Ray dole out the punishment. The sound of the leather strap striking her skin would serve well to work his men into a frenzy. Yes, that should do it nicely. With a skip to his step, he opened the front door to his house and walked back to his office. He shuffled papers on his desk, emptied the overflowing ashtray into the trash can sitting beside the desk and yelled for Amy.

"Amy! Bring me a beer!" When she didn't respond, he yelled again.

"Girl! You'd better be moving your ugly little ass, pronto!" Still, he got for no response. Curling his lips into a sneer, he stormed out of the room and searched each room for her. He found her in the last place he looked.

"Arrrrggggggg!" he screamed as he saw her sitting in the corner, head tilted forward, hands splayed wide open on her lap like pale starfish dying in the sun. She had two ragged gashes in each wrist. Blood, bright and fresh, pooled on the legs of her jeans staining them crimson. He felt his mind snap and a blind rage take over. He welcomed it as he walked over and yanked her dead body up by her long hair. He felt a roar rip from his throat, and he slung her across the room.

"You bitch! You bitch!"

She landed in a tumbled heap on the cream plush carpet, face turned up, and eyes wide, vacant, and accusing. His bladder let loose, and he felt hot urine leak down his leg. He tossed every bit of furniture in the room, splintering a wooden chair, turning over the double bed they'd shared, smashing the nightstands as the splintering of wood filled his ears. Panting, furious sobs ripped his chest apart and his fury drove him to his knees.

He lost it and somewhere, deep in the recesses of his mind, he knew he had.

"See Bobby, even your whores would rather die than be with you," his mother's voice whispered.

He placed his hands over his ears and howled like a wounded animal and rocked himself back and forth, willing her voice to go away.

"No! No! You're wrong!" he sobbed staring at the floor. It was filthy with dust and dirt, dead bugs, empty beer cans, and cigarette butts.

A hard pounding on his front door shook him to his feet, and shaking, he stumbled out of the demolished room and away from Amy's accusing eyes. Snot clung to his upper lip, and with a shaking hand, he wiped it away. He opened the door to see Ray standing on the front porch.

"What!" he snapped.

"Boss, I think you need to come to see this," Ray stuttered, his eyes shifting nervously. Bobby groaned.

"What! What do I need to come to see?"

"Boss, well, ummm, Tim and the girl, ummm…"

"Spit it out, man!" Bobby growled.

"Well, I dunno how they got the knife but, they killed themselves."

Bobby's fist swung out before he even thought about it. He felt his knuckles crack against Ray's jaw. The man stumbled backward.

"You left them unguarded, you idiot!" he screamed. He felt his face flush with rage and his gut clench. Pacing like a caged animal, he stopped and stood over Ray who cowered on the ground.

"Why did you leave them unguarded? Of all the stupid, idiotic things for you to do!"

"I'm sorry boss. I didn't think! I'm sorry!" he stuttered. He looked up into Bobby's wild eyes. He'd screwed up.

"Well, we are having a hanging tonight, so you'd better find me someone to hang!" Bobby snarled then he turned and stormed back into the house, slamming the door behind him.

"It's falling apart, Bobby. It's all burning down," his father crooned softly and then cawed with laughter.

Bobby drove his fist into the wall and stumbled over to his desk. He pulled a baggie of cocaine from the top drawer and snorted up a line. A burning and buzzing sensation filled his mind as the drug worked its magic.

Chapter Nine

Ray stumbled down the street, muttering to himself. He wrung his hands nervously. He moved to the sidewalk and kicked a chunk of broken cement from his path. The town was falling apart, and Bobby had lost his mind. His train had finally run off the rails. It worried him. There were too many people counting on him for him to go and jump off the deep end now. The Alliance wouldn't be happy about his behavior. And where in the hell did Bobby think he'd be able to find a body for hanging tonight? A woman would be easy enough to get; he'd grab one of the whores from the brothel but a man? What man deserved to die for nothing? There were no traitors among Bobby's gang. They were all loyal to him. He'd have to grab one of the town's people. Perhaps the storekeeper over on Ridge Street? Shaking his head, he grimaced.

What a nasty piece of work this turned out to be. He would gladly participate in the hanging of a criminal and a traitor, but to hang an innocent man? It turned his stomach, and he swallowed hard, tasting the saltiness of his blood. He brought his hand up and wiped a trickle of blood from the corner of his mouth and winced. Pouting, he muttered under his breath. Bobby shouldn't have sucker-punched him. That was just wrong.

With a determined tightening to his lips, he made his way to the library. He'd at least cover one problem first. He'd grab the first woman he saw for tonight's little show. But what he didn't know, was that his second solution waited there for him too.

Entering the library, he made his way down through the gloom of the steep stairs to the basement. A musty, putrid smell assaulted his nostrils, and he gagged. These were deplorable conditions, even for an animal. Cells, made from rebar, lined each side of the room. Each cell housed five to seven women. The men were still there, still enjoying the playtime Bobby gave them. Whimpers, cries, and husky laughter echoed through the dank room. Ignoring it, he walked over to the first cell and grabbed a redhead by her hair, dragging her out. She struggled against him, and he backhanded her.

"Don't!" he threatened, his eyes narrowing.

"Hey, Ray? What'cha doing, man?" Jared yelled from one of the cells. He was happily wrapped up in some woman's arms.

"Mind your own!" Ray barked. His eyes scanned the room. He spied a puddle of blood on the floor outside of the third cell in the row and walked toward it. A blonde of about twenty-five, lay sprawled naked across a dirty mattress on the floor, her mouth wide open in a silent scream and her eyes staring vacantly at the ceiling. A leather belt looped around her neck and blood trickled from her mouth. Her head lay at a funny angle. Johnny sat on the floor beside her with his head cradled in his hands, his fingers splayed through his greasy hair.

"What did you do?" Ray roared. He took in the grisly scene in front of him.

Johnny raised his eyes to Ray's and shrugged.

"I didn't mean to man. I didn't mean to kill her," he moaned. "She just wouldn't stop screaming."

Ray smiled bitterly. He'd just found his hanging victim.

∞

Bobby moved slowly, cleaning up the mess in the bedroom. Depression clouded his mind, leaving him feeling sluggish, and his shoulders slumped in defeat. What in the hell was going on? Why was his game so off these past few days? He had so much going for him; his business was thriving, his manpower tripled and grew significantly. The gangs of the Alliance were finally coming together, and the whole of the North East sat there for the taking. So why did everything feel so wrong? A puddle of blood on the floor sparkled garishly as a ray of sunshine from the window cast a glow on it.

A growl formed in the back of his throat. It wasn't! He was just tired. He just needed a moment's peace to regroup. Once they took over the compound, then he'd be able to rest and bask in the glow of victory.

"But boy, you will fail. You are a loser, always have been," his mother's voice whispered.

"You're dead, nothing you say matters anymore," he snapped.

The bonfire lit up the darkness. A crowd, loud and boisterous, gathered in the town park. People crowded the grassy areas, sitting on a mixture of lawn chairs and blankets. The night held a celebratory feel to it and the many voices combined, making a dull roar, while the beer flowed freely. Stars glittered in the black sky, and a breeze cooled sweaty skin as people milled about. Henry stood beside Bobby in the center of the gazebo. Cathy stood front row in the audience; her eyes shining with pride, and her hands clasped in prayer against her chest. She wore a pretty pink sweater and had her hair braided into a coil on the top of her head.

"People! We are gathered here tonight," Henry said, his voice booming and bringing silence to the audience. The boys had cleared the park of picnic tables and in the center of the horseshoe pit stood a pole with a woman bound to it, naked from the waist up, her bare back exposed. Left of the horseshoe pit stood a tall maple tree, its limbs thick, and its branches just greening up with spring buds.

"Because we have a thief in our midst! This man," he yelled pointing to Johnny, who lay hogtied on the floor in front of him, "dared take from all of us. A thief who wanted to have for himself, denying all others! This is a sin of the greatest proportion in these times when everyone must work together for the common good of all! He has been found guilty, along with his whore, and they shall suffer the punishments earned tonight," he continued. A roar rose from the crowd as his voice boomed righteousness.

"A man who shall gather for only himself is immoral! A sinner of gluttony and greed! God sent this great plague to wipe out the heathens, the sinners, the whores, and the wicked. But HE needs our help in raising a righteous community. HE needs our devotion to do HIS work no matter how distasteful it might be. HE asks of us only obedience. We are blessed, my brothers and sisters, blessed that our God spared us the plague that took so many in the early days. His judgment upon us is one of love and compassion. And we cannot fail in our duties to carry out his punishments for those who sin against HIM."

Bobby stood behind Henry and smiled. It was going beautifully. The man pumped up the crowd to an almost frenzied fever. He gazed out over the faces and saw the growing bloodlust. Yes, this was going perfectly.

"For the whore, she shall receive thirty

lashes for that is what the Lord commands of me. For the gentleman, he will receive death by hanging."

The crowd exploded with cheers and fist pumps. Henry smiled widely, and behind him, Bobby grinned and laughed while rubbing his hands together in excitement.

Part Two – The Reckoning

Chapter Ten

Beth awoke from the thick haze of sleep, to the sounds of hurried footsteps and hushed voices. It took her eyes a moment to focus, and she slowly inched her legs off the bed. Her hip protested by sending a jolt of nauseating pain up through her back. Something was going on. Something was wrong. She could tell by the hushed voices outside of her closed door and the rattle of medical equipment as it clanked onto a table with an ear jarring clang Sucking in a deep breath, she grabbed for her crutches and struggled onto her feet. Her hospital gown blew open in the back with the movement, and she fought with the ties to cover herself as a chill moved over her skin.

Careful not to put any weight on the injured hip, she hobbled on her crutches to the door and swung it open with a grunt. The bare tiles of the floor were cold on her feet. Jill, seeing her, rushed over to her side and Beth could tell, by the expression on the nurse's face, that it pissed her off that she got up and came out of her room.

"No, you need to go back to your bed

right now."

Beth grimaced, ignoring her order. "What's happening?"

Jill rolled her eyes and threw up her hands in frustration.

"They're back. Brian and Spike are back, and they have Sarah. She's injured though. Let me help you back to your bed. I'll let you know how she is the moment I examine her," she said. "I promise, Beth. As soon as I know anything, I will come and tell you."

Beth spied a chair in the corner of the exam room and shook her head. Stubbornly, she pointed to the chair. "No, help me to that chair. I'll stay outta the way, I promise."

Jill knew this was an argument she wouldn't win; she guided Beth to the chair with a frustrated sigh.

"Doc is on his way. I'll be right back. Don't you dare move, you hear me? I swear you're one stubborn woman."

Beth nodded. Anxiety pulsed through her, and she absently chewed on her fingernail. They were back with Sarah. Tears stung her eyes, and she brushed them away.

The room smelled of bleach. Weak, early morning light filtered through the window and Beth could see the rising sun in the distance. Where were they? Why did it take them so long to carry Sarah in? Impatiently, she drummed her fingers on the arm of the chair, fighting the temptation to get up and hobble her way outside. Before she could give in to that temptation, Brian came rushing into the room with an unconscious Sarah in his arms, Jessie padded in right behind him, her nails clicking on the tiled floor. Seeing Beth, she went over and sat beside her. Beth curled her fingers in the dog's hair then stroked her head. Brian glanced at her quickly, nodded, then laid Sarah on the examination table. Beth could see the blood staining the front of Sarah's shirt and her breath caught in the back of her throat.

"What happened?"

"She's been shot. I patched her up, but she's lost a lot of blood," Brian replied, grimacing.

Doc rushed through, his hair tousled from sleep and a shadow of stubble on his cheeks and chin. Jill stood right behind him. With gentle but quick movements, he cut the shirt from Sarah and pulled away the bandage to reveal a four-inch-long, deep wound. It already showed signs of infection. Brian stood helplessly by the table until Jill ushered him over to where Beth sat.

"Brian, take Beth back to her room. We need room to work, and you two are just in the way."

Brian nodded and reached to help Beth up. She glared at him in protest.

"No, I want to be here when she wakes up!"

Brian clenched his teeth in frustration.

"Damn it, Beth! For once don't argue." As tired and stressed as he felt, dealing with her stubbornness was the last thing he wanted to do right now.

Glaring at him, she brushed his hand away and struggled to stand. With an awkward hobbled gait, she made her way back to her room, feeling him close behind her.

Sitting on the bed, she sighed deeply. She felt a pang of guilt wash through her. She glanced at Brian standing by the window. He looked exhausted. Tired lines framed his eyes and his mouth. His shoulders slumped with fatigue.

"I'm sorry," she murmured. "I've just been so worried about both of you."

Brian nodded, his gaze falling on the common center of the compound, watching the darkness of night slip away, into the gray light of early morning. His eyes burned with grit from the trail, and he rubbed his hand across them. Turning to Beth, he gave her a tired smile.

"It was a hard trip and once I scrounge up a cup of coffee and wash up a bit, I'll come back and fill you in. Be patient, Beth, please."

She nodded pulling the blanket from her bed across her chilled legs and feet.

"I will. Go get some coffee."

While Brian went in search of a cup of coffee, she pulled a set of clothes from her backpack and struggled into them. They smelled freshly washed, and she smiled. Mary Anne must've laundered them for her. The shirt proved easy to put on; the pants were a different story. Biting back tears of frustration, she maneuvered her bad leg in first. She clenched her teeth against a moan of pain while she got her other leg in. Slowly she pulled them up over her hips, being extra careful not to brush the bandages that lined from her hip to mid-thigh. She couldn't believe how much the simple task, of putting on pants, exhausted her. She sat on the edge of the bed and panted from the exertion.

A light tap on her door startled her, and she glanced to see Jill poke her head through.

"Sarah's fine. Doc stitched her up and gave her a starter dose of antibiotic. She's sleeping comfortably now."

Beth breathed out a big sigh of relief and smiled.

"Can I go see her now?"

Jill nodded. "Yes, you can." Then she raised an eyebrow as she saw Beth fully dressed.

"You're gonna end up busting those stitches wide open, Beth. You gotta take it easy. Give yourself a chance to heal," she scolded. Beth nodded.

"I'm fine. I feel fine."

Jill helped her to Sarah's room to wait.

Beth crooned softly and smiled when

Sarah opened her glass blue eyes.

"Hi, baby girl," she whispered.

Sarah hitched back a sob and reached her good arm toward her. Beth hugged her back tightly.

"I'm so sorry, so sorry, baby," she cried bending her face into Sarah's hair.

"It wasn't your fault, Beth."

Snapping her head up in shock, she looked deep into Sarah's eyes and squealed.

"You're talking?" Sarah laughed and nodded.

"Yes, you noticed," she teased then yawned. The pain medication that Doc gave her started to kick in. Beth smiled and laughed in delight.

"I knew you could talk. I just knew it!"

Sarah nodded sleepily. She felt Beth pull and tuck the blankets around her.

"Go to sleep, baby. We'll talk later. I'm just so thankful you're back and safe now."

∞

Brian stepped into her room, and Beth saw that he'd showered and shaved. The scent of lavender soap clung to his skin. He carried two cups of coffee and placed one on the bedside stand for her. She saw that he looked much better, not so scruffy and a lot less frazzled.

"I missed you. I've been so worried," Beth said. Her legs were tired from pacing, or in her case, hobbling around trying to get some strength built back up. She now had them propped up on a pillow.

"I'm glad you missed me," he teased, but his eyes reflected more. Did she see hope? Longing? Beth couldn't tell.

"C'mon outside. We're having a meeting with Roger to discuss what we've found out about Bobby and his gang. We'll fill you in on what has happened. There are some things we all need to think about." Brian said then drained his cup and set it on the stand beside hers.

Raising an eyebrow in curiosity, Beth nodded then glanced toward Sarah's room.

"She's still asleep," Brian said. He wrapped an arm around her to help her off of the bed. She leaned into him heavily. The strong smell of lavender soap drifted up to her nose. It felt good having his arm around her.

"She's gonna be fine, that is one strong girl."

And it was true. For someone so young, so abused, Sarah possessed the fighting spirit of a warrior. He admired her for that.

They approached the table and Beth saw some faces she recognized, and several she didn't. Roger, who sat in a chair next to the picnic table, jumped up to pull a chair over for Beth. Mary Anne had her face buried in her notebook, and she looked up and smiled when Beth sat down. Cain sat next to a woman Beth didn't know, and Spike leaned against the opposite end of the table sipping on a cup of steaming coffee. Two other men sat on chairs next to the table along with Julie and Jill. Doc stood off to the side, his eyes staring off into the distance and she could tell, his mind was far away.

Introductions were made all the way around, and Beth nodded and smiled at each person.

"Rose helped Sarah escape," Brian said as Beth glanced at him in question. As if hearing them, the young woman smiled shyly and nodded.

"Nice to meet you, Rose, and thank you so much for helping us get our Sarah home," Beth murmured.

She gently hugged the other woman. She wrinkled her nose at the rancid, sweaty odor that wafted from the woman and into her nostrils. How long had it been since this poor woman had seen a shower she wondered? Her breath caught in her throat as she felt the thinness of her. They'd all lost weight over the past months, but this girl was skeletal! It was apparent she hadn't probably eaten a good meal in quite some time.

"Okay, let's get started," Roger announced. He took a stand at the head of the table. "Now, Brian and Spike have filled me in quite a bit on what happened and what they'd learned of Bobby and his gang. We've got quite a shitload of trouble heading our way."

All eyes were on him, and Beth studied each face while he talked. She saw expressions of fear and anger.

"So? We go at them sooner!" Julie snapped. As part of the defense team, she portrayed a no-nonsense, get it done type of attitude.

"That would be fine, if we knew what we'd be walking into, but going in blind is only gonna get us killed," Calvin replied.

Julie, Calvin, and Thomas were the leaders of the defense teams. All strong personalities, all with military backgrounds. They were instrumental in planning and executing the plans that kept the compound safe.

Brian stood up and coughed lightly. He held a cup of coffee in his hands. "I can help with that."

All eyes turned to him.

"Right now, I know Bobby's group is at least a hundred plus strong. They are confident almost to the point of reckless. They will be heading this way. So, the question is, do we take the fight to them? Or do we hold our ground here?"

Spike nodded and stood up.

"We're thinking an ambush—the same way they did to us a few weeks ago. Like Brian said, this man and his gang are reckless, bold. They don't believe anyone can stop them. So, let's surprise them. One thing we did learn when we were forward observing the town. Bobby is lazy, and so are his men. They won't take the trails to come here and trust me; he is coming here! They will stick to the main road. And it is there that we should attack and keep them from ever reaching the compound."

Beth listened and watched. Murmurs spread around the table, and heads nodded. Mary Anne pressed a hand over her eyes tiredly, worry showing on her face.

Rose stood up, drawing the attention of the group. "I have spent the last four months as a prisoner of Bobby and his gang. They came into my town in February. They killed my parents and took my younger sister and me. My younger sister is still there. She is only seven years old, and my heart is shattering just thinking about what is happening to her! You have no idea of what they are forcing the prisoners to do. Mainly women and children," she said then shuddered. Her eyes filled with tears. Mary Anne reached over and grabbed her hand gently, nodding her head for her to continue.

"He uses women and children for slaves, trade, and, sex trafficking. The men he uses as part of his force. They have no choice. Either join him or die. He's going from town to town, killing and pillaging. I spent a long time in his house for what he calls training," she spat, red-faced with shame, "and I saw the map on his wall, listened in on his meetings with his men. He intends to take this compound and the whole of the North East one way or another. He's part of a bigger group called the Alliance, and they have gangs from out of Boston and New York. They've not yet formed into one group, but when they do, they will number into the thousands," she finished.

Beth saw dark scowls, anger, fear, and shocked expressions around the table.

Spike stood up and cast a warm glance at Rose. On the journey, he talked with her about what she'd been through. She spoke to him of her life before the event, about her little sister. What she'd told him gave him chills. Bobby and his gang were animals. The cruelties, the tortures of the women and children, of the town's people they held prisoner. Just to name a few things he'd done.

"So, do we agree? We ambush them?" Spike asked.

Julie, Thomas, and Calvin all nodded. Roger, seeing their agreement nodded as well.

It's time they took the fight to the enemy. It's time to free the town.

"We'll meet back here at noon. We've got to gather our groups, fill them in and outline our strategy," Thomas said. His eyes were those of a soldier preparing for war.

Beth's mind spun with turmoil. She

wanted to grab Sarah, Jessie, and Brian, and just run! She wanted to be back on the trail and didn't care about the hunger, the exhaustion, the cold, and the mud. Part of her wanted to believe this problem was not her problem. Another part of her knew and felt guilty, because she felt it was because of her that Bobby and his gang were now planning an attack. She felt guilty that she brought this miserable excuse for a human being, Bobby, directly into the path of this compound.

Hatred burned deep in her heart and she clenched her fists in anger. Why couldn't people pull together and form communities? Why did people like Bobby feel the need to harm and destroy? She thought of her neighbor and how he attacked her in her kitchen so long ago. How many did he hurt before her? And why hadn't she paid attention to her neighborhood—tried to pull her neighbors together to help each other survive? Had she been buried so deep in her misery that she couldn't see the forest for the trees? Shaking her head, she gritted her teeth until they ached. The early morning sun failed to chase away the chill that coursed through her body.

Brian moved beside her and crouched in front of her chair. He looked deep into her eyes and saw the turmoil there. "You know I have to do this, right?"

Beth nodded. Yes, he did have to do this.

She knew that. He would help stop Bobby and his gang, once and for all. For her sake, for Sarah's sake, and for all those others that this man had hurt.

"You just promise me. Promise me you will come back!" Beth hissed with tears in her eyes. Brian looked at her with an expression of determination and nodded. It was a promise he intended to keep. He hadn't wanted this war. But he felt he had no choice but to fight it. Too many men like Bobby touched his life in one way or another; touched it in ways that seared pain into his soul. He'd be damned if he would let Bobby ever hurt Sarah or Beth again. And the only way to ensure that would never happen again would be to take care of the gang for good, in the only way he knew how. With blood!

Mary Anne sat beside Beth. She grasped her hand and squeezed it.

"I know you're scared. I'm scared too. But trust me when I say, this is what our men have trained for. They won't let this gang within ten miles of us here. My Roger will see to that!" she assured Beth.

When the others got up to leave, Doc moved over beside Jill, and Beth listened in on their conversation.

"I want you to grab Grace, Eli, Max, Evan, and Tillie. We're gonna need them," he murmured. Jill nodded, set her lips into a firm grimace, and rushed off to do what he asked.

"Mary Anne, can you assign three people to put together medical trauma bags for us? We'll need four of them for each medic."

Mary Anne nodded.

"Who are you sending out?"

"Grace, Eli, Max, and Tillie. Evan will stay here with Jill and get the hospital ready. We'll do triage out in the field. God help us," he said softly then swore.

Beth groaned. They were sending medics along with the army. She felt helpless and useless. As an EMT, she could've been helping out in the field. But because of her broken hip, she could do nothing! Pulling herself up from the chair, she turned to Mary Anne. Nervous anxiety crawled through her like an electric current.

"Is there anything I can do to help? I can't stand this! I can't stand to sit back like an invalid and do nothing!" she growled.

Chapter Eleven

Bobby led the men out into the early morning darkness. A heavy mist dampened the air, and he pulled his jacket tighter around him. The festivities of the night before left them all sluggish and tired. Many angry, petulant glares met him while they all assembled at the crack of dawn. The public hanging and whipping lasted long into the night and pumped the men up for the fight ahead of them. A smile curled his lips as he thought of the night before. The drinking, the cocaine flowing, the screams with each strike of the lash as it hit the whore's bare back. The faces of his men while they watched greedily and hungrily. And then the faces of the townspeople, the horror and fear of their expressions as he forced them to attend and observe. It served a good lesson to those who might entertain the idea of ever crossing him.

He'd left twenty-five men to stand guard in town. The rest were with him. They would make their way through town after town on their way to the compound. They were a show of force that would instill fear in everyone who saw them pass through. He knew that the mute bitch and Rose would not be able to reach the compound before him and his men. They were traveling on foot. He and his men traveled on horseback. No, he didn't worry about them tipping off the compound. Licking his lips, he thought of the strategy he and his commanders had laid out. They came up with plenty of surprises and the perfect plan. Feeling pretty pleased with himself, he kicked his horse, sending her into a run. The damp wind hit his face and he grinned.

He thought of his plan. It was simple really, he would burn the compound down! By the time he finished, it would be nothing but a pile of rubble, ashes, and dead bodies. A few miles outside of the compound, his group would split into four teams: north, south, east, and west. They would attack from all sides simultaneously.

At first, it would be with Molotov cocktails, sending fire into the heart of the compound, which would be followed by the little explosive surprises Ray had made for him. The firebombing would send the men, woman, and children scurrying like little vermin. Then he and his men would move in, take down any resistance, and the compound would be theirs. All of its supplies, and all of its whores. Then he would wait. He would wait for that mute bitch to arrive. And boy, did he have a surprise planned for her. She would pay dearly for killing six of his men.

Laughing softly, he pulled a cigarette from his pack, lit a match, and took a deep drag; enjoying the burn in his lungs. He stared off into the distance. His mind teased him with ideas of what he planned to do to the girl. On either side of the road the thick woods hummed with the call of birds and insects, and the dark inky night faded into the gray of early dawn. The air felt crisp, misty and cool; perfect for the early morning ride.

∞

Mitch Smalley tossed a cracker over his shoulder and watched the rooster dive for it. Shaking his head, he laughed. How in the hell had he ended up with this freakin bird? Stuffing the remainder of his lunch in his saddlebag, he mounted the nag and gave her a soft pat on her neck before kicking her gently on the flanks to get her moving. Before they'd gone even a hundred yards he heard the pounding of hooves coming from behind him, around the bend in the road. With a quick nudge, he led the horse into a thick stand of brush at the side of the road and crouched low. He looked at the rooster and hissed a warning. The scent of pine filled his senses. The thick, green leaf cover hid him, and he peeked through the branches of a low hanging limb.

"One squawk and I'll ring your neck."

The rooster looked at him with its beady eyes and growled.

"I mean it, Peckerhead!" Mitch whispered.

He watched a large group of riders pass a

few yards away from him. His gun loosely grasped in his hand but ready, just in case. He didn't like the looks of this. Many of the men he noticed wore gang tats on their bare arms. His stomach sank. He intently observed them from his hiding spot. Disjointed conversations met his ears, snippets of information, and laughter. He wondered where they were going, and his gut told him that wherever they were headed would soon see a whole lot of trouble.

He considered himself a soldier. He'd seen war, tasted it in his soul; not any war overseas, but the war in his homeland. Years of nightmares plagued him from what he'd experienced on the streets. He'd been in law enforcement and was fully aware of the horrors and realities of what humans were capable of. His experience included SWAT and Anti-Human Trafficking. He had fought in the trenches, on his own soil. And it had left a lifelong stain on his soul.

Never did he think the United States would fall. Never did he think he'd have to see combat again. His heart hardened at the thought, how the many towns he traveled through had now become nothing but ghost towns. Filled with violence and destruction, the towns had an aura of hopelessness that hovered in the air like a heavy, black cloud. Rubbing a thumb across his lips, he continued to watch the riders pass.

This group before him reminded him of the gangs he'd seen in the inner cities. Every town they touched burned, along with the slaughter of every man, woman, and child.

Peckerhead growled softly by his side and he looked down at the rooster.

"Yup, wonder what these folks are up to? Methinks something stinks about this. I say we mosey on back a bit and follow. What do you think?"

The rooster, dubbed Peckerhead, hissed and bobbed his head.

"Yeah, I agree," Mitch whispered then laughed softly.

"You know? I love fried chicken, right?"

Peckerhead growled and fluffed his white feathers.

As he waited and watched he drifted in a swamp of memories. He hailed from Herington, Kansas; spent his law enforcement career in Kansas City. When the event had hit, he'd been traveling across the United States visiting his brotha's and sisters, friends that he considered family. He'd met with Claude out of California, Joe in Wisconsin, Alan in Kentucky. They were all members of the Truth Seekers. The event hit when he was far up into the North East, where he'd spent weeks in New Hampshire at Naomi Stilters' compound. Every one of the Truth Seekers, and their families, had all built compounds. They were scattered from one end of the country to the other. Except for him. He was a nomad, a wanderer. His feet had had a tough time staying planted in any one location. But that didn't keep him from adding to his experience and knowledge, or in the helping others.

Now he found himself on his way to see Roger at his compound in Connecticut. He'd left Naomi's compound two weeks ago. He started his journey driving his old beat-up Ranger until that ran out of gas, somewhere on the border of Massachusetts and New Hampshire. After walking for several days, he happened upon a farm. That was where he had picked up the old nag, along with the tag-along rooster. The farmhouse he'd stopped at had been abandoned and ransacked. But he'd been able to find enough supplies to hold himself over. If worse came to worse, he'd cook the damn rooster if he got hungry enough.

He followed the group for miles, staying just a bit behind, ghosting them from the deep woods. He watched with growing horror, as in each town they stopped, they attacked anyone unlucky enough to be in their path. They were the worst kind of animals—the dangerous kind, ones who relished in the gang violence mentality.

Stopping for a rest, he pulled the map from his jacket pocket and swore softly. He traced the route they were on with his finger and saw it led straight to the compound where Roger lived. There was nothing he could do to warn Roger about the danger coming his way.

He looked at the rooster and shook his head and muttered under his breath. "I wish the heck you could fly!"

Peckerhead gave an indignant squawk and glared at him.

Climbing on his horse, he stayed hidden in the shadows, trailing them. He sent up a silent prayer that they would veer off in another direction and head away from his friend's domain. But as prayers would have it, it seemed that no one was awake and listening.

∞

A fluttering of activity flowed through the compound as everyone scattered, getting prepared. Mary Anne looked at Beth, who was hobbling back and forth, her eyes darting everywhere trying to see where she could be of help. The girl was as nervous as a cat on a tin roof.

"Beth!" she snapped, getting the woman's attention.

Beth turned to her.

"You can help with dinner. We've got fifty chickens to slaughter and pluck."

Beth's eyes widened in horror. Slaughter and pluck? She'd never seen a chicken, other than the ones in the little Styrofoam packs at the meat department of her local grocery. Was this woman serious? She wanted to help, but the idea of handling a live chicken made her cringe. Not to mention the fact that they were on the brink of war and all hell was about to come raining down on the whole compound. She thought it was crazy, thinking of food at a time like this! They should be doing something, but slaughtering chickens was not the something Beth had in mind!

"Are you serious? Food? Chickens? We're about to go to war!"

Mary Anne nodded her head.

"Yup, you are right, Beth. But, in spite of all this, in spite of our men and women going off to fight, we still need to eat! Work still needs to be done here, in the compound! We can't and won't just sit here, twiddling our thumbs and worrying. It does no one any good. When those men and women get back, they're going to be hungry and tired. If they bring back any prisoners, they too are going to be hungry and tired. We need to prepare!"

Beth nodded, feeling the heat of shame redden her face. Mary Anne was right. Life didn't stop because of her panic.

"I'm sorry. I'm just overwhelmed, stressed, and freakin out."

Mary Anne laughed. She too was freaking out, but she wasn't about to let anyone else see that. If she gave in to the panic that chewed at her stomach, she'd end up just sitting down and crying, and that wouldn't do anyone any good.

"Okay, back to the chickens then?"

At the look of horror that crossed Beth's face, Mary Anne burst out laughing.

"It's not hard, and you can do it sitting down."

Beth nodded and rolled her eyes. Good God, what had she gotten herself into?

Jenny set up the table for the chicken duties. She smiled at Beth shyly. She placed a sharp knife on the table in front of her. Beth grimaced. A kettle of water set over an open pit, boiling furiously. On the table were knives of every size, a basket for the feathers, and a plastic cooler, filled with cold water from the well. Beth slipped an apron over her head which Mary Anne had handed to her. The coolness of the morning gave way to searing afternoon heat and Beth found herself sweating beneath the cotton apron. She peered up at the cloudless blue sky and sighed. It was turning out to be a hot day.

"Okay, it's a simple process. We kill the chickens, cut off their heads, eviscerate them then dip their bodies in boiling water to help loosen the feathers," Mary Anne instructed. Beth wrinkled her nose.

"I don't have to kill them, do I?"

Mary Anne laughed softly.

"Well honey, I think they'd be mighty upset if we tried to pluck them while they are alive!" she said, shaking her head. Beth grinned sheepishly.

"You know what I mean."

Mary Anne laughed and placed the first dead chicken in front of Beth. She then began to show her how to cut into it.

"First we cut off the head. I won't make you kill them, but you do need to know how to dress them out. Once the head is off, we hang them upside down over here, "she said. She took the bird and hung it by its legs, attaching it to a long pole, between two sawhorses. "This is to drain the blood. We save the blood in this pail so we can feed it to the hogs later. Once done, we then turn it over on its back, find the Y between its breastbone and anus. We make a small incision like this," she said. Taking the point of her knife, she made two small vertical cuts that met in a vee at the bottom of the tail section. Sliding two fingers in, she tugged and pulled out the anus and intestines. Beth felt her stomach jump with nausea as she watched.

"We do this so that none of the excrement gets into the meat. Then we take our knife, make a longwise cut right up to the breastbone, open it, and bring out the rest of the intestines, heart, liver, and stuff. The heart, liver, and gizzards we save and use for stews."

Beth watched intently, biting back the urge to get up and hobble away. The odor of the dead chicken hit her nose. Blood stained Mary Anne's small hands as she made quick work of the bird. It took her from start to finish about ten minutes to gut, clean, pluck, and dash the body into a cold bath. The screech and death squawk of another hen met Beth's ears. Part of her was fascinated with the process, but another part of her recoiled in horror. She knew she would never look at another chicken the same after this.

Grimacing, she set to work helping Mary Anne, Ginger, Connie, Jenny, and Tempy harvest the chickens that would be the group's supper that evening. It was hot, hard, sweaty work, but once she got past the gruesomeness of it, she found herself loving every minute of the work. Smiling to herself, she couldn't wait for Sarah to wake up so she could tell her all about it.

Wiping her hands down after rinsing them in a basin of cold water, Beth set to help by cutting the chicken up into more manageable pieces. There were four large plastic coolers filled to the brim with whole, fresh birds. Mary Anne and Jenny brought large cutting boards to the table and handed Beth a chicken. Chatting, they set to work and for the first time in a very long time, Beth found she enjoyed herself. These women were knowledgeable, kind, and friendly. And her hands were busy. It felt good.

They took the chicken pieces; put them in a big pot of boiling water and cooked them until the meat fell from the bones, the meat then would go into a hearty stew that would feed the community. In another pot of water, they threw the bones, skin, and organs in to simmer for the day. It would cook down into a savory bone broth for future meals: bean soups, pastas, and rice. It would also be good over the coming winter for those who might fall ill to colds and flu. Nothing would go to waste. The bones would then be ground up and used to feed the hogs. It demonstrated an efficient use of the chickens, and Beth shook her head in amazement.

"Dang, I can't believe all of this will come from just these birds?"

Mary Anne smiled and nodded. "Yup. Waste not, want not. That's what I was always taught."

"I was never taught this. When we ate roasted chicken or fried chicken, what we didn't eat got thrown into the trash," Beth replied a bit guiltily. She slid her shoes from her hot feet and curled her toes in the cool grass beneath the table. She thought of how much she had wasted in her lifetime, and it made her cringe.

"I'll teach you how to can the bone broth tomorrow if you're up to it," Mary Anne said. Beth nodded eagerly. She would love to learn to can. Anything that would up her skill in survival.

"I would love that."

∞

Brian sat with one hip propped on the

edge of the table, sipping a cup of coffee, staring down at the map spread out in front of him. Spike circled in red where he thought the men should position themselves. Everyone murmured and nodded. The first wave would head out in an hour followed by two more groups of men and women an hour later who would station themselves a mile below the first wave just in case any of Bobby's gang slipped through the initial ambush. They planned their ambush up on Diamond Ridge, which looked down onto Pyson Gap Road, the only road leading to the compound. They bet that Bobby and his men would be traveling it. They were far too confident and lazy to go over the trails.

Moving from the edge of the table to another table, Brian laid his rifle, a Ruger AR-556 semi-automatic, to clean it. He could feel eyes on him, and he turned to the group and smiled.

The rifle had belonged to one of the guards at the prison. He didn't need it anymore, Brian shrugged. "Dead men can't shoot." He quipped to himself.

Noticing how they looked at his strange expression, he quickly recovered. "Don't want no mishaps out there, right?"

After he finished, he got up, slung the rifle over his shoulder, grabbed his empty cup and rinsed in the barrel of water at the edge of the lean-to, and cut his eyes to Spike.

"I'm gonna go and see how Beth is

doing." Spike nodded. They would be in the first wave to leave, along with fifty others. He could see Brian was edgy, nervous. They all were. He thought of Rose and her sister, of his promise to the young woman. He hoped he could keep it. A cough from Roger brought his attention back to the group.

"So, I think Mark stays here with one group to protect the compound in case any of Bobby's boys slip by us."

Mark shook his head, arguing.

"No! I want to be out there with you all. Leave Cain here. He's better at organizing things than I am."

Roger turned and scowled at the young man.

"Boy! You'll do as I say!"

Mark grimaced. He didn't want to be left behind. But he'd do what Roger said.

"Bella can stay too. She's not experienced enough to be in this fight," Roger instructed. Bella was a twenty-one-year-old hot head. She trained day in and day out for the past few months along with twenty others. Max worked them hard, but Roger had his misgivings about their battle-ready status. He thought her too green, too quick-tempered and too impulsive to be out there in the field with them.

"I think she's ready. And hell, Roger, all of them are ready. Yes, they are green, but they gotta get their feet wet sometime," Max replied sternly. Roger nodded and squinted his eyes at the glare of the mid-day sun. The man was right. But they, the trainees, only knew of mock battles. The real shit hadn't hit the compound yet. Dying was real. The bullets and blood would be real. It would not be the minor skirmishes they faced in the past. It would not be a training session where everyone got to get up after the mock battle and walked away. Good Lord, some of the trainees were barely eighteen, and then others were well into their sixties and seventies! These folks should not have to fight. The kids should be out dating and raising hell, the older folk sitting home on their porches enjoying retirement. Shaking his head, he rubbed a tired hand across his face.

"You're right. Get them all ready," he murmured. "And God forgive us."

Brian smiled. He watched Beth at the picnic table with Jenny and Mary Anne, glad they gave her something to do. She was a funny woman, at once fierce and independent but on the other side, unsure and doubtful, quite the combination. His heart gave a small tug as he gazed at her, the sun shining on her shoulders and her hands busily working. Why did she intrigue him? She was the biggest pain in the ass, mouthy and stubborn, and had a fiery temper. But he also saw something else. Her fierce protectiveness for those she cared for, her unwavering persistence. Shaking his head, he walked over to her and sat beside her. She smelled of soap, barnyard, and sunshine — quite the curious combination.

"I'll be leaving soon. If things go bad, and Bobby's men get through us, you do what you have to and protect Sarah." He then slipped one of his knives into her hand. Beth nodded. Her fingers slid around the smooth grip of the knife handle. She had two guns that she wouldn't hesitate to use, and if she needed to, she'd use the knife. It wasn't like she hadn't stabbed anyone before, she thought. Images of her neighbor lying on her kitchen floor floated back to haunt her.

Her throat constricted with tears. This man, he saved her and Sarah from certain death, he fed them and stayed with them through the mud, the rain and the cold. He had walked miles alongside them. He didn't have to; she knew that. He could've just walked away. But he hadn't.

"I don't care what happens out there. You come back to me."

Brian smiled and nodded. "I'll do my best, and I will try."

With that, he bent and kissed her lightly on the cheek. Yes, he would do his best. There was something here he wanted to explore a little more. He bent and whispered into her ear.

"Take care of Sarah and yourself," then standing, he glanced at her one more time before turning and walking away. She watched as he walked back to the group of men getting ready to leave. A single tear slid down her cheek, and she hastily wiped it away. Mary Anne wrapped a warm arm around her.

"My Roger will make sure they all come home, Beth," she whispered. Beth nodded. She sure hoped Mary Anne was right.

Chapter Twelve

Spike, Brian, Roger and their group set to the woods just before dusk. Shadows broke, long and heavy. The men scattered, behind hills, brush, rocks, and trees. Brian chose a large boulder about fifty feet off the road and settled in behind it, sitting on a soft bed of dried leaves. If his estimation proved correct, they should be hearing the clip-clop of horse hooves coming their way soon. He'd estimated a good two days by road from where Bobby had planted himself in the small town of Lee, Massachusetts. He reached down and slid his knife from its sheath, pulled the stone from his saddlebag, and with slow, methodical movements brought the blade to a glistening sharpness. There would be wet work ahead. Of that, he could be sure.

The scent of earth, grass, and pine filled his nostrils, and he breathed deep, filling his lungs till they felt like they would burst. For so long, he'd yearned for the smell of just this. In prison, the only scents that he smelled were of the cleaning solution they used on the floors and toilets. His stomach clenched with anticipation, with anxiousness. He'd always been this way before a fight, even in prison when he would plan an attack against a foe who threatened to unseat his position, he'd gotten this same uneasy, nervous, gut-clenching feeling. He continued sliding his knife across the stone, calming himself with the soft, monotonous sound of it, feeling his shoulders and back relax.

"We've got everyone in position. You ready for this?" Spike asked. He kept his voice low and soft.

Brian gazed up at him with a chilly expression, then let his eyes slide into the darkening shadows of the forest.

"Ready," he replied, then ran his thumb across the blade and watched as a fine bead of blood appeared. With a quick movement of his hand, he slid it back into the sheath.

"You kept the medics back a bit, right?" Brian asked. Once the bullets started flying, he didn't want to worry about any of them getting caught in the fray. Max possessed enough experience that he could, and would, handle a combat situation, but the other two were reasonably green.

Spike nodded.

"Yup, they have radios. They'll come when the fighting's over. Hopefully, it won't be any of our men they have to help."

Brian shook his head. It would be their men and Bobby's men. Battles couldn't be fought without casualties from both sides. But he could understand Spike's wishful thinking.

He replied with a sigh. "To God's ears, my friend."

Spike stood and moved back to his

position fifty yards or so to the left, behind a tall and thick oak tree. Closing his eyes, he sent up a silent prayer and hoped God had his ears tuned in. And he asked for forgiveness for what he was about to do. It needed to work. With Roger and his group on the left side of the road, himself, Spike and their group on the right, there would be no way Bobby and his men would be able to escape the hell that was about to rain down on them.

Coming into this fight, Brian had two goals. One, to take down as many men as he could whether it be through bullet or knife, anything, to keep them from reaching the compound. Two, and the most important to him, to make sure Bobby would die by his hand. For what he did to Beth and Sarah, for what he'd done to so many others like them. He hated the Bobby's of the world. He hated them with a blackness that often dragged him to the depths of blood lust. Talia, his baby sister, she had suffered at the hands of men just like Bobby. And those men paid dearly for her suffering. If this meant he'd go to hell when he died, then so be it. He'd gladly suffer the fires of hell and shake hands with the devil if that's what it took to scrub this earth of all the men like Bobby.

∞

Mitch followed about a quarter of a mile behind the group. Shadows danced among the trees as the sun sank below the horizon and the woods around him darkened. He glanced up at the half moon as it drifted in and out of the clouds. It would give just enough light for him to guide the nag through the obstacles of the woods. Peckerhead followed a few yards behind stopping every so often to peck a bug from the ground.

He carried an AK-47 across his back and a Glock 22 on his hip. Strapped in a sheath on his chest was a 13-inch tanto blade. In his boot, he carried another knife, this one smaller but no less deadly in his experienced hands. Law enforcement taught him that. Always be prepared. A growl from Peckerhead brought a smile to his lips, and he turned his head.

"Stay quiet! You give us away, and I swear, I'll be the first to fry you up in a hot pan of grease, my friend." The rooster peered at him and fluffed his feathers.

The volley of shots in the distance sent him jumping down from his horse. With a quick flick of his hands, he tied the reins of the horse to the nearest tree and grabbed the rifle from his back, running up the embankment on the left of the road.

"Stay here," he hissed to the rooster.

With silent steps, he made his way through the woods toward the sounds of the gunshots. The group he had been following was now taking hits from either side of the road. He watched as men scrambled from their horses, looking for cover. Spying a log, he rested his rifle on it and laid flat on his stomach. Peering through the scope, he looked up into the woods on the left side of the road. A tug, then pouncing on his legs startled him, and he whipped around to see the rooster perched on the back of his legs.

"Oh, you listen well, you foolish Peckerhead!"

Turning back, he scoped one side of the road and then the other. He swore softly as his sight set on none other than his friend Roger's face peering out from behind a tree.

"Well, I'll be damned. What have you gone and gotten yourself into this time, my friend?"

He chuckled shaking his head. Well? Guess the time had come to help a friend out. With that, he sighted his rifle in and joined the fray. He didn't know why Roger had mixed it up with this group, but he knew his friend well enough to trust that he had a good reason. With each shot from his gun, the rooster sitting on the back of his legs growled softly, drawing a chuckle of laughter from Mitch.

∞

When the first shot rang out, Bobby dove from his horse and hit the pavement. His head swam as it rocked off the tar. Scrambling to make sense of what was happening, he clawed and crawled his way to the ditch while his men and their horses screamed around him. How did this happen? Could that mute bitch have made it to the compound to warn them? Did someone help her? Did he have a traitor in his group? Breathing hard, he drew his gun. He didn't know in which direction to shoot. He could see no target. Crawling along the center of the ditch, through the mud, the slime, and the wet leaves, he had only one thought, run. Get out of the midst of the bloodbath.

∞

Brian took down one man after another, each shot hitting its mark. He saw the man in the lead dive from his horse and crawl into the ditch. Screams erupted from below. Coming out from behind the boulder, he walked parallel to the man in the ditch staying behind trees and brush for cover but keeping his eyes trained on him. Lead rider? He assumed it must be Bobby. Crouching low, he made his way across the road and up into the woods in the direction he saw Bobby run. Bullets screamed off the pavement and sent up clouds of dust hitting the dirt behind him. His breath burned in his lungs as he sprinted, climbing the steep hillside.

He hadn't gone a hundred yards when he came to a dead stop. Blinking his eyes rapidly, he shook his head in confusion. Before him, just on the other side of a stand of brush, lay a man with a rifle resting on a log and shooting. He didn't recognize him. But that wasn't what stopped him in his tracks, what stopped him was the rooster standing on the man's outstretched legs. He took another step and winced when he heard a branch underfoot snap loudly. The rooster turned its head and stared at him.

"Shit!" he whispered under his breath. The large white bird, all claws and beak, launched itself right for his face in a fury of white feathers and beating wings. Instinctively he threw up his arms and in doing so, dropped his rifle.

The blow hit him hard in the stomach, knocking his breath away. He fell to the ground. He flailed one arm to throw the rooster from his face and chest while reaching for his knife with his other hand. He felt the rooster's spurs dig into the side of his neck, and he grabbed a handful of feathers, struggling to pull the rooster off of him. Another blow from the man rocked his head back, and Brian saw sparkles of light. Pain sang through his jaw. Gasping, he backed up and swung wide, connecting and knocking the man back. Bringing down his knife, he sank it into the man's thigh. The man staggered back and drew his knife, stabbing it wildly. Brian felt it graze the top of his forearm, and he hissed. Burning pain traveled clear up to his shoulder.

He needed to end this fight. The longer he screwed around with this man, the better chance Bobby would get away. His breath rasped in and out in gasps, as he dove toward the man. He felt a hard kick to his chest that knocked him backward. Another burning pain seared his chest and the man's blade kissed his skin. Crouching low, he thrust for the man's stomach only to miss. His knife blade instead bit into the man's hip. He heard a low groan of pain as the man pummeled his stomach and face with hard jabs from his fists.

A loud shout from Roger brought him to a halt and he staggered to catch his breath. He looked at the man opposite him. Blood ran down the front of his jean-clad leg and trickled from the corner of his mouth. He watched in confusion as Roger stormed toward him.

"Boys? We're supposed to be fighting the enemy, not each other."

Confused, Brian cut his gaze to Roger.

"He's not one of us," he spat angrily.

"No, he's not. But he is a friend," Roger said then smiled. "Mitch meet Brian."

A grin split Mitch's face, and in two steps, he folded Roger into a bear hug. It then dawned on him that the shooting stopped.

"Did we get them all?" he asked.

"Most of them. A few turned tail and ran, but we've got guys out hunting them down now," Roger replied.

"How many of ours hurt or dead?"

Roger grimaced.

"We lost four men. We've got six wounded. Max, Grace, and Eli are tending to them now. Once they say they're ready to be moved, we'll load them up and get them back to Doc," he replied. Turning to Mitch, he shook his head.

"Man, what the hell are you doing here? And what is up with the chicken?" he asked, then chuckled. Brian turned and glared at the rooster who sat near Mitch's feet.

"Well, my friend, it is a long story, a very long story," Mitch said then chuckled. Turning to Brian, he stuck out his hand.

"I'm sorry man; I thought you were one of them, the enemy."

Brian nodded but didn't take the man's outstretched hand. He glanced at Roger and mumbled. "I'll go help with the wounded."

He could smell a cop a mile away, and Roger's friend was most certainly a cop. As he limped back to the group, he thought of Bobby. He'd gotten away. He knew the coward would probably head back to Lee, and Brian intended to be right behind him. Tiredness washed through him and sweat stuck to his skin as he peeled off his shirt and shoved it in the saddlebag. He pulled a clean one out and slid it on as he gazed off toward the woods. He had a score to settle with Bobby, and he wasn't about to let up until he collected on it.

∞

Roger called the men to gather around him. He looked into the eyes of his men and women and sighed. Tiredness, shock, and disbelief were expressions that met his gaze. A lot of them had never seen battle before. And Roger knew this wouldn't be the last; he feared there would be many more battles ahead of them. His heart sank with dread.

The wounded were tended, and he planned to send them back to the compound with half the group. The other half would be heading to the town of Lee to free the townspeople. They'd killed all but ten of Bobby's gang, and the prisoners would be brought to the compound for the time being until they could figure out what to do with them. They would hunt down the few who escaped into the woods. He was confident his men would find them; either killing them, or taking them prisoner. Either way was fine with him.

Chapter Thirteen

Roger and his group set up camps on either side the road. Several in the group laid out bedrolls at the edges and sat, resting on them. Spike gathered wood for a fire and Brian sat with a stick of wood between his teeth while Max stitched up the nasty gash on his arm from Mitch's blade. Trevor Darling pulled sandwiches and chips from the packhorse and handed them out to everyone while Jeremy Watts followed behind with plastic water bottles filled with sweet tea. Roger, between bites of food, thanked God for Mary Anne's preparedness, of sending along an extra horse with food and drinks stuffed into its saddlebags. They would camp for the night and then head toward Lee come first light. They had a town to set free and a little girl to find, whose sister waited for her back at the compound.

∞

Brian breathed a sigh of relief as Max taped a bandage to his arm. Taking the sandwich handed to him, he bit into it hungrily. He grunted. Spike sat down on the tar beside him.

"I talked to the prisoners. Bobby got away."

Brian nodded. Anger curled and burned in his stomach.

"We'll find him," he replied between mouthfuls. "And when we do you can bet, he won't be getting away again."

Brian gazed around the camp, so many faces. Across the fire from him sat Mitch, who talked quietly with Roger. Firelight danced and flickered across their faces. The night darkened around them. He wondered about the freaking rooster. Why did the man have a rooster for a pet? He gave the man, Mitch, credit; although older than him, he still gave a good fight. He looked at the bandage covering his forearm and grinned. Yeah, he did have a lot of experience for an old guy.

Ellen Beasly, Kay Genner, Doug Francis and Kenny Washton all sat in a group, eating their sandwiches and talking in low voices. Although Brian didn't know any of them well, he had the highest respect for them. They fought a good fight. Each one kept their wits about them when the bullets started flying. Roger created a good thing with these people. In providing them a stable place to live, security, food, and housing, they in turn provided him with loyalty and hard work.

He thought of Sarah and Beth. As much as he was growing fond of Beth, as much as he wanted to explore that relationship further, he knew in his heart that life for her would be better at the compound than it would be with him on the trail. The compound would be the best place for them to plant roots. A place they could settle in and find community. His heart gave a tug of sadness at the thought of leaving them behind. But he wanted to return home. To his family, to see if they managed to survive the event. And would it be fair to ask Beth and Sarah to go along with him? Especially when Roger's compound offered them so much... more than he could? Shaking his head, he leaned back on the saddle he'd removed from his horse and closed his eyes. His body screamed with fatigue, with pain from his fight with Mitch, and with a longing to go home so deep, it made his heart ache. Yes, once they freed the town from the grips of Bobby and his men, he would be heading out. Tennessee called to him.

∞

Beth sat by Sarah's bed and watched her sleep. A fragile sadness caressed her heart. So much had happened to this young girl. The thought of this made Beth's heart weep. Too much happened to all of them these past months. The flu taking loved ones, the violence, hunger, and worst of all, the not knowing. Every day was not a given anymore. Jessie lay at her feet, and she reached down and stroked her fingers through her soft fur. The dog looked up at her gently, with chocolate eyes.

"Yes, girl. Even you, you've been through a lot too."

Yells from outside brought her up off the

chair, and she hobbled with her crutches to the window. Looking out, she saw a group of riders coming in, headed toward the infirmary. Shooting a glance over her shoulder to make sure Sarah still slept, she quietly let herself out of the room. Jill met her in the hallway.

"We've got wounded coming in!"

She quickly began setting up medical trays and rolling in empty stretchers.

"What can I do to help?"

Jill looked at her and brushed a stray strand of hair from her face. Her long hair, pulled up into a haphazard bun fell from its band and onto her shoulders.

"Can you start loading these trays? We'll need bandages, scissors, tape, and surgical kits. I don't know yet how many, or how bad the injuries, so let's plan for the worst and hope that we don't need to use all this stuff."

Beth nodded and started digging in drawers for the items Jill mentioned. As an EMT, trauma events were familiar, and she knew what the doc would need on the medical trays. Using one crutch for balance, she hobbled around the small room and gathered I.V. poles, extra sheets, and blankets, sterile gloves, gowns, and masks. If the doc needed to do surgery, he would do it in this room. While she worked, she couldn't help but be amazed at the equipment and supplies in this little hospital infirmary. They had everything needed to do minor, or even more complicated surgeries. Roger and Doc must've spent years stocking away this stuff.

She looked up when Jill came running back into the room.

"You did well," she quipped. She dumped an armful of I.V. plastic solution bags onto the nearest table.

"Do you know if Brian is among those injured?" Beth asked, nervously. Jill shook her head.

"I didn't see him out there. That tells me he is still with Roger's main group."

A sigh of relief escaped Beth's lips.

"How many wounded?"

"Six, two will need surgery immediately. The other four have gunshot wounds but are not critical. Doc is out there now triaging. He'll be rolling in here soon to get to work."

Beth nodded. Jill sighed tiredly and turned to prepare two stretchers. Having only one doctor meant back to back surgeries, hours of standing on her feet.

"I can help with the triage. I can take the non-critical cases." Beth offered. Jill turned to her.

"Well, shit, woman! Gown up! I don't care if you have a license to practice or not! And neither will those folks who are wounded," Jill said and smiled. She knew Doc would welcome the extra set of experienced hands. He's been a one-man show for far too long, and Jill knew it wore him down.

Beth stared down into the face of Bella Mitchell. She clenched her fists by her side to stop her hands from shaking. Bella, not even twenty years old and wounded in a battle that she should never have been a part of. The bullet lodged deep into her shoulder, and the field medics did an exceptional job of stemming the blood flow and bandaging her up for the journey back to the compound. Her deep brown hair spilled over the white of the pillow. Her face was drained and pinched in pain. Her brown eyes stared up at Beth.

"It's okay Bella. I'm giving you something for the pain, and it should kick in shortly."

Bella nodded, compressing her lips. Her eyes filled with tears. Beth could tell she was trying to put on a brave front but starting to crumble.

"Doc will have that bullet out of you in no time." She swiftly inserted an I.V. line and pushed in a dose of morphine. She watched Bella's lids grow heavy then close. Her heart broke for the child. The pain she must've endured on the journey back. Preparing her for surgery, Beth cut her shirt off and swabbed around the wounded area with a disinfectant that smelled pungent and strong. She then lightly draped her with sterile squares. She felt Jill's eyes on her as she worked, and she smiled at her.

Jill nodded and turned back to help Doc, who worked on Elroy Blinter, and it wasn't going well at all. The man took a bullet to the chest that had punctured his lung and exited through his back. Beth could see Doc was sweating beneath his mask and every few moments she'd hear a muttered curse. She could see he was struggling to repair the hole in Elroy's lung. He stood in a puddle of blood that pooled near his feet and squares of bloody gauze bandages littered the floor.

Beth's good leg shook with fatigue. She peeled off her gown, gloves, and mask and sat on a chair in the corner of the room. Mary Anne sat beside her on another chair, waiting for the next patient to be carried in on the stretcher.

"Are you gonna be okay to do this next one or should we wait for Doc?"

Beth grimaced and nodded. The night gave way to early dawn. The shadows receded and weak light filtered through the window.

"Just need to give my leg a moment then I'll be ready to go," she replied. She took a sip of the coffee Delilah brought to her. Mary Anne served as Beth's helper. She didn't have medical experience, but between the two of them, they were managing quite well. The door banging open served to tell Beth that break time was over. Doc finished up with Elroy, and the prognosis looked grim. He now worked tiredly on Thomas Greene who took a bullet in the knee, shattering the bone. Although he did his best to put the pieces back together only time would tell if Thomas, or Tommy as everyone called him, would be able to keep his lower leg. The hospital infirmary had a considerable amount of supplies, equipment, and medicine but not everything a full surgical unit would have. And rebuilding a knee was tricky even in the best of times, which this certainly wasn't.

Beth spent the next four hours alternating between standing on one leg, and sitting, resting while waiting for the next patient. She groaned at the deep burn in her hip each time she climbed back to her feet. Although exhausted, she felt a sense of accomplishment and joy that she'd been strong enough to be able to contribute to those who did so much to help her, Sarah, and Brian. With a yawn, she washed her hands.

"I'm gonna be glad to lie down and get off of my feet for a while," she murmured. Jill, Mary Anne, and Doc all nodded in agreement. It had been a long night for all of them.

"Do you need some pain medication?" Doc asked. Beth shook her head. She'd make a cup of herbal tea. It would help her sleep and provide anti-inflammatory actions. She hated the drugs she'd been on after her surgery but knew the importance of them. They did help her through the worst of the pain of her own surgery.

Stopping on the way to her room, she checked in on Sarah. Jessie lay next to her bed and lifted her head when Beth entered the room.

"She's still sleeping, eh, girl?"

Sarah's voice startled her when she spoke from out of the darkness.

"No, I've been awake for a while. Are you okay?"

"Yeah, baby girl, I'm fine. Just tired," Beth replied.

Sarah nodded.

"Jill stopped in. I wanted to help, but she made me stay in bed."

Beth laughed. She could see in her mind's eye, Jill's stern expression. The woman was a force to be reckoned with for sure.

"She's right. You've lost a lot of blood and are still weak. You need to rest."

She laughed when Sarah rolled her eyes.

"And look who's talking, gimpy!" Sarah replied. Beth bent and tousled her hair and gave her a peck on the cheek.

"You have a beautiful voice, baby girl. I love hearing it. Please don't ever go silent on me again," she whispered into her ear. Sarah smiled. Beth straightened up and sighed. She pulled the blankets and tucked them around her.

"I'll see you in a few hours. I need to get some shut eye. You listen to Jill!" she teased as she turned and made her way to her bed.

∞

Bobby stumbled through the dark, tripping over roots, brush, and fallen logs. The ambush had dealt him a hard blow, and he wondered how his men fared. The woods sang with the night creatures around him. The moon slipped in and out of clouds. How long had he been walking? He lost track of time and didn't know. The plan had gone FUBAR. His stomach ached with tension, and his nerves sang on the edge of hysteria. He plowed ahead in the dark, batting branches out of his way. He winced at the sting as they scratched bloody lines into his bare arms. His breath roared from his lungs. He fought the terrain. Every step brought pain. Shadows, dark and menacing, haunted him from behind every tree. No direction, no clear path, just running to get away. He knew if the compound's men found him; they would kill him. Fear ripped into his throat and he struggled to hold back a scream. Ghosts chased him, demons of regret, of anger, all his doubts, haunting him.

"I told you, boy. You're a loser, worthless, a coward!" his mother's voice sang. With an anguished cry, he clapped both hands over his ears and stumbled over a rock, falling to his knees. He felt the warmth of blood soaking his pant leg.

"I am not! I am not worthless!" he moaned. Snot and tears ran down his face. Picking himself up, he drew a deep breath. His mother was dead. She couldn't hurt him anymore. But in his heart, he knew. She would never stop hurting him. That had been his life with her. All the beatings, the verbal abuse, the cruel taunting he got from her came back to haunt him each time the silence crept in. He wished he could scrub his mind clean of her and his old man. He wished he could turn back time and kill them both again and again until he cleansed himself of the memories.

Pushing himself along, he let the darkness swallow him. He may be down, but he wasn't out. He could recoup from this. He just needed to make it back to Lee. Once there, he'd start over with the twenty-five men he'd left behind. Once they hooked up with the Alliance, then he'd make the compound pay for what they'd done. But first, he needed to get home. Gritting his teeth, he pushed his aching legs forward.

"Boy, you never learn, do ya? There ain't no one in their right mind gonna follow a loser, a coward like you. Once they find out what a coward you are, they'll turn on you. They will rip you apart like a pack of hungry hyenas. You should lie down here in these woods and die, just like you let your baby brother die!" his father's voice shouted. Bobby grimaced and stopped long enough to pull a little baggie of cocaine from his pants pocket. Shoving a snort up his nose, he let the drug drive the voices away.

Chapter Fourteen

When the first light broke over the night sky, Brian crawled out from his sleeping bag on the ground and rolled it up. With a soft groan, he threw the saddle back onto his horse. His breath puffed white in the chilly early morning air. He looked around at the sleeping group and at the fire that had burned down to low embers. Silently, careful to not wake anyone, he grabbed the horse's reins and led it up the road a bit before climbing into the saddle. A cough from behind him made him sigh in frustration.

"Ya didn't think I'd let you go off by yourself now, did ya?" Spike asked. He nudged his horse up alongside Brian.

With a shrug of his shoulders, Brian swore softly. "Just ain't no getting rid of you is there?"

Spike laughed. "Nope, not a chance buddy. I want a piece of him too. Can't let you have all the fun."

With a soft kick, Brian set off, jumping over the ditch and climbing the hill where he'd seen Bobby running off. Even if the man traveled through the night, Brian knew he probably hadn't gotten far. Five or six miles at the most. Brian intended to get a head start trailing him. Alone. It irritated him that Spike seemed one step ahead of him with this idea.

"They need your help with the town. I don't need you," Brian snapped.

"No, but I need to see this Bobby character finished! It isn't just about what you need; he took my family too, remember?"

Guilt tugged at Brian's gut. He hadn't thought about that. All he'd thought about was his hatred for the man. He hadn't given one thought to what agony his friend had been going through. Yes, it was Bobby's men who'd viciously and savagely killed Spikes family.

"I'm sorry, man," he murmured.

Spike nodded. "You aren't the only one that has a stake in this dog fight."

The trail Bobby left was easy to follow for the experienced eyes of both Spike and Brian. He gave the bastard credit; he was moving fast. A broken branch, a scrape on a moss-covered log alerted Brian that he veered off northwest. Puzzled, he stopped. Northwest would take him away from Lee, not toward it. Following Bobby's trail another mile or so, Brian stopped, slid down off the horse and knelt beside a scuffled area in the leaf litter. He spied several drops of blood on the ground. Looking over to his left, he saw a small, discarded baggie with remnants of white powder clinging to the plastic. He shot a glance up at Spike and shook his head, grimacing.

"Our boy is higher than the proverbial kite." He waved the tiny baggie in the air and chuckled. Spike smiled and shook his head. It answered the question that had been nagging him. Why Bobby's trail had been weaving to and fro like a drunken sailor on payday? The man was jacked up; that's why.

The trail veered back to the south and Brian squinted riding into the glare of the sun. It was apparent Bobby was lost, and Brian shook his head and laughed as he followed it. He gazed up at the blue sky overhead through the heavy canvas of leafy branches. They'd been on Bobby's trail for several hours. Turning in the saddle, he motioned for Spike.

"It's a good time to take a break."

Spike nodded. His back felt like a mule had kicked it, and his ass was burning from the rub of the saddle. Sweat trickled down his back and into the crack of his ass. Black flies bit at him without mercy, he swatted them away, but they were relentless.

"Yeah, I'm starving, man."

Pulling his horse to a stop, he climbed down from the saddle. He dug into his saddlebag for two sandwiches which he'd grabbed the night before, along with two plastic bottles of the sweet tea. He had an idea that Brian would set out, so he'd prepared. Tossing one to Brian, he sat on a log and bit into his own. Thick peanut butter and sweet jelly, his favorite. His stomach growled noisily. Between bites, he mumbled.

"He can't be that much further ahead of us."

Brian nodded.

"I agree, keep your head on a swivel. He still has a gun, and he'd think nothing of blowing either one of our heads clean off," Brian warned. Spike let out a chuckle and he tipped his head back and took a deep draw from the bottle of sweet tea. He moaned with pleasure.

Would he kill Bobby if he got the chance? Thinking of his wife and children, a chill ran down his spine. Yeah, he would take pleasure in killing him. And he knew soon he'd have his chance.

He hadn't always been this man. As a cop, he'd taken his oath to protect and serve very seriously. He'd always followed the rules. Even when he'd watched as the same criminals skirted the law. Ones he had arrested repeatedly, time and time again; he'd still followed the rules, fully and completely. But the event, Bobby, and his men, they all changed that. The old laws no longer applied in this new world. Now…the only law was to survive, and to do it by taking down any who posed a threat to that survival.

Hatred burned in his heart like a match to kerosene; explosive and consuming. Memories of his beautiful wife's eyes, staring at him, vacant and accusing. The blood, all over her body, from what Bobby's animals did to her. And his two boys, innocent and murdered. The memory made him lose his appetite, and he wrapped his half-eaten sandwich back up and tossed it into the saddlebag. He saw Brian's questioning glance and turned his face away. Tears tugged at the corners of his eyes.

"You bout ready?" he asked. He climbed into the saddle, not waiting for an answer.

They followed Bobby's trail long into the afternoon. Brian let his mind wander. The woods, the crisp air, and the rocking motion of the horse lulled him into a relaxed state. When the sound of a gunshot echoed in his ears, it startled him, damn near stopping his heart.

He dove from his horse, hitting the ground. Crawling quickly, he took cover behind a fallen log. Peering out, he released a pent-up breath. Spike did the same as he hid behind a large pine tree. He met Spike's gaze and made a motion with his hand. Spike nodded that he understood; crouching low, he made his way off to the left and into the woods. Brian crawled, staying behind the thick cover of the brush and trees. He made his way to the right.

Flanking the shooter, Brian spied Bobby curled up behind a large boulder, and Spike, out about a hundred yards or so, moving in on him from behind. He took a shot, knowing he wouldn't hit him but keeping Bobby's attention to the front. Spike moved in closer while Brian watched from behind a tree.

"I got him!"

Brian stood and walked toward where Spike held his gun on Bobby. The man looked pitiful. His eyes were glazed over and wild. Vomit soaked the front of his shirt. His weapon lay empty across his lap. His face, bright red with sweat and fear. A cloud of black flies swarmed around the man's face and head. He sat with his back against the boulder, his leg lay twisted and bent at an odd angle. Brian swallowed back a roll of nausea when he saw the white splinter of bone sticking up through the leg, in an ooze of blood and flesh.

Shaking his head, he looked at Spike and grinned. "Well, well. Ain't this a sweet turn of events." His eyes shone cold.

He glanced back down at Bobby. Weak sun filtered down through the trees, bouncing off the tears in Bobby's eyes.

Spike nodded at Brian and smiled. He looked down upon the pathetic wreck before him. Tears streamed down Bobby's face and he clutched his leg, writhing in pain. He glared up at them both with hatred.

"You won't shoot an injured, unarmed man," he hissed. Spittle flew from his lips, and his hands clutched at the leaf litter on the ground.

"No, I ain't planning on shooting ya," Brian said, then grinned. He pulled his knife from its sheath. The blade glinted in the sunlight, a wicked indication of what he planned to do. He laughed when he saw Bobby's eyes widen in terror. Glancing at Spike, he saw disgust in his eyes.

"Brian." Spike murmured.

Brian shot him an angry glance. He could hear his own heartbeat, as hatred and bloodlust made his hands shake with want—the knife beckoning to him to complete what he'd set out to do. Moving in closer, he brought the knife down to Bobby's throat, and ever so lightly, he slid the blade across it while staring into his terrified eyes. He jerked his head up when Spike shouted at him.

"Brian, he's as good as dead already. Don't become the same animal he is!" Spike snapped. He couldn't believe he was saying it. His lust for this man's blood was as intense if not stronger than Brian's. He wouldn't allow himself to be a murderer though.

"He's dying. Can't you see that? Why make it quicker for this piece of trash? He will suffer long and hard if we walk away. Let the coyotes have him." Spike said. He looked down at Bobby. He saw the man's eyes widen in shock as the truth of what he said hit home.

"No, you can't! You can't leave me here to die like that!" Bobby screamed.

Spike smiled; his eyes cold with hatred.

"Oh yes, we can," he purred softly.

"Please. Please." Bobby begged then started sobbing. His begging and crying fell on deaf ears.

Brian shook his head, what Spike said made sense. If they left him, he'd die slowly and painfully. He couldn't go anywhere with his leg shattered. He was sick; he was weak. The coyotes would smell the stench of his weakness, and they would move in for the easy prey. His hands shook with temptation and he slid the knife back into its sheath. Bobby, seeing this, snickered through watery eyes.

"You ain't got the balls," he spat challenging him. His eyes glistened with hatred and insanity as he howled with laughter. Brian turned his back and stared out into the darkening woods. His mouth burned with dryness and his hands opened and closed as he clenched and unclenched his fists. He wanted to rip and tear into Bobby, to make him suffer endlessly for what he'd done to Sarah, Beth and all the others he'd hurt. Sucking in a deep breath, he cast a disgusted look at him. It took every ounce of willpower to still the rage inside of him.

"I had her, you know. That mute, sweet little piece of ass? I hurt her in ways that you couldn't even imagine, and she begged me for more." Bobby hissed then chuckled, goading Brian on. "Then I gave her to my men, and they took turns with her too. I left a stain on that girl's soul that she will never be able to wash off."

Brian winced. The words hit him, their

bite as sharp as a sword. He turned when he heard a thud, then a grunt, as Spike drove his fist into Bobby's face.

"You're not worth it, man! Not worth the blood staining my hands to kill you." Spike said, his lips curling into a snarl as he crouched down and stared into Bobby's eyes. "You are gonna die hard. When those animals are ripping into you, and you feel their teeth against your skin when you smell their breath as they are eating you alive? That's dying hard, man. And you deserve every misery you suffer." Turning, he nodded to Brian.

"Let's go, man. We've wasted enough time on this piece of trash."

With that, both Spike and Brian walked away to the sounds of Bobby's screams of rage and terror ringing in their ears.

Chapter Fifteen

Roger slid into the saddle and guided the horse off from the road. To get to Lee in decent time, they would be making their way through the woods; along trails that would cut both miles and travel time by hours. Mitch Smalley rode beside him, and the rooster followed not far behind. Roger shook his head and laughed. They didn't have time to talk much yesterday about Mitch's travels. Today they would have plenty of time to catch up. The sun warmed his shoulders and back, the air heavy with the scent of rotted leaves and pungent pine.

It didn't surprise him when he woke up to find Spike and Brian gone. It surprised him they didn't leave the night before to hunt Bobby down.

They had hit Bobby's gang hard, wiping most of them out, taking the few that remained as prisoners. His stomach had turned nauseously at the information he'd gleaned from his interrogations. Bobby, the gang leader, had been quite busy these past few months. And his business not only meant a whole lot of trouble for those small towns nearest Lee. This also meant a whole lot of trouble for Roger and his compound.

He'd found out from one particularly chatty prisoner, David, who had gladly spilled his guts at the sight of Roger's knife when he held it against his throat, about the plans of Bobby and the Alliance: about the tanker trucks that were moving into the northeast, loaded with fuel and weapons; about the convergence of two very well-known and nasty gangs escorting the trucks; about the plans for a complete take over to create a new territory run by them.

The sun filtered weakly through the dense cover of the forest. Birds chirped and squirrels chittered noisily. He let his mind drift as the horse gently rocked under him. If the town were in as poor of shape as the prisoners told him, then there would be a lot of people wanting to come to the compound for refuge. He would have to get a work detail together to build more shelters. It wouldn't be a problem; he had plenty of lumber for such projects. Long before the event, he had scavenged every board he could find. He became known in the town as the junk man. If a house or building were torn down, he'd be there with his truck, pilfering through the lumber and grabbing what he could.

Over the years he'd collected enough boards and beams to build every small house on the homestead plus outlying sheds and barns. He figured by the size of his lumber piles he still had enough for at least twenty tiny houses. And he hoped he wouldn't have to build that many. Shaking his head, he sighed.

He knew, without a doubt, the town was

guarded by more of Bobby's men. The prisoner, David, a sour little man with a fat face, had informed him that Bobby had left twenty-five of his men behind. They would put up a fight.

Turning to Mitch, he grimaced. "You know, when we enter the town, we're probably going to have to fight our way in right? You don't need to be a part of this. The compound is only a short ride away. You could go there and wait it out."

Mitch grinned.

"Awww buddy, you know me better'n that. From what you've told me about this gang, they need to be taken out. If not, you'll only end up having more problems with them down the road if they reorganize."

Roger nodded. He'd come to the same conclusion. Better to completely wipe them out than need to deal with a resurgence at a later time.

"Just as long as you're sure. It ain't your fight, my friend," he replied.

"It became my fight yesterday," Mitch said then laughed. Roger smirked. Leave it to Mitch to wade in neck deep.

"So, what's up with the rooster?" he asked, changing the subject. Laughter met his ears. He watched Mitch tip his ball cap backward.

"Well, my friend. That is a story." For the next two hours, Roger listened to Mitch's tale of traveling across the nation, of visiting Naomi Stilter in New Hampshire, of his truck running out of gas and of him finding the old mare and the rooster who decided to adopt him and follow. Laughter brought tears to his eyes as he listened to Mitch spin his tale, throwing in dirty jokes, bad jokes, and just plain sad jokes into the mix.

"So that is how I came to be a prisoner of this rooster I named Peckerhead," he finished. "Now, speaking of prisoners, let me ask you a question and if I'm stepping out of line, just let me know."

Roger nodded.

"Why are you friends with Brian, the Butcher?"

Roger turned to him, eyes widening. "What? Man, what in the hell are you talking about!"

"Brian. Don't you know his story? That man was front-page news. He is one nasty piece of work. He hunted down and killed how many men? I can't even remember. He's a wet worker...with his knife. How did you end up with him in your life?"

Roger shook his head. It was the first he'd heard of Brian the Butcher. Mitch must be mistaken.

"I think you got the wrong guy, my friend. Brian is a decent man," he replied. Mitch shook his head.

"Nah, I don't think so. You can't forget that face, those eyes. The man is a killer. Last I heard he was doing a life sentence out in Vermont."

Roger worried his lower lip with his teeth. Could that be true? If so, did Spike know about Brian? How about Beth and Sarah? Did they know they were traveling with a killer? He needed to think about this. Having a killer, a convict, at the compound? His gut told him that Brian was a decent man, a good man. And in all his sixty some odd years his gut very rarely steered him wrong. He would have to talk with Spike about this; find out what he knew of Brian's past and of the story of Brian the Butcher.

Turning to Mitch, he scowled. "Let's keep this information just between us kay?"

Mitch nodded. "Sure thing, I just figured you'd wanna know about the kind of man this Brian character is."

He could see that Roger wasn't entirely convinced of how dangerous his relationship with Brian was. But that was okay; he'd be watching him closely enough for them both. Smiling coldly, he nudged his horse into a trot.

The main street was eerily quiet as Roger, and his men sat on a high bluff and looked down upon it.

"Keep your eyes open and heads on a swivel. We know there are twenty-five more of

Bobby's gang here. And they won't go without a fight," he instructed his men. Heads nodded in agreement. Mitch pulled his rifle to the front.

"Okay, let's go in and let them know we're here," Roger announced. He nudged his horse down over the grassy embankment and onto the road. His men split off into several teams, each going left and right. They would flank Roger and his small group in case things got gnarly.

Roger entered Main Street; a desolate strip of black tar hemmed in by cement sidewalks on either side. He saw a group of five men walking slowly toward them guns held at the ready. He slowed his horse to a halt and cut his eyes at Mitch on one side of him and Cain on the other. Buildings lined the street. Some run down and shabby, others newer and well kept.

"Be ready for anything," he murmured. Both nodded in reply. Pulling away from the group, Roger rode a few more paces.

"Give it up, boys. Bobby is dead, and we've taken the rest of your boys out. There's no one left but you few. Do ya really want to get into this?" he shouted.

He saw several expressions of anger, disbelief, and fear.

"You ain't taking our town!" one of the men shouted back. He lifted his rifle and pointed it dead center of Rogers' chest. Roger smiled coldly. Both Cain and Mitch lifted their guns. He shook his head and glared at the man.

"Don't be stupid, man." He saw a momentary flicker of fear shadow the man's eyes.

"Give it up. There's been enough bloodshed," Roger replied. He watched the other four men. They were all backing up with their hands in the air and their guns on the ground in surrender.

"Look, even your men know it's a losing battle."

Although Roger smiled, it didn't reach his eyes. He saw the man swallow hard, his Adam's apple bobbing up and down.

"You gonna kill us if we do! I ain't a stupid man."

Roger shook his head.

"No, we won't." he lied. "You will become our prisoners. We will treat you as fairly as you've treated the people of this town," he replied, his eyes squinting in anger. And that was a promise. He would give them the same consideration they gave the people of this town. The man glared at him suspiciously for a moment then bending, he placed his gun on the ground and raised his hands above his head in surrender. Screw that. Bobby wasn't here to help them, and he'd be damned if he'd die to defend a leader who might already be dead.

"Smart man," Roger murmured. He motioned for the rest of his men to converge.

"Where's the rest of the gang?" he asked. His men gathered up the five and slipped zip ties over their wrists.

"Hiding out in the library," one of the men replied. Roger turned and looked at him. He shook his head. The boy couldn't have been more than nineteen at the most. He wore ratty, filthy jeans, and an oversized gray sweatshirt. His hair hung long and greasy over his shoulders. Hell, he didn't even have facial hair yet. What on earth was this kid doing involved in this gang?

"What's your name, boy?"

"Jimmy," the boy replied.

"Okay Jimmy, you're gonna run ahead and tell those men at the library that we outnumber them ten to one. You're also gonna tell them we're coming in and it can either be peaceful or bloody, it's up to them."

Jimmy nodded.

"Will do." And with that, he took off running with one hand holding up his pants.

They made their way toward the library and Roger drew his horse to a halt in front of the town common. The grass, bright and green, was littered with lawn chairs and blankets, beer cans and empty booze bottles. But his eyes set on a sight that curled his stomach and made his heart sink. In a large maple tree hung the body of a man, bloated and dangling, covered with flies. In the center of the gazebo, hung a woman, naked from the waist up, wrists tied to upright posts, with her head hanging limply onto her chest. The hot sun beat down on her bare back, and her hair matted with sweat and blood, her back a crisscross of bloody lacerations. Swearing, he climbed down from his horse, followed by Mitch and two others.

"Cut her down!" Roger snapped angrily.

"She's still alive," Mitch said. He cringed when he heard a low moan escape from her lips. Carefully and gently, he held her while Terrance, one of Roger's men, cut the ropes from her wrists. She sank into his arms, and he laid her gently on a blanket that Warren, another of Roger's men, brought over.

"What kind of animals are these people?" Warren muttered. His eyes glistened with angry tears. He covered her with the blanket. His breath caught in the back of his throat when she opened her eyes and looked up at him through a glaze of pain and despair.

"You're gonna be okay. We've got ya, honey," Warren murmured. The woman nodded, licking her lips.

"I'm thirsty."

Looking up at Roger, Warren motioned for his canteen. Roger grabbed it from his saddlebag and brought it over. He watched as Warren held it to the woman's lips and she drank greedily, choking and sputtering.

"You stay here, take care of her," Roger

instructed. Anger burned in his chest and crawled up his throat. He mounted his horse. If this gang would do this to a defenseless woman, he couldn't even imagine some of the other things they may have done.

Kicking his horse, he moved ahead with a murderous glint in his eyes. Rage sang through his veins.

The library, a massive, two-story brick behemoth, sat in the center of Main Street. On one side of it lay the police station and on the other side, what appeared to be a town office. His eyes took in the fifteen or so men standing in a group in front of the steps leading into the library. Guns lay at their feet in a pile. He motioned for his men to collect up the weapons and to shackle the prisoners.

"Any others?" he shouted at the group. Head shakes and quiet 'No's" echoed through the group.

"All the women, where are they?" he asked. A tall, gangly man of about fifty stepped forward. He bowed his head and kicked at a pebble on the pavement.

"In the basement," he replied. Roger nodded. Climbing down from his horse, he motioned for Mitch, Cain, Dennis, and Joey to follow him.

They descended the dark stairwell and opened the door. The smell, the horror that greeted them was enough to send them all screaming into the night. Cages, filled with women and children of all ages, lined the basement walls. Mattresses lay on the floors, stained and filthy. Plastic buckets sat, filled with human excrement. Hollowed expressions of pain, despair, and, hopelessness as the women and children peered out from between the bars at them.

Roger turned his head and gagged. He heard retching, coming from several of the men with him. Tears filled his eyes. He couldn't help but see the enormity of human desperation before him. Sucking in a deep breath, he looked at Mitch who wore an expression of horror.

"My God!" he whispered.

∞

Bobby watched the woods darken around him. He pulled the last small baggie of cocaine from his shirt pocket and stuffed it in his nose. He knew he was dying. He could feel his heart slowing down and a weakness flowing through him so consuming that even moving his arms caused him to gasp for breath. He could smell the stench of himself as his bladder let loose, then his bowels. And he sat in his putrid excrement.

"Look at you now? You! Thinking you were so much better, so much smarter. Nothing but a punk sitting in your own shit, boy!" his father shouted then laughed. Bobby shook his head and wept softly.

"I'm so sorry," he murmured. And he was. Sorry for all he'd done, for all he'd been in his entire miserable life.

"You're such a whiny baby. Always whining, always whimpering. No wonder I hated you," his mother hissed. And Bobby nodded sadly. She had always hated him. Every day of his life, she'd remind him of just how much.

"Stop! Just stop!" he screamed into the darkness. The ghosts of his parents tormented him. Howls and yips erupted in response to his scream, and his heart lit with terror.

"They're coming for you, Bobby. They are gonna tear you apart piece by painful piece, boy!"

With the last remnant of strength, he pulled the knife from the sheath on his side. Looking at the blade, the memories of screams and cries, of tortured moans and guttural whimpers plagued his mind. The face of every woman he'd ever abused floated in front of his eyes. Smiling, he leaned his head back and with one quick motion, drew the blade across his own throat. He sucked in a gargled breath. Blood flowed freely down over his chest and pooled in his lap. And finally, finally, the voices of his parents quieted.

Chapter Sixteen

Henry watched the strangers, as they passed by, from behind the white linen curtain. His heart jolted with anger. Bobby must've failed. He stepped to the side of the window so not be seen and hollered to his wife. He motioned for her to sit on the sofa. She looked up at him with adoration in her brown eyes.

"Mother," he sighed sadly, "the sinners have come. We've lost the battle."

His wife nodded.

"God will see us through this. Fear not. Fear nothing that is not of our Godly ways," he continued. With a fevered breath, Cathy cast her eyes downward and made the sign of the cross.

"Amen, husband," she whispered. They would do what they needed to do. Henry pushed up from the couch and drew the blade from its sheath on his side. He walked over to their slave, a female child of fourteen. With one quick motion he slit her throat and turned, ignoring her gurgles and gasps, as she bled out and slowly died. Cathy smiled.

She followed him to the cellar and smiled deeply into his eyes. With gentle hands he taped the explosives to her chest. They were doing the Lord's work, and it made her proud. She, in turn, helped Henry with his belt of explosives. They had lost the battle, but not the war. The sinners were storming the town, setting all the whores and criminals free. It was their duty to the great Father to make one last stand. And they would take as many of the sinners with them as they could.

Henry turned his face toward her. With a soft moan, he kissed her deeply.

"With God's grace we'll see each other again soon, my love," he murmured.

∞

Roger sat on the steps of the library with his head hung low. Exhaustion flooded every cell of his body. His heart ached with the extent of misery before him. Women, in tattered and stained clothes, wandered in circles, eyes wide with shock. Several children, ages ranging from as young as four years to young teens, clambered in groups; searching and seeking desperately to disappear from the sunshine, the crowds of prisoners, as well as any others around them. A mass of misery and desperation tinged the air, and Roger held his breath, overwhelmed with a rush of anxiety. What would he do with all these people? There were twenty women, and God knew how many children that Bobby turned into orphans.

Additionally, there were twenty-five prisoners. If it were up to him, they, the prisoners would be lined up against a wall and shot for what they'd put these poor people through; for the misery they'd caused. But then that would have put him on the same level with Bobby. And he would never be able to live with himself if he let himself become that kind of man.

His men, Cain, Mitch, Dennis and Joey, and the others, were standing around, not knowing what to do or which way to turn. They had their hands in their pockets, staring at the crowd with mixed expressions of horror, sadness, and overwhelming shock, covering their faces. Coughing, he stood up and whistled loudly, causing everyone to stop and stare at him. He motioned for his group to gather around.

"We need to find horses. You men will have to double up. These people can't stay here. They will need food. Many of them will need medical care. We can't do that here. We'll have to get them back to the compound; where we can sort this mess out," he said. He gazed out at all the tortured faces.

Mitch nodded and turned to Cain. "Grab one of the prisoners, that Jimmy boy. Get him to take you to the stables."

Then turning to Dennis and Joey, "You two, grab a couple of the guys. Go house to house and gather up whatever supplies you find. Meet back here in an hour," he instructed.

Turning to Roger, he grinned. "You and me, we're gonna go and talk to a few of these townspeople and see if we can find us a good old-fashioned wagon. There must be a farm nearby with an old hay wagon or something that someone knows about."

Roger nodded. He liked this idea. If they could find at least two hay wagons, then they could hitch some horses up and transport these wretched souls to the compound. He highly doubted that many of them would be able to walk or even ride on the back of a horse that far. Many were near starvation, skeletal, completely emaciated.

The prisoners could walk, he didn't care if their feet bled and fell off. He didn't care if they died on the long walk to the compound. If they were representative of what humanity had become, then they deserved death and misery. But the women and children, he'd be damned if he'd put them through any more suffering than they'd already seen.

Two hours later they had gained three hay wagons and teams of horses to pull them. One of the wagons held plastic coolers of food which they'd retrieved from the houses of Bobby and his men, enough to feed every woman and child for many days to come. They'd also found a cache of weapon and ammunition. Blankets and pillows lined all three wagons to help make the trip more comfortable. Roger nodded with satisfaction. They helped the women and children load up to the back of the wagons when an older blonde woman approached Roger.

"I know where they are keeping all the medicines and medical supplies. There are several in this group that are sick. Can we take the time to grab the stuff?"

Roger looked into her blue eyes and smiled. "Of course we can, Miss... errrr..."

She grinned and held out her hand. "Melissa. Just call me Mel, everyone else does," she replied. "I'm sort of the adopted mama to everyone here," she sighed sadly.

Bobby and his gang had murdered many of the women and children's families. She took them all under her wing, caring for them after the beatings, the rapes, and the other abuses they'd suffered at the hands of the men Bobby had pimped them out to.

Roger called over Cain and told him what the woman suggested. He watched the two of them stroll toward the police station. Bobby used it for a clinic of sorts. After a few minutes, they both returned with two boxes stuffed full of bandages, assorted medications, antiseptics and bottles of various products. Mel held her hand up with a bottle in it and smiled timidly.

"We've got many with lice. I'll treat them along the way. Don't want to be bringing that nasty bug home to your folk."

Roger nodded. Lice? What else would they find with these refugees? Scabies was a good possibility along with venereal diseases. He shook his head sadly. He couldn't imagine what some of these women and children had been through and he didn't want to. If he thought too long and hard about it, he'd probably lose his mind.

Just before dusk they slowly made their way out of town; his men on horseback, along with the prisoners on foot, and the three wagons following behind. It would be a long and arduous trip. He estimated it would take probably triple the time it normally would. Roger glanced over his shoulder at the parade of faces behind him.

He glanced at Mitch, who rode beside him, and smiled tiredly. "I don't know how these people survived this," he murmured.

The last thing he saw were two more people running toward him, an older man and a woman; waving their hands and smiling. The explosion propelled him from his horse, and he landed on the ground, hearing screams of terror erupting around him.

Cain ran up from behind the wagons. His ears rang with the concussion of the explosion, and his heart beat rapidly in his chest almost to the point of panic. The air smelled of sulfur and burnt flesh. Acrid blue-gray smoke hung in the air, stinging his eyes, making them water. In shock, with wild eyes, he took in the carnage in front of him.

There were so many men and women on the ground. Screams of pain, of agony, ripped into the air. Spying Roger, lying twisted and broken, he ran to him and knelt. His heart sank when he looked down upon the man who had taken him in as one of his kin. A thick wedge of bone protruded from his chest, and his legs were splayed out at an awkward angle.

"Roger, don't move," Cain muttered. He looked down at him and placed gentle hands of his shoulders.

"You've got a bone broken in your chest; I think it's a rib that punctured through."

Roger grimaced. Funny, he felt no pain. Craning his neck to look, he let out a soft cough of laughter.

"Oh, boy. That ain't my bone," he murmured. He watched Cain's eyes widened in horror. Milton, one of his friends, moved up beside him.

"Cain? What do we do?" he muttered, with shock written all over his face. Cain sucked in a deep breath and swiveled his head, taking in the carnage that lay all around him. He didn't know. Panic sucked at his breath. He watched as men and women who hadn't been hurt by the explosion began to pull together and tend to the wounded. Looking down at Roger, Cain's eyes filled with tears.

"Hang on Roger. Hang on," he choked. He saw the life slipping from Rogers' eyes. Roger looked up at him and smiled.

"You take care of the compound, boy.

And Mary Anne, she's gonna take this hard," he whispered. With one last rattling breath, he gave into the death that waited for him.

Cain howled in agony, and he felt strong hands on his shoulders. He cried as he bent over Roger's body. He turned his head and looked up into Milton's sad eyes.

"C'mon, boy, we need help with the living," he murmured. There would be time for mourning later. Cain stumbled to his feet and shaking; he turned to those who were still standing.

"Check the wounded. There are medical supplies in the wagon. Let's get it together, people!" he shouted. His heart shattered with grief.

∞

Mitch opened his eyes. The blue sky danced with puffy white clouds and he stared up into it. His chest pounded with pain, and he groaned as he rolled onto his side. He smelled heavy smoke and coughed. Screams filled the air around him. Using his hands, he pushed himself up off the pavement, where he had landed after the explosion. He sat stunned, his eyes wildly searching for Roger. A gash on his head was leaking blood, down over his face, causing his eyes to sting. Another trickle of blood ran down the side of his neck from his ear; his eardrum had ruptured. Sucking in a deep breath, he struggled to his feet and staggered toward

Roger. He looked down at his dead friend, and his heart exploded with rage.

∞

Cain staggered on shaking legs through the bodies that littered the ground. He saw Joey laying near the damaged wagon that took the brunt of the explosion. His left arm dangled uselessly by his side, hanging by a flap of skin below his elbow. He looked up at him with a helpless, scared expression on his sweaty face. Cain bent, pulled his belt off, and tied a tourniquet just above the elbow.

"Just hang on, brotha. We'll have you right as rain in no time," Cain lied. Getting up, he stumbled to the next person.

Jason moaned and clenched and unclenched his fists. Pain etched deep lines around the outside of his mouth. He grit his teeth to keep from screaming. Cain saw that Dennis bent over him with a blanket folded into a square pressing down on his stomach. Blood soaked the blanket a bright red. He looked at Dennis, and the man shook his head. It wouldn't be long before blood loss would take twenty-five-year-old Jason's life. He looked into the man's eyes and smiled sadly.

"I'm dying, ain't I?" Jason moaned. Cain nodded.

"Man, that just sucks," Jason whispered. Cain turned his face away. Tears, hot and pressing stung his eyes.

A scream from the back of the group drew his attention to two women standing over a child: seven-year-old Stella, Rose's baby sister. Her body lay twisted and mangled, her eyes staring skyward. Sobs and shrieks met his ears. He looked down at her small frame, pain heavy on his heart. Shock tore through him when he saw the extent of the damage the explosion had caused. It looked like a war zone: bodies, blood, body parts, the smell of sulfur filling the air, the sounds of screams, prayers, and moans.

When all was said and done the death toll had reached twenty-four. Fourteen of them were Bobby's men, three of the rescued women and little Stella and six of Rogers's men. The carnage of the two bombs painted Main Street a grisly and garish red.

∞

Brian and Spike heard the explosion from a mile away. They'd traveled all night to catch up with Roger and the men. Throughout the night, Brian chewed over and over in his mind how they'd left Bobby; weak, broken, and pathetic. The man didn't stand a chance of surviving the night. Part of him wanted to go back and check. Just to make sure and to watch the coyotes chewing on that miserable excuse for a man's body. But he knew, Bobby was getting what he deserved, and karma was a bitch. When they had left him, Bobby had been as good as dead; his body just didn't know it.

When the explosion echoed in the distance, Brian shot Spike a glance and kicked his horse into a run. He prayed Roger and the men were not in the line of fire, but something in his gut told him they were. Racing along the road, side by side, they came upon the carnage — a gruesome puzzle of bodies and body parts, screams, and moans. Jumping quickly from his horse, Brian kicked himself into action. He swung his head around, eyes frantically seeking the enemy except there was none. No bullets were flying, no firefight. Just bodies. Everywhere.

He spied Cain and Mitch across the street, bending over Roger. Walking toward the two, he motioned to Spike.

"It's your granddad!" Cain was covering the old man with a blanket. Brian looked around with wide, shocked eyes. It looked like a scene out of the old war movies he used to watch on T.V. Bodies and body parts everywhere, scattered from one end of the street to the other. Faces, shocked with horror as people realized the extent of the damage. Spike ran past him and roared in anguish, pushing Cain out of the way he knelt beside his grandfather. Lifting the blanket, he about passed out at the sight before him. A large bone protruded from his grandfather's chest; blood pooled brightly on either side of him. His eyes, lifeless and hollow, stared up into the bright blue sky.

"What in the hell happened!" He came up off his knees and advanced on Cain. Cain retreated a few steps and shook his head. When he replied, his voice choked with anguish.

"I don't know. I don't know, man!"

Mitch coughed and with a raspy voice, spoke to Spike.

"It was an explosion. We never saw it coming."

Brian stepped over and laid a restraining hand on Spikes' shoulder. He whirled on him angrily, growling with murderous rage in his eyes.

"Get away from me!"

Brian stepped away and dug his hands deep into his pockets. He would let the man have his grief. He walked away and began to assess the situation, helping with those he could and saying a brief but silent prayer for those beyond help. He bent over a man he didn't know and felt Spike move up beside him.

"It was a bomb. Cain said two people rushed them while they were heading out of town with the prisoners and refugees. They carried home-made bombs strapped to their chests. What the hell is the matter with these people; suicide bombers, and gang bangers? I just don't get it!" His voice choked with emotion. Brian shook his head. He could find no words. No advice. He didn't get it either. They, Roger and his men, were there to help save these people. This shouldn't have happened.

"I don't know, my friend. I just don't know."

Chapter Seventeen

Beth woke just before the first rays of light emerged behind the mountains, off in the distance. She limped her way quietly past Sarah's room and out into the yard. The air tasted of morning dew and fresh grass. It tasted, to her, green, if green could be a taste. With her limping gate and one crutch, she made her way to the community kitchen. Her sneakers, bright neon purple ones that Mary Anne had given her, were soaked through, chilling her toes. Thinking about the sneakers on her feet brought a smile to her face. When Mary Anne had presented them to her, there was a story that went along with the gift.

Long before the event, when Roger and Mary Anne decided to create the compound, Mary Anne had taken it in her head that lots of clothing would be needed. So, for years, she'd visited the town dump and its swap shop to bag up shoes, clothes, blankets, sheets, and other such items. Friends, she'd told Beth laughingly, had thought she'd lost her mind as her weekly trips to the dump became well known. They would whisper about her being a hoarder and other such things.

But Mary Anne would just smile and gather for her storage. Curiosity created quite the buzz about her activities, and soon, townspeople would bring their clothing and household items to her, rather than the dump. Thus, Roger dedicated one entire barn to Mary Anne's collection of clothing and other items. Beth remembered seeing it for the first time. Boxes and boxes, reaching high up into the loft, filled with everything one could need. Clothing of all sizes, bedding, curtains, pots, and pans. It was an incredible sight. Shaking her head, she laughed softly. It amazed her; the thriving community Mary Anne, and Roger had built. She approached the kitchen, where she got a waft of freshly brewed coffee.

The kitchen bustled with activity from the three morning cooks, Mary Anne being one of them. On the old cook woodstove sat a large square pan of scrambled eggs and in the oven two pans of home-made biscuits. Bacon sizzled in two large cast-iron frying pans. The aroma tantalized Beth's stomach and her mouth watered.

She looked at Mary Anne and grinned, pouring a cup of coffee for herself. "How do you do it?"

Mary Anne smiled. "Do what?"

Beth waved one hand around the room at the trays and trays of eggs waiting to be scrambled once the pan emptied. She pointed to the biscuits just coming out of the oven, fluffy and golden brown. "This, all of this. Cooking on a woodstove? I am amazed!"

She struggled enough cooking on her electric stove at home, never mind trying to keep the temperature of a woodstove where it didn't burn everything.

"Oh, that's easy. C'mon over and I'll show ya," Mary Anne said, smiling happily. It had taken her many months to figure out the tricky temperament of the old cookstove, but once she had, cooking on it'd become second nature.

"See these?" she said, pointing to the little glass thermometers on the front of the oven. Beth nodded.

"Well, this stove has two chambers, or ovens, and it has a water boiler which helps cool the temperature down when we need to. The wood goes here." She pointed to a small door on the top left where the wood fed into the stove. "Now, oven number one gets really hot because the wood burns closer to that oven. The oven next to it stays just a bit cooler. So, with the biscuits, I use oven number two. I can keep the temperature around 375 degrees, perfect for baking. When I want to do large hunks of meat, like say a turkey, I need the hotter side." She paused and looked at Beth, who stared back at her blankly.

Her eyes smiled at her as she patiently continued. "By controlling what wood I feed into it, I can easily control the temperature." She pointed to what looked like a handle on the stovepipe running up through the roof. "And this here? This is the chimney bypass. With just a push or pull of this lever, I can heat or cool the oven. Sometimes all I need is a good bed of coals and other times; I need longer burning wood, like oak, which doesn't burn as hot or fast as say pine. It takes a bit to get used to, but once you've gotten the hang of it, it is easy. Now, the top of the stove has eight burners. It's just a matter of moving the pans around to either heat them more or cool them down," she explained. "And these drawers down here, these are the ash drawers, where the wood ash filters to. These need to be emptied several times a day."

Beth shook her head and laughed. Mary Anne made it sound so simple.

"I'll be making pies this afternoon. It'll be a good opportunity for me to teach you, if you'd like," Mary Anne offered. Beth nodded eagerly. Someday she'd have to do this all on her own when she left the compound. The more she could learn now, the more she'd be able to survive on her own later.

"Sure. I'd love that, Mary Anne."

"Okay, then. It's a date. We'll start right after the breakfast crowd is done and the plates are delivered to the prisoners," Mary Anne said with a smile.

Beth scowled, and it was on the tip of her tongue to ask Mary Anne why she bothered to cook twenty prisoners such a good breakfast.

She should just throw cold bread and water at them and call it good. Why waste precious food on swine?

Before she could voice her opinion, Mary Anne turned to her and smiled. "We cannot let ourselves become like them. We need to treat them with the same grace we treat others."

Beth nodded, embarrassed. "You're right. I've just seen the harm and the evil those men have done and caused."

"So, you go grab a plate, have some breakfast. Let me finish up here, or we're gonna have a lot of workers unhappy that breakfast isn't ready."

Beth laughed. She couldn't imagine anyone being mad at Mary Anne. The woman worked three times harder than anyone at the compound. Without her, in Beth's opinion, this community wouldn't run nearly as smooth as it did.

"Why don't you let me help before I eat? I can start setting up the prisoner's plates," Beth offered.

"Sure thing, many hands make simple work, my friend," Mary Anne said happily.

Beth used an ice-cream scoop to measure out scrambled eggs on to each plate, in a row of plates. She then added two strips of crispy bacon and a hot biscuit slathered with homemade butter. A dollop of strawberry jam and they were ready. Thanks to Mary Anne, they would eat well. Not that they deserved it in Beth's opinion.

Sliding the full plates onto trays, she loaded them onto a child's red rider wagon which one of the men had brought into the kitchen. Beth put several carafes of coffee and stacked cups in the cart.

The prisoners were held in one of the barns. One way in and one way out, and heavily guarded. Mary Anne worried about what to do with them. They were a ratty-looking group and hostile. Many were addicts and this, in and of itself, represented a huge problem for Doc. To let them detox cold turkey would mean round the clock care. They were already stretched thin with the recent wounded filling up the small infirmary. Shaking her head, she made a mental note to meet with Doc and discuss the issue of the prisoners. Thinking of this, she turned to Beth. "In your experience as an EMT, how often did you deal with addicts?"

Beth shook her head in sadness and disgust. "Too many times, why?"

Mary Anne sighed. "Because, a few of the prisoners that came in are showing signs of withdrawals. They are shaking, puking, have diarrhea, they're sweating, and restless. I need someone to take charge of their care. Doc is straight out, and so is Jill with all the wounded. So…." she murmured, leaving the question un-asked.

Beth scowled. Yes, she did have experience with addicts and with withdrawals. But did she want to spearhead the care for those who at one time would have killed her and Sarah? Or worse, made prisoners of them?

"I can't force you to help, Beth. But I'm pleading with you. These are human beings. No matter what they've done, it is our responsibility to treat them humanely," she said.

Beth rolled her eyes in annoyance. "I know, I know. I sound like a bleeding heart, right? But I just can't let anyone suffer needlessly. And some of these men, well they might have been good men at one time, but because of the event, they got into a bad situation," she went on stating her case.

Beth sucked in a deep breath. How could she say no? How could she argue against a good heart such as Mary Anne's? Hell, Mary Anne and Roger took her in when she'd been shot, they cared for her, and Sarah, and Brian, and asked for nothing in return. They didn't have to. They did it because they genuinely cared for all men and women. Sighing in defeat, she looked at Mary Anne. She would do it for her.

"Yes, I'll help. But Mary Anne, please, I know your heart is in the right place but listen to me. These men, Bobby's men, they are dangerous. Do not let your guard down for one minute. They would easily think nothing of killing you, me, and everyone in this community if given the opportunity," she warned softly.

"Oh, girl, I know that. You may think I'm naïve, soft-hearted and yes, I probably am. But I also believe, one kindness will conquer even the hardest of hearts. I just have to believe in second chances. If I lose that, then what's left? And everyone deserves a chance to redeem themselves. I'll ask three of our medics to assist you."

Beth nodded. If even half of the prisoners were withdrawing from addiction, then three medics plus herself, well they would be very busy over the next few weeks.

Beth helped Sarah out of bed and held her arm until she stabilized and found her balance. She looked ten times better than she did the day before. Jessie pranced around their legs, eager to take a walk with them. Twenty-four hours of bedrest had worked wonders for Sarah.

"Are you okay? Dizzy at all?"

Sarah shook her head and smiled. "Stop worrying. I feel good."

"Okay. I'll stop," Beth teased then smiled.

Today Sarah would have lunch in the community kitchen. She wanted to get out of the small infirmary room, to breathe some fresh air, and to explore the compound. She wanted to stretch her legs. She wanted to see, feel, and taste the freedom she thought she'd never see again.

They walked toward the community kitchen. Beth set her eyes on the horizon in the distance. She felt Sarah squeeze her hand gently.

"You're worried about him, aren't you?"

Beth nodded. Yes, she did worry about him, about Roger, about all the men. It had been three days since the initial battle. Three days since the first group came back with the prisoners and the wounded. They should have been back by now. A feeling of foreboding filled her stomach, causing it to ache uncomfortably.

"Yes. I am, Sarah, I hope they return soon."

After Sarah finished her cup of coffee, Beth walked with her and they explored the compound. She'd been here, going on three weeks, and still had yet to see it all. There were thriving honeybee colonies which gave them fresh honey. There were root cellars, smokehouses, and two more outdoor kitchens where a lot of the food prep and canning took place. It blew Beth's mind as her eyes took it all in. There was a laundry area where a few old antique ringer washers sat on platforms with buckets beside them and long lines strung to hang the clothes. There were also several rabbit colonies along with chicken flocks. Goats, milk cows, beef cows, and horses. They walked past the large gardens where men and women were working, weeding, and tending to the tender new crops. Beth squealed in delight when she came across some impressive herb gardens, she stopped to inspect every plant to see what they were growing for medicine.

The extent of this community almost overwhelmed her. This is what should have happened to all of society after the event. Rather than the misery, the violence, the starvation, and sicknesses, if only people had had the foresight of Roger and Mary Anne; then things may have turned out a whole lot different for everyone. Even herself, if she'd given thought to the future and prepared, she wouldn't have been a refugee looking for a home and a community. She would've started her own. How stupid she had been. How very foolish.

Turning to Sarah, she smiled. She watched the expression on the girls face turn to delighted surprise as her eyes took it all in. "Wow, they've thought of everything!"

Beth nodded. They had, and hopefully they'd have a chance to learn from them.

"Well, are you ready to head back? Mary Anne is teaching me how to bake pies today," Beth said. Reaching down she plucked a mint leaf from a flourishing plant and popped it into her mouth. It tasted fresh and sweet like a watermelon on a hot summer's day.

"Yup, I think I'll just sit outside on a lawn chair in the sun while you work with her if that's ok." Sarah sighed. Although she felt much better, she found she was still a bit tired and weak.

"Sure thing," Beth replied. She looked

sideways at her and frowned as she took in the paleness of Sarah's skin. The girl had pushed herself too hard, too fast.

"Yes, I think that's an excellent idea." She smiled. "I'll bring you out a glass of sweet tea."

Sarah nodded and smiled. "I wish I'd had a mom like you. Your daughter; your Sarah, was very lucky," she whispered.

Beth felt the burn of tears sting her eyes and she hugged Sarah tightly. "Although I didn't give birth to you, Sarah, I consider you my daughter."

She turned her face away as she choked on unshed tears. With an impatient swipe of her hand, she brushed the tears from her eyes and smiled a watery smile. She had a date to make pies; sweet and tart strawberry rhubarb pies.

∞

Rusty McNeil sat on a stump outside of the prisoner barn with his long legs stretched out in front of him, cleaning his rifle. An old Winchester, his grandfather had given it to him. He knew there were better and more powerful guns, but this one had a history for him. It was the first rifle he'd ever owned. The wooden rifle stock was as smooth as glass and worn to a light, caramel color from so many years of handling. The weight of the rifle felt natural, as fitting as any firearm he'd ever handled. The sun warmed his shoulders, and he sighed. It felt good after the long, frigid winter they'd had. The air sang with the soft hum of insects, and the smell of hay drifted from out of the barn door.

He thought of the prisoners and shook his head. What were they going to do with them? If it were up to him, he'd string them up out back from a sturdy limb off the tallest maple tree. But it wasn't up to him. The decision belonged to Roger and Mary Anne. He'd known the two of them going on forty years and they considered him their right-hand man, and the person in charge in Roger's absence. But this decision needed the agreement of all three of them. It couldn't and wouldn't be just up to him.

He glanced up when he saw Beth and two others approach the barn. They were pulling two red rider wagons loaded with plates of food for the prisoner's lunch. He grimaced worriedly.

"Mmmmm…you might not want to go in there."

Beth raised an eyebrow in question.

"At least half of them are puking and shitting. Sick. It smells like an outhouse in there," Rusty muttered in disgust. Shaking his head, he gazed out over the fields then turned his head and spit onto the ground.

Beth shook her head. Damn! This was worse than she thought. Turning to Tanya, she instructed her to go back to the community kitchen and ask Mary Anne for buckets of bleach water. They would need to clean and sanitize the prisoner quarters. Then she instructed Jamie, a young boy of sixteen, to find some more hands that were willing to help, and then go to the infirmary and gather six sets of gowns and gloves. He nodded and ran off toward the infirmary, leaving Beth alone with Rusty.

"They've got to have food. Is it possible they can eat out here?"

Rusty sighed in irritation. Yes, possible, but that would mean more guards to watch them. He nodded.

"Give me twenty minutes to gather up some more men."

What a shit show. Sick prisoners required extra guards, extra food and medicine, and extra hands to care for them. They were tying up resources that were sparse to begin with. They should 'a just shot them all on the road and been done with it. Getting up from the stump, he whistled for Sammy to stand guard.

"I gotta go and find us some more men to help," he muttered. Sammy grimaced and nodded. Guard duty, he hated it. He would much rather be out helping with the farm animals.

Chapter Eighteen

Brian rode lead beside Spike. His head pounded furiously as he squinted into the sunshine. His entire body screamed with fatigue. A dark pall hung heavily over everyone. Cain stayed in the rear, quiet and lost in his thoughts and beside him rode Mitch who was followed by Peckerhead. The night before, they all camped alongside a river where Mel and two other women spent the night tending to the wounded. Brian learned from helping her with the injured that before the event, she'd been a nurse. Even with her dedicated attention, they'd lost two more men through the night—one from internal hemorrhaging and the other, Joey, from blood loss.

The sadness of losing Roger, Joey, little Stella, and so many more pressed down on his shoulders like the heaviest of iron yokes. He should have been there rather than off chasing Bobby. He should have stuck with Roger and his group and finished this job once and for all. Guilt ate at his gut. Yes, they'd freed the women and children, freed the town from Bobby and his gang of thugs, but at what cost?

They left the dead prisoners, back in town, rotting right where they'd landed from the explosion. The animals would take care of the bodies. Brian and Spike agreed, they didn't have enough time or men for burials, and really, why should they bother? They took their own dead and loaded them onto one of the hay wagons to bring them home where they could bury them with honor.

"We need to take a break. Mel has to check bandages and give the wounded some water and food and more medicine," Spike said.

He glanced back over his shoulder at the two wagons carrying the women, children, and wounded. Brian nodded back at him. They were stopping every couple of hours, and this slowed them down significantly.

The remaining prisoners were keeping up but, if he were to be honest, he didn't give a rat's ass about them. He'd walk them into the ground and watch them bleed to death before he'd lift a finger toward helping them. It was the children and the women he was most concerned about. And he knew they all needed to take a break and stretch their legs.

He glanced back at those they'd rescued and his heart broke. Hollow eyes filled with shock stared back at him. What have those children and women been through? He'd heard bits, and pieces from Mel and what he had learned curled his stomach. If Bobby were standing in front of him right now, he'd skin him alive, one strip of skin at a time. His suffering would be nothing though, compared to what he'd done to those poor souls. How could a man be so evil, so twisted? Shaking his head, he swallowed back the anger that clogged his throat.

The medicine Spike spoke of was a joke at best. Tylenol was the most potent pain relief they had. Brian guessed it was probably better than nothing, but some of the wounded were in considerable pain. At best, they tried to make them comfortable while riding on the bumpy, rickety, hay wagon. It was better than walking but this was not ideal.

"Okay, we'll rest over this next rise." The pounding in his head grew worse.

Spike saw the pinched expression on Brian's face and laid a friendly hand on his shoulder. "I'll have Mel dose you out some Tylenol."

Brian nodded. Anything to help knock back the pain throbbing behind his eyes.

They traveled another two hours after resting. The sun hit the five o'clock position or somewhere near that. A cool breeze sang up from the east, and Brian tasted it on his tongue. Although the weather was nice enough, sweat beaded on his forehead and chills racked his body. He was sick. And his body screamed at him. It hurt to turn his head and focus his eyes. Sharp and agonizing pain flared, sending waves down his neck and into his shoulders. It was more than just a mere headache. It was excruciating. His stomach roiled with nausea, and his bowels felt watery and weak. Looking over at Spike, he muttered. Sparkles danced before his eyes just before darkness spiraled him down.

Spike swore and pulled his horse to a halt, quickly jumping down from the saddle. Running over, he knelt beside an unconscious Brian and turned him over onto his back. The sheen of sweat on his face and the moaning shocked him. He looked around helplessly. Mel saw what happened and jumped down, springing to action, from the moving wagon.

She pushed Spike out of her way with one curt word. "Move!"

Spike shot her a glance and moved aside while she checked Brian out.

"Shit! He's burning up. We gotta get him cooled down, right now! Get me the water, soak down a blanket! Hurry!"

Spike ran to one of the wagons and dragged a blanket from it. Taking a jug of water, he poured it onto it until it dripped and ran it back to Mel. He saw that she'd peeled Brian out of his shirt, and she was struggling, working to remove his jeans. Kneeling, he grabbed the bottom cuffs of both legs and tugged hard after she'd finished undoing his belt.

"Let's move him under that shade tree over there."

Spike motioned for Cain, Mitch, and Earl to help. Gently, they lifted Brian and laid him on the wet blanket under the shade tree.

"What's wrong with him?"

Mel shook her head. "I don't know. He's got a scorching fever. The only thing I can do is cool him down and give him Tylenol. Hopefully, we can wake him enough to swallow the pills with some water. Did he complain of not feeling well?"

Spike nodded. "Yeah, he complained earlier of a bad headache. I gave him some Tylenol. But other than that, not a peep."

The sound of Brian gagging sent Mel moving fast and she turned him onto his side. Instantly, he began to projectile vomit. Spike moved up behind him and held him there until he finished. Once done, Mel took two fingers and swiped his mouth to clear it. With a start, she pulled back and ducked when Brian's fist swung out. He opened his eyes with a roar of anger.

"What the hell!"

Spike grabbed him from behind and pinned his swinging arms so he wouldn't accidentally hurt Mel.

"Easy, friend, easy," he murmured. "You're sick. Mel is trying to help you."

His voice quieted Brian down, and he felt him sag with weakness.

"I don't know what happened. We were talking, then nothing! Bang, I went out like a light," Brian murmured.

"You have a fever. And you've been vomiting. We need to make camp here for the night so that you can rest. You need fluids and a bit of broth. I saw a can or two in the stash we took from the town coffers." Mel explained.

Brian nodded. The sickness came on so quick and fierce that it drained every ounce of energy from his body. The thought of pushing through and climbing back into the saddle almost crippled him with dread. He looked down at his nearly naked body under the blanket and gave Spike an odd stare.

"Don't look at me, man," Spike laughed, "she did it." Waving his hand, he pointed at Mel.

Brian's face turned red with embarrassment.

"Ain't nothing I haven't seen before," Mel teased.

His thoughts raced; did he have heatstroke? He hadn't thought the temperatures were that bad, the mid-seventies, typical for late May. Leaning back on the blanket, he closed his eyes and sighed tiredly.

∞

Jerry Miller smiled behind his hand. The arrogant and self-righteous Brian, sick. It pleased him. Now all he needed to do was wait for the others to fall. He'd take as many as he could before they reached the compound. He was as good as dead anyway. As a prisoner, he could only imagine his fate once these whores started blabbing their big mouths. After all that he and the others did to them, with them? He'd even surprised himself with how deep his taste for perversion went. Well, not that they didn't deserve it, but others would see it differently. He was sure that once they did, he, along with other members of the gang, would hang for their parts in it. He twisted his wrists against the zip ties that bit painfully into his flesh and felt the sting of his raw, tortured flesh. Yup, tonight would be fun to watch. They all drank from the water jug, even the wounded. He laughed and scanned the faces around him. Maybe this would turn out better than he thought.

∞

His nausea passed, and the headache kicked back a notch. Brian sat with his back against a tree and sipped slowly on the cup of broth Mel fixed up for him and thanked God for the supplies they'd taken from the town before they left. They had enough food to keep them all going for several days. Spike and Cain built a small campfire, boiled up some water to bathe and redress the wounded. On another campfire, the women cooked and dished out food. The children, all sat subdued and quiet, in a circle.

It surprised Brian when the little one, Stephen, strutted over to him and plopped down on the ground beside him. The little boy smiled up at him and reached over and grabbed his hand. Brian smiled back. The child's hand in his felt strange.

In a normal world, one without the horrors; they would be playing ball, teasing, laughing, and getting into mischief. Brian's heart jolted with sadness. This world was anything but ordinary. These kids would probably have nightmares for the rest of their lives from the ordeals of living and being prisoners of Bobby and his gang. Bitter bile rose up in his throat. He hadn't seen the cages. But, Cain, when telling him about them had clenched and unclenched his fists and wiped tears from his eyes, which told him all he needed to know. It was bad. Worse than bad; it was horrific.

Plucking a blade of green grass from the ground, he chewed on the stalk. Saliva filled his mouth and turning his head, he spat onto the ground. Life. It sucked big time right now for so many people. Glancing at the wagon that held the bodies of those killed by the explosion he felt a sharp ache in his heart. How could he tell Mary Anne that her husband of forty-some odd years was dead? That he'd been taken down by a crazed suicide bomber. And the wives of the other men dead men, how would he tell them...and Joey's girlfriend...Joey's mother and father?

Anger flushed his face as he thought of all those who lay dead and covered with blankets. They shouldn't have been in this battle. They had no business fighting against the ruthless thugs of Bobby's gang. Hell, they were lawyers and businessmen, young kids, waitresses and bankers. They weren't trained soldiers, but this world forced them to become so. The event had forced them to pick up guns and fight for their survival against the thugs and criminals that would try and take advantage of them; who would try to take what little they possessed. No law to stop them, no Army, Navy, or Marines to fight for them. Just everyday people that were struggling in a life that was nothing but struggle and hardship. It was enough to want to make him scream in frustration and rage.

Chapter Nineteen

Beth worked long into the afternoon. Cleaning, sanitizing, and laying fresh bedding for the prisoners. She wished there was more that she could give them for their withdrawals besides chicken broth and ginger tea. It was decided after a lengthy discussion between her, Jill, Mary Anne, and Doc that the medicine they needed was something that the compound couldn't spare. They would have to suffer through their illness, withdrawing, cold turkey. It wasn't that they didn't have the medication that would help; they did. But they couldn't use it on the prisoners. If they did, it would be taking it away from their community. A tough decision, as it was human nature to want to help to alleviate suffering; but in the end it was a decision they all made together, right or wrong, they would adhere to it.

Weariness nagged at her mind, and her hip screamed with burning pain. She knew she had been pushing herself too hard. It had only been three weeks since her surgery. Doc told her she could put weight on her leg, but to go easy. Easy was not part of her make-up and the work with the sick prisoners demanded that she dig in and get things done.

The lodging in the barn was not an ideal set up. The wooden floors had soaked up urine, vomit, diarrhea, and God knew what else. It was a breeding ground for bacterial infections. But they had no other place to house them, so she made do.

One prisoner particularly worried her, a young man named Devon. He looked to be barely twenty and was severely underweight. It was evident from the needle marks on his inner arms, between his toes, on his stomach and neck; he had been using drugs, heavily. His body bore open, weeping sores that led her to wonder about what diseases he carried. Could he possibly have AIDS? And if so, bleach would eradicate it from the surfaces? With the wooden floors, she highly doubted she would be able to get rid of it completely. If it was AIDS, like she suspected, then he was already dead. But should she quarantine him from the others or leave him be? She'd have to talk with Mary Anne and Doc about it. To be on the safe side, she told Tanya and Jamie that they were not to go in his stall or work with him in any capacity. They had neither the proper personal protective equipment for this type of infectious disease, nor the training.

She'd sent them out for dinner over an hour ago. They both had worked alongside her with grim determination the entire afternoon. They were troopers; not having to be asked but instead just jumping right in and doing what was needed. Jamie had made her laugh several times through the afternoon with his comical antics and silly jokes. She found herself liking the boy a lot. Through the midst of raunchy smells that gagged them, handling gross and soiled bedding, cleaning up vomit, spoon feeding the ill, fetching fresh bleach water, and listening to the moans of the sick, he'd kept a smile on his face the entire time. She didn't know how he had managed it.

Shaking her head with a tired sigh, she looked bleakly at the faces of the prisoners. Hard, cold eyes stared back at her. Those that were sick lay on blankets with hay bedding underneath. She'd found buckets for them to vomit in and made them comfortable. Rusty stood at the ready in the doorway, gun at hip level. If one of them, sick or well, made a move toward her, she knew he would not hesitate to shoot. With one last glance at the seven sick men, she made her way out of the barn and into the fresh air. Three sets of hands would not be enough. She headed to the infirmary to talk with Doc about getting more help and about what to do with Devon. With the hollow, empty look in his eyes, she figured he wouldn't last too much longer. No amount of care and medicine would help that young man.

∞

Sarah lifted the coffee carafe and set it on the table. She winced as her shoulder zinged, an electric pain shooting down through her chest. She didn't care. It drove her crazy not helping.

She couldn't stand one more minute of inactivity. Mary Anne stood at the stove, stirring a large pot of chicken and dumplings. The table was laid with fresh bread and butter, and strawberry jam for people to help themselves. The community kitchen buzzed with activity, serving up dinner for those who worked all day at the compound and for those who spent their nights patrolling the perimeter. So much work to do every day kept everyone busy, and hungry. Her mind drifted. She set another pot of coffee on the stove to percolate.

The hand on her shoulder startled her, and instinctively she turned, her fist curling as she swung. A steady hand blocked her strike and grabbed her arm. She looked frightened and panicked. Looking up, she stared wildly into a set of hazel eyes.

"I didn't mean to scare you, I just wanted to grab a fresh cup," a man who looked to be about twenty-five said softly. Sarah bit the inside of her cheek and felt her face heat in embarrassment. An image of Gregory's face, snarling, flitted across her mind and she willed it away. She needed to stop this. She needed to pull herself together and stop jumping at ghosts.

She took a step back. "I'm sorry."

The man nodded and smiled. "No worries. We're all on edge. I should have announced myself."

With a grimace, Sarah nodded. He should

have.

"I'm Billy," the man said. He held out his hand.

She glanced down at it and then back up at him. "Nice to meet you. I'm Sarah."

"Well, Sarah, I'm sorry again that I startled you."

She watched as he grabbed for a cup on the shelf behind her and made his way over to the fresh pot she just put out. She watched him pour himself some coffee and she muttered to herself. "Not all men are monsters. Stop being a baby!"

But she knew, it would take a long time for this truth to sink in. The only men she trusted were Brian and Spike, they had both earned that trust.

With shaking hands, she went back to work brewing the coffee and helping Mary Anne at the stove. A soft shout from Beth alerted her to her presence.

"Hey, kiddo. I sure could use some coffee," Beth said, then held up the empty carafe. Smiling, Sarah brought the fresh pot over and refilled it. She gazed worriedly at the dark circles shadowing Beth's eyes and the faint lines around her mouth.

"You need to take a good, long break. You're working too hard," she scolded.

Beth smiled tiredly. "There's so much to do. But Doc is getting me more help."

Sarah hated that Beth helped with the prisoners, and she voiced her opinion loudly.

"Someone's gotta do it. I'm trained and have the experience, so I guess I'm it," Beth replied.

Mary Anne, overhearing their conversation, came over and sat beside Beth at the table, wiping her hands on her apron.

"We are grateful that Beth can help, Sarah. Although these men hurt a lot of people, it is still up to us to care for them, to feed them. Once my Roger gets back we will decide what to do with the prisoners, but until then it is up to us to make sure they are taken care of," she scolded gently. Sarah nodded, and her eyes darkened with anger.

If this woman only knew what these men had done, what they were capable of doing. She might then change her mind about how much compassion she gave them. They were rabid animals, and in her mind, rabid animals needed to be put down. With a grunt, she got up and walked back into the kitchen, leaving Beth and Mary Anne staring after her. Anger boiled in her blood, and she wished Brian were here. If he were, he'd have no qualms about shooting every one of those prisoners, none whatsoever.

∞

Beth looked at Mary Anne and sighed sadly after the girl left. She could only imagine what Sarah went through at the hands of Bobby and his men. So yes, she could completely understand her anger, her outrage; she could also understand Mary Anne's reasoning for doing so. To not help, to let them suffer would make her and Mary Anne no better than Bobby or his gang. Suddenly the bowl of chicken and dumplings in front of her didn't look so appealing. With a gentle nudge, she pushed it away and instead sipped at the hot coffee. Digging in her pocket, she took out two Tylenol and popped them into her mouth. Her hip screamed with pain, and she rubbed it gently. This day could not end soon enough.

Mary Anne grabbed her hand and squeezed it gently.

"You're tired. I've got a surprise for you." With a smile, she helped her up. Beth looked at her questioningly.

"Come with me."

Hand in hand, they walked through the compound to a small cottage next to the infirmary building. Mary Anne smiled and opened the door.

"I figure it's time for you and Sarah to have a place of your own. It's only got one small bedroom, but I got a few of the guys to move in a trundle bed for Sarah," she said. She led Beth into the small living room. Beth laughed in delight.

"This is wonderful!" She turned and hugged the other woman tightly. To be able to move out of her small room in the infirmary, and into this with Sarah, made her rough day all the better. Sighing, she sat on the small, blue-flowered print couch and leaned back.

"I can't thank you enough, Mary Anne." She swallowed past the lump of joy in her throat.

Mary Anne laughed. "You don't have to."

After Mary Anne left, Beth sagged into the couch and closed her eyes. Having a space of her own, no matter how temporary, set her heart at ease. She loved this community and what Mary Anne and Roger created here. And if her heart hadn't been set on the south, she could easily make a permanent home here. She knew Brian wanted to go home to Tennessee. He wanted to see his parents again. And she wanted to be with him. Sighing, she let herself drift into a soft sleep. Jessie curled up beside her and laid her head on her lap.

Chapter Twenty

The night unfolded around them. Sleep came quickly to the children in the group. The wounded were tended to and made comfortable. Brian nodded when Mel sat down beside him and sipped a cup of broth.

"Thank you." She turned her face up toward him and smiled.

"For what?"

"For helping with the wounded and for taking care of me." She nodded.

"It feels good, Brian. Feels good to know I am free to help without looking over my shoulder in fear. These people?" she said, waving her hand around at the group of refugees, "they've been through more than you can ever imagine. The conditions they have lived under, the abuse they have suffered. Life became hard enough after the event, but to go through this? No man or woman should ever suffer what Bobby and his gang did to them. It's gonna take a long time for some of them to heal, some of them never will. Not physically, but emotionally and mentally. But these women, they were all someone's wife, someone's sister, someone's mother or daughter! And they were all ripped from their families in the most vicious and brutal way. And the children, God, my heart screams out for them. I don't know what happened to compassion, to kindness, but those kids ain't seen that in a very long time."

Brian nodded, and he swallowed past the sadness in his throat. "And you. Don't forget what you've been through," he murmured.

Mel shook her head. "I've been through nothing better or worse than any one of them. I'm a tough cookie. Yes, I have my nightmares and demons to battle. But ya know what? I won't let those demons destroy me. I don't want your pity," she replied with a stubborn set to her jaw.

Brian smiled. "Pity is not what I'm giving you, compassion, yes."

Mel shrugged her shoulders. "I do what I do. I've learned that the hard way."

∞

Mitch moved in the tree line, waiting and watching. Peckerhead pecked the ground near his feet and he hissed at the rooster to get out of the way. He sucked in a deep breath when he saw Joseph turn his back on one of the prisoners, diverting his attention to another. He watched Jerry Miller use the diversion to pick up a water jug, look around then insert something into it.

Swearing, he exploded out of the darkness and threw himself at the man. "What did you just do?" he screamed. He pinned him to the ground.

The man, Jerry, struggled to get up. Joseph quickly moved beside him and drew his gun, pointing it at Jerry's face. "What's up? What's happening?" he asked in confusion.

Mathew and Earl came running over. Quickly, they gathered up the prisoners and pushed them into a tight group. Brian and Spike walked over.

"This man put something in the water!" Mitch snarled as he drove a fist into Jerry's face. The crack of his knuckles against flesh resounded in the air, and Jerry threw his arms up in defense.

Brian reached down and hauled the prisoner to his feet. Turning to Spike, he ordered him to search the prisoner.

Spike searched both pant pockets and found nothing. Moving to the upper shirt pocket, his fingers fell onto a small cellophane packet. Pulling it out, he held it up.

"What is this?" he growled menacingly.

"Nothing," Jerry mumbled. His eyes darted wildly looking for a way out.

Mel came walking over and opened the packet. With a dampened finger, she tasted one of the little crystals and then spat on the ground.

"It's rat poison. We now know why you were so sick, Brian. This sick bastard has been poisoning our water supply!" she growled. Before anyone could stop her, she stepped up to Jerry, curled her hand into a fist and punched him in the face. A satisfied grin spread across her face when her fist connected, and his nose spurted and gushed blood.

"You've been poisoning us?" Brian hissed. The look in his eyes sent a wave of terror spiraling through Jerry's gut.

"I gave you just enough to make you sick, not enough to kill you, I swear!" Jerry whispered, pleadingly.

He watched in horror as Brian lifted his gun from its holster.

"No! No man, don't!" he screamed.

Brian grinned coldly and pulled the trigger. Spike, standing beside the prisoner, jumped when part of his head blew off and spat bits of flesh, bone, and brain out. He swore loudly and looked at Brian.

Brian shook his head and turned on his heels.

"Problem solved."

Mitch watched Brian walk away. He looked at Spike, who wiped the gore from his clothes, and he shrugged his shoulders. He'd of pulled the trigger if Brian hadn't. He wondered if Spike knew of Brian's past. He hadn't had much of a chance to talk with him but made a mental note to do so soon. Although he'd seen nothing from Brian that sent up warning flags, he knew the man was a stone-cold killer and warranted close watching.

The rest of the night passed in bouts and fits of uneasy sleep. When the first light of dawn broke over the night sky, Brian got up and fed the campfire and put on a pot for coffee. Today they should easily make the compound. His headache had subsided, along with the nausea and cramping diarrhea. Other than tiredness from the broken sleep, he felt pretty good. They had lost another of the wounded overnight, and this weighed heavily on his heart. The man's name was Timothy. He had a wife back at the compound along with two small children. Now they would be fatherless and his wife, a widow. He shook his head sadly. Mel moved up and sat beside him.

Spike stirred in his sleep a few feet away and grumbled. "Shit! I didn't sleep worth a dang!"

Smiling, Brian held up a cup of coffee. "It's ready. Get your ass up and rouse the others. We need to get an early start today. I don't want to lose one more of the wounded on this bloody road."

Spike grimaced and crawled out of the blanket. His hair, wild and unruly, stood on end.

"Yup, I hear ya," he muttered. Mel handed him a cup of coffee. He smiled at her gratefully and took a sip. Leslie, Barbs, and Karen stumbled sleepily over to the fire and grabbed cups of coffee to get them started. Mel looked at each of the women and nodded good morning. Mitch and Cain joined them a few minutes later.

"Little Stephen is sick this morning. He

drank a lot of water yesterday in this heat, so I'm thinking he's suffering from the poison," Barbs said. She lifted the cup of coffee to her mouth and peered over the rim at Mel.

"I've got some activated charcoal. That should help absorb the poison. We'll have to watch him through the day for dehydration if he starts vomiting and experiences diarrhea," Mel replied with a shadow of concern on her face. Damn, the children had been through enough, and now this? She didn't know how much more she or they could take. With a sigh, she got up and pulled a bottle of activated charcoal from a bin in the back of one of the wagons. The stuff would go down hard, but not all medicine was meant to taste good. Activated charcoal would act as a binder for the poison and grab onto it. It would then transport the poison from the body through feces—a simple, effective remedy for mild poisoning.

Brian, Spike, and the rest of the men moved in single file making their way across the last few miles to the compound. After several rest stops and emergency stops for Stephen to run off into the woods with Mel hot on his heels, the rise of the road brought them within sight of their destination. A deep sigh escaped Brian's lips as he moved the group ahead. He dreaded bringing the news of the deaths to the community. The trip caused a lot of heartaches and had taken a toll on all of them. It would be a relief to hand the reins over to the others. With Roger gone, he and Spike took responsibility for the ragtag group of refugees and prisoners. Now he could let that responsibility go.

A shout from the watchtower near the gate of the compound brought his head up and his horse to a halt.

"It's me," Spike shouted back. He raised his hand. "I've got wounded, refugees, and prisoners. Open the doggone gate, please."

Brian watched several men come running toward the heavy iron gate and push it open. Cheers and clapping erupted when they filed through and he watched as several women and men from the community began helping with the refugees. Mary Anne stood at the back of the chaos and gazed through the crowd for her husband. Her eyes met Brian's, and she let out a shriek of pain when she read the expression on his face. From behind, a large and grizzled man caught her as she collapsed to the ground. Brian's heart shattered with agony hearing her sobs, and he bit down on his tongue to keep the tears that stung his eyes at bay. With a sigh, he hung his head. He'd seen too much death in his lifetime. His heart sank with the truth of this.

Chapter Twenty-One

He sat at the table in the community kitchen with Beth and Sarah. Jessie lay by their feet, sleeping, her belly full of all the treats she had begged from them. His gaze roamed the room. All the refugees sat quietly eating. The kitchen staff had prepared dishes of baked ham, bowls of rice with chicken gravy, hot biscuits from the oven, pitchers of fresh water, and plates filled with a variety of vegetables. His dish, laden with food, sat untouched.

"How bad was it?" Beth asked. Brian grimaced. His hands played with the fork, tapping it against his plate. About as bad as any human situation could be. Even in prison, where it was almost unbearable, it hadn't been this bad. What Spike told him about the condition of the cages that housed the women and children gave him chills. He said this to Beth and saw her face whiten with shock.

"Oh, my God! Those poor women and children," she whispered. Sarah shook her head, and a tear slipped from her eyes. She quickly brushed it away. The days she'd spent as a prisoner in that town made her count her blessings that she hadn't seen the inside of the library. What she'd went through seemed mild in comparison to what Spike and now Brian described. The filth, the confinement, the stench, the abuses, how did they all survive it?

"How's Mary Anne?" Brian asked. Spike was the one who broke the news to her about Roger's death. He and Rusty helped her to her house and stayed with her for hours until she finally threw them both out.

"I just checked on her. It's gonna take some time," Beth replied sadly. Her voice caught on a sob, and she buried her face in her hands. She knew full well the pain Mary Anne suffered.

"There will be a mass burial tomorrow. Several men and women are tending to the dead now, and Tony Milsed along with a few other boys are making coffins. Mary Anne wants to have a full service up on the hill behind the compound. This way, she can look out her back window and see Roger's grave. I think this will bring her some comfort."

Brian nodded. "Understandable. I've got to meet with Rusty and several others today. We will be deciding what to do with the prisoners," he said.

What he wanted to do was have a few moments alone with Beth. Moments where he could sink into her calmness and feel her skin against his own. Pushing this thought away, he grimaced. One day there would be time for that. But not today.

He knew Beth was taking care of the sick prisoners and running herself ragged in the process. He planned to vote to remedy that situation. None of them, in his opinion, deserved the least bit of care from the decent people in this community. Spike, he knew, would agree. Mary Anne may be the opposing vote; either way, he'd let them hear his opinion. If they chose his method of dealing with the scum, then good for them. And if they decided not to, then it would be on the people of this community and not his problem.

Brian sat on a stump outside of the prisoner barn while Beth tended to the sick. Rusty sat on another stump beside him and pulled a cigarette from his pack, lit it, then handed one to Brian. Although Brian never picked up the habit of smoking, occasionally he enjoyed one if given to him. Taking a deep drag, he sighed with enjoyment as the smoke filled his lungs. His eyes drifted into the gloaming, and his mind chewed over the upcoming meeting. He'd been inside the barn; he'd seen the prisoners. And at the cost of how many those men had murdered and tortured, he had to use every ounce of willpower to quell the urge to take out his sidearm and start shooting them. The hatred burned in his gut like a wildfire, causing his hands to shake.

"We'll soon be finished with them. The prisoners won't live to see the sunset, tomorrow evening. Your woman won't be running herself ragged taking care of those scum after today," Rusty said. He turned his head and spit onto the ground. Brian raised an eyebrow.

"It doesn't matter what the vote is. I'll tell ya that right now! You should have executed them on the road. Not brought them back here!" Rusty growled angrily. Brian nodded in agreement, but would he go so far to ignore the vote if the group decided the prisoners should live?

"I hear ya. But the vote will decide," Brian replied. Rusty shook his head.

"No! It won't. Because if they all vote to keep them alive and try to rehabilitate them? Then I'll take matters into my own hands. They are animals! And I won't tolerate them at this compound that Roger and Mary Anne, and yes, I built! I do not care what the majority says. I will have the final say!"

The group could vote for the prisoners to live. But Rusty, second in command behind Roger, would have the final say. He would, Brian knew, go against the group if he needed to. The hatred he felt for the prisoners lay evident on his face. The cruel twist to his lips, the dark anger in his eyes, and the tenseness of his shoulders showed Brian just how adamant he was that the prisoners should die. Brian was surprised that he'd let them live this long.

"Roger was my best friend. I have known him since I was a young buck. They," he said, waving his hand toward the barn, "took my best friend from me! We'd been through the war together, sat in the mud and muck, swamped through the most inhospitable of countries, bled together. And now he's gone. Because of what? Those scum, in there, who are eating our food, being cared for by our community!" he shouted. "Because they decided, rather than help each other and those around them after the event, they would rather rape, murder, and steal from others! Well, I'll be damned if I'm gonna let Roger's hard work benefit those who deserve only my disgust and a bullet." His voice broke, and he grimaced.

Brian nodded. "I'll vote with you. And when the time comes, I will stand beside you to put these animals down."

Rusty nodded and smiled weakly. "Thank you."

Brian walked with Beth, back, toward the infirmary. The small white building stood next to the community kitchen. Roger had been smart when setting up the design of the compound. A large grassy area surrounded by a circle of buildings: a community kitchen, an infirmary, bathhouses, and an outdoor kitchen. The main house where Mary Anne lived stood just off the center next to the supply barn. In the center of the circle of buildings, Roger had constructed a playground with swings, slides, and monkey bars for the children of the community where they could play safely. He'd also set up a dozen or so picnic tables where everyone could relax and gather.

When they neared the infirmary, Beth slowed. She wanted to check on the wounded and discuss with Doc what was happening with the sick. Devon had died during the night and his body, they decided would be burned rather than buried. Doc couldn't be sure that he had AIDS, but he wasn't going to take any chances.

Mel greeted them both when they entered the small waiting room. "Hi."

Although her journey was long and hard, despite all she'd been through in captivity, the woman still insisted that she would help with the wounded and the refugees. Many of the children suffered from scabies and lice. She had used one of the exam rooms to bathe them in an old washtub then treat them with Ivermectin, a powerful insecticide. Then she sat with each child and combed the eggs from their hair. Several of the women helped her with the process. She was bound and determined that there would not be an outbreak allowed to run rampant throughout the community. Brian, smiling, knelt in front of Stephen, whose face was bright red and scowling. He could smell the pungent odor of the insecticide drenching the boy's hair, and he wrinkled his nose.

"Easy, boy. It'll soon be over then you can shag butt and get away from these girls!" he teased. The young boy grinned and wiggled in the chair, fighting Leslie, when she picked another nit from a strand of his hair.

"I'm not a boy. I'm big!" he answered. His face squinched in pain when once again Mel pulled his hair through the nit comb.

"Yes, I guess you probably are," Brian replied with a laugh. The boy, Stephen, had a tough go of it. First, with what Bobby and his gang put him through; second, with the excruciating pain of being poisoned; and now, this.

"You're done. Now go play until it's time to rinse that stuff out of your hair," Leslie said. She tapped him on the bottom and ushered him out the door to play with the other kids who'd been treated. Wearily she wiped her hands on a towel and walked over to Mel who worked on Jaden, a girl of about twelve with waist-length hair.

"I'm gonna take a quick break. My back is killing me, and I need a drink,"

Mel smiled and nodded. They'd all been going at it for hours. "Sure, can you bring me back a glass of water?"

Leslie nodded. "I'll be back."

Once Beth finished, they decided to go to the community kitchen and see if there was any coffee brewing. It had been a very long day. They sat at the table, each with a cup of fresh coffee in front of them. Brian turned and gazed into Beth's eyes. The banging of pots and pans, the aroma of food while it cooked, and the voices and laughter of the women in the kitchen made it so that he had to raise his voice to talk to her.

"You're walking much better. How is the hip feeling?" He hadn't found a chance to talk much with her since his return.

"I'm doing good. Doc says another three or so weeks, and I should be good as new."

He nodded.

"You like it here, right?" he asked. Beth nodded and looked at him oddly over the rim of her coffee cup. She took another sip of the dark brew.

"Ummm, yeah. I guess, why?"

"Well, I want to make sure. After things get settled, probably in a few weeks, I've decided to head out. I need to get home, Beth. I need to know if my parents are still alive," he murmured, breaking the news to her. It had been on his mind, troubling him a lot this past week. He knew here, Beth and Sarah were safe. He also could see that she was happy here with this community. As much as he wanted to beg her to come with him, he wouldn't. He didn't have anything to offer her other than a long, hard journey with an uncertain future.

Beth sucked in a deep breath. His words settled painfully on her heart. Did this mean he didn't want her to go with him? That he no longer wanted her and Sarah, that they were holding him back? Tears filled her eyes, and she turned her head away from him. Angrily she brushed them away. She felt him sigh deeply beside her.

"Beth?"

She turned back to him.

"I'm happy here, yes," she lied. Her heart shattered. Getting up, she slammed her cup down on the table, the coffee sloshing over the side and spilling. Not bothering to clean it up, she turned on her heels and walked away from Brian, ignoring his pleas for her to stop.

Chapter Twenty-Two

She walked back to the cottage, struggling to hold back the sobs trapped in her throat, and fought against the tears that wanted to rip her apart. She'd trusted him. She thought they would always stay together. She thought he felt the same way. How could she have been so wrong? The grass beneath her feet soaked into her shoes, and she kicked them off in anger; preferring to feel the grass on her bare feet. Opening the door, she walked past Sarah, who sat on the couch with Jessie and went to her room and closed the door. Only then did she let herself cry. Hugging herself, she crouched on the floor with her back against the wall as sobs ripped into her. Confusion chased itself around in her mind. Did she imagine that Brian had been attracted to her? Shame flooded her face. A soft knock on the door brought her to her feet, and with a trembling hand, she hastily wiped her eyes. Pasting a smile on her face, she opened it.

"Beth?" Sarah asked, seeing her swollen and puffy eyes.

"It's okay, baby girl. I'm just having a moment. Stress, ya know?" she lied. She watched as the other girls' eyes narrowed.

"Bullshit! What happened?"

Shaking her head, Beth choked on her

words.

"Brian is leaving in a few weeks. He doesn't want me, us to go with him," she stuttered through tears. Sarah swore softly, and anger flitted across her face. How could he? How dare he hurt Beth after all they'd been through together? With clenched fists, she stormed from the room and out of the house. Well, she had a few choice words for him for sure!

Marching across the compound, past the children playing on the swings, past a few people sitting at the picnic tables, she made her way to the community kitchen where she found him sitting by himself at a table. His head bowed, and his hands were wrapped around a cup of coffee in front of him. Without missing a beat, she stormed over and tapped him on the shoulder. When he turned, she slapped him hard across the face.

"You bastard!" she spat angrily. Brian jumped up, knocking over the chair behind him. He blocked her hand when she swung at him again.

"Stop!" he roared angrily. Sarah stared up at him defiantly, angrily she clenched her fist by her side. She didn't back away when he took a step toward her. Mitch, who sat across the room eating, got up and made his way toward the two. His hand rested lightly on the butt of his knife.

"Everything okay here, Miss?" he asked giving Brian a warning glance. Brian smiled coldly.

"Not your business, man," he growled. Mitch shook his head.

"Well, it kinda is. When I see a young girl being threatened by a grown man twice her size, then I kinda get a little concerned."

Sarah moved in between the two men.

"I'm fine," she snapped. She glanced at Brian from the corner of her eye and could see the dangerous glint in his eyes as he stared down the other man. "We are just having a disagreement."

Mitch nodded, leveling a look at her.

"Okay. I guess then I'll be moseying back to my table," he replied. He shot a warning glare at Brian. Something about him didn't sit well with Mitch. The man was cocky and overconfident.

After he left, Brian whirled on Sarah angrily.

"What in the hell is the matter with you, Sarah?" he growled. He towered over her. She reminded him of a small terrier as she stood her ground in front of him. Her eyes flashed angrily and her body was tensed like a coiled snake, ready to strike. Fierceness radiated from her in waves.

"Matter with me?" she hissed, "What is the matter with you? Telling Beth, you didn't want her to go with you? Telling her, you didn't want Jessie or me? We are family, you asshole! And family does not leave each other behind!"

Brian shook his head in shock. Is that what Beth thought? That he didn't want her? That he didn't want her to go with him? That he would just leave them behind because he didn't care? Turning on his heels, he shot a sharp look over his shoulder at Sarah.

"You both cannot possibly be more wrong!" he snapped.

He didn't even bother to knock. He just pushed through the door with a bang. He found Beth curled up on the couch with Jessie's head on her lap.

"We need to talk! Now!" he shouted.

Beth glared at him from swollen eyes.

"There is nothing to talk about. You made it pretty clear earlier!" she shouted back. Brian sucked in a deep breath and rolled his eyes. God help him in trying to understand this blasted woman.

"What exactly did I make clear, Beth? Because, you and me? We're not on the same page here!" he growled. The tone of his voice, the stance of his body, set off a wave of threatening growls from Jessie and Beth grabbed her collar. Brian's face darkened and he glared at her.

"Get that mutt under control, Beth."

"It's okay, girl," she purred. She glared

back at him.

"You made it perfectly clear that you didn't want Sarah or me around anymore. That you were tired of carrying us, that you want to be rid of us," she replied. Brian grimaced and shook his head. He wanted to throttle the woman in front of him. He had said no such thing! How could she even think that?

"You're wrong," he murmured softly, "I wanted to know if you were happy here. If you were, then devil be damned if I would ask you to drag yourself and Sarah back onto the trail with me. I want you, Beth. I have grown very fond of Sarah, and yes, even that mutt next to you. And I think I've made it pretty clear how I feel about you. So much so, that I didn't think it right to ask you to come to Tennessee with me. How can I uproot you when you've finally found a community, a home? That would be the most selfish thing I could ever do," he finished tiredly. He ran his hand through his hair in frustration.

Beth stood and walked into his arms. She hugged him tightly and leaned her head against his chest. She breathed in deeply of his scent, a mixture of sweat, smoke and lavender soap. His arms tightened around her, pulling her closer and she felt the beat of his heart against her cheek.

"Then damn it, be selfish, Brian. Ask me to go with you," she whispered. Brian smiled and gazed down at the top of her head. This woman was enough to make him crazy. Stubborn, fearless, crazy, inept at most survival skills, but he loved her. He didn't know when or how it had happened, but this woman he held tightly in his arms meant everything to him. His life would not be complete without her in it. He groaned softly and rubbed his face in her hair.

"Will you come with me, Beth?" he asked softly. She raised her face to his and smiled.

"Yuppers! You would 'a had a hard time making me stay here," she replied. "After all, we are family. You and me, Sarah and Jessie."

Brian bent and kissed her long and hard. He didn't know where their road would lead, but he would be more than happy to continue his journey with this woman.

∞

The meeting came to order, and Brian looked around at the faces at the table. The kitchen was empty and quiet although he smelled the aroma of chicken stew simmering on the stove. Spike sat in the chair next to him. His long, slender fingers were playing nervously with the handle of the coffee cup sitting in front of him. Cain sat across the table from him, and his eyes were staring vacantly ahead. His expression bore his grief and sorrow. Rusty sat at the head of the table beside Mary Anne, like he was trying to protect her from her pain. Then there was Danny, Jacob, and Mathew and the new man, Mitch.

A cough from Rusty brought all attention back to the matter at hand. What to do with the prisoners? "You all know how I feel. And we've all had a chance to speak our peace. So now we need to vote. All those in favor of execution, raise your hands."

Brian glanced around. All but Mary Anne raised their hand in favor of executing the prisoners. He looked at her. She stared vacantly at the far wall. He could tell her mind was a million miles away from where she sat.

"Mary Anne? Do you have anything you want to say?" Rusty murmured. She chose not to vote on the issue; explaining that in her grief, in her anger, she didn't feel she would be able to make a decision that wouldn't be based on her emotions.

"I do." She stood and addressed the group. "I know what these men did. I know the horrors they put those women, those children, and others through," she choked through tears, "but I want you all to remember. We do what we must—to survive. If that means executing those men, then so be it. Their deaths will fall on us all equally, though. We will each carry that stain on our souls for the rest of our lives equally. I do not want one person at this table to say they didn't have a part of this! This is a tough decision to make, to take another's life. But for the good of all, I feel we have no choice. We can turn them loose, and I will bet my bottom dollar it will come back to haunt us. But, know this; we are still condoning taking a life. God help us all," she finished then she looked each person in the eye. Heads nodded in agreement around the table. Yes, if the law were around, they could turn them into the nearest cop and be done with it. But there was no law other than what they decided.

Brian got up from the chair and stretched tiredly. They had decided. Tomorrow morning, he and six others, Spike, Rusty, Cain, Danny, Mitch, and Jacob, would roust the prisoners. They would take them to the far end of the compound and execute them. Tonight, they would dig a mass grave, and tomorrow, they would bury them in it. No headstones, no graveside prayers. Just dirt. Although he didn't feel an ounce of compassion for these criminals, he did take to heart the seriousness of the situation. More stains on his soul that he would one day have to account for. He prayed God would find it in his grace to forgive him.

∞

Mitch sat on a lawn chair with his legs stretched out in front of him, staring off into the distance. The vote bothered him. To openly execute the prisoners didn't sit well with him. Although he understood the reasoning and knew it needed doing, he still had misgivings. Since when had they all become judge, jury, and executioners? And Brian? He watched him while the vote went down. He watched the cold fury in his eyes while they talked about the prisoners. That man was a true killer at heart, and he didn't trust him one bit. His reputation for leaving a bloody trail in his wake made Mitch uneasy and on edge. Leaning back, he let the sun warm his face and listened to the noise of children playing on the playground fade away as his body relaxed.

∞

When the first light of dawn broke over the mountains, Beth heard the gunshots, and she winced. Crawling from the warmth of the blankets, she quickly dressed. The chilly morning air raised goosebumps on her skin. Brian had told her what the committee had decided. She didn't know how she felt about it. Relief? Sorrow at the loss of even more lives? Anger that they all were forced into this situation by the event? Would these men have led different lives if the event never happened? Or were they just inherently evil and the event unleashed their restraint of hiding it? Shaking her head, she closed her eyes and said a quick prayer. This was life now. A criminal didn't go to jail, didn't have a trial. This community, people everywhere couldn't afford that luxury anymore.

With exaggerated quietness, she tiptoed past Sarah, who slept in the living room on the trundle bed and made her way out into the morning. The air held a late May chill, and she breathed deeply of the scents of grass, earthy moisture, and fresh, clean air. No fumes from vehicles or factories polluted it. No airplanes overhead buzzed to break the silence. No smog clouded the horizon. It was as though nature was healing itself from the thousands of years humans had assaulted it.

Stepping into the community kitchen, it surprised her to see Mary Anne in her usual place in front of the stove. Tantalizing scents of frying bacon wafted through the common dining area. She walked over and stood beside Mary Anne at the stove and grabbed her hand, squeezing it tight.

"Mary Anne, what are you doing here?"

Mary Anne turned and through a watery smile, sighed.

"Where else would I be? I mean, this is it," she replied. Her voice choked with tears.

"You don't need to be here. People will understand if you take a day or two, or five, off," Beth said softly.

"I know. I know everyone will. But Beth, Roger would not have wanted me to curl up and die because of this. He and I built this together. No matter what happens in this world, this matters. I need to keep busy. I mean, these people, they depend on me holding it together. All that Roger and I have done here depends on me keeping it together."

Beth hugged her and tears filled her own eyes.

"I'm okay, or I think I will be okay, yes, I will be okay. Maybe not today, maybe not tomorrow, but eventually. For now, though, it's one breath at a time until I am okay again." Mary Anne whispered. Turning, she stirred a big pot of bubbling oatmeal. Leslie, setting bowls out on the long table, glanced at Beth and smiled. Her lip quivering, she brushed away a tear.

"Well, I agree. You will be okay. I speak from experience, just please, let others give you love and support. Don't try to bear this all on your own." Beth whispered. Mary Anne looked into her eyes and nodded.

"Okay, enough of this dripping and weeping. I've got work to do so get the hell out of my kitchen." Mary Anne quipped through her tears. Beth nodded and made her way to the coffee pot. Pouring herself a cup, she carried it with her while she helped Leslie set out the dishware for breakfast. She knew the men who'd stayed up most of the night digging the long mass grave for the executed prisoners would be ravenous and wanting breakfast.

∞

Brian made his way back to the cottage to wash up before heading to the community kitchen for a cup of coffee. The prisoners had been executed, and the burial detail had placed the last shovel full of dirt over them. Many of the men were deeply affected. Acting the executioner would never be an easy task. He hadn't any qualms about pulling the trigger. Did that make him cold and unfeeling? No, just practical. Men, especially men such as those they'd shot, needed to be dead. They gave nothing to society other than hardship and sorrow. He thought of them the same way he had thought of those who'd destroyed his sister Talia. They did not deserve his compassion or mercy. He would someday be judged by the Almighty for his actions. It would be only to Him he would answer.

The day unfolded in front of him. The funeral for Roger would be in the early afternoon. After that, he would meet with Rusty to help with defense details. Although Roger was gone, the compound still needed to run. And when Rusty found out that Brian was ex-military, he cornered him for help. There were still plenty of threats out there that they had to deal with. The Alliance was still making its way to the northeast. Still hell-bent on taking the compound for themselves. Just because Bobby's gang was no longer a concern; the Alliance still was. Brian wondered if they'd gotten word yet of the annihilation of Bobby's group. He was sure they probably did. Sure, that someone in that God-forsaken town had set off to warn them of the resistance they would find at the compound.

He'd promised his help to Rusty for the next three or four weeks. He and Beth hadn't yet told anyone of their plans to leave and head south. He dreaded having to tell Mary Anne. He knew she had become very fond of Beth and Sarah. Sighing deeply, he kicked a small stone in front of him. These long thoughts did nothing to improve his mood.

∞

Mary Anne made her way back to the house. They'd finished breakfast, and lunch was in the works with the many hands, pitching in to help. The morning sped by fast, and she thanked God it did. Staying busy kept her mind from wandering too far into the sadness that hung heavy on her heart. Doubt rode her like a bucking pony, and she wondered if she could keep up with all that Roger used to do at the compound. Tears slid slowly down her face, unchecked. She opened the door to her home. A home now without her husband of forty-some odd years. It felt lonely and very empty, like it missed Roger too. With a huff, she swiped at her face and made her way to the basement where Roger kept his HAM radio equipment. She sat tiredly in his leather chair, a chair that smelled like him, and it brought on a fresh onslaught of tears which angered her.

Picking up the mike, she dialed into Joe's

handle. She would inform him of Roger's death and ask him to send it out over the radio to all their other friends. It was the hardest conversation she thought she'd ever had. Once done, she made her way back upstairs and to her bedroom. She rifled through the closet for the prettiest dress she owned, and after a quick sponge bath, she put it on. Numbness lessened the grief that had been cloaking her like a shadow throughout the day.

Rusty walked beside her, up the long hill, toward the old oak tree at the top, holding her hand tightly in his own. The hole gaped darkly, and Roger's casket sat beside it. Her eyes glazed over with pain. She gently placed a sprig of lavender on the top of it. Roger always loved the smell of lavender. It was only fitting she bury him with some.

Charlie Sims gave the eulogy with the entire community gathered round. Tears flowed freely when Roger's casket was lowered into the ground, and the first shovel of dirt was tossed on top of it. Beth held Brian's hand and she bowed her head in prayer. Spike stood behind Sarah and placed his hands gently on her shoulders while she wept softly. Cain stood beside Rusty, Mitch, and Mary Anne, an expression of deep sorrow in his eyes. Mary Anne stood stoically, her face stricken with grief as members of the community filed by with words of condolence and warm hugs. Her mind screamed in agony and she silently pleaded for solitude. But she stayed, stayed until the very end. She let Rusty help her back to her house, where she closed herself in. Once alone, she felt something inside of her tear loose and break. Sobs tore her heart apart. Images of Roger's face danced before her eyes, his goofy smile, and the mischievous sparkle in his eyes. These were the memories that hurt and crippled her. Sinking to the floor, she cried herself to sleep.

Chapter Twenty-Three

The next week flew by with a flurry of activity at the compound. Beth worried about Mary Anne, and how hard she pushed herself. This morning, they planned to slaughter pigs, twenty-five of them. The community raised a herd of about one hundred and fifty, with several new litters being born over the past week. A group would begin the slaughtering process, another group would be butchering the meat, and another group would be preparing it for winter storage. In the center of the compound, several men had constructed another temporary outdoor kitchen where large pots hung over fires to boil water. On a long plank wood table, jars were set up for canning. Two temporary smokehouses sat waiting while two men tended the wood chips to begin smoking hams and pork butt roasts.

Beth sliced bacon from a large side of meat and watched the chaos of women and men. They each stood at their stations chatting and laughing while their hands stayed busy. Hundreds of pounds of pork would be processed.

Mary Anne sat beside her and with a sharp knife, expertly and quickly sliced large swathes of meat, then cut it into thinner strips. She then laid these strips carefully in layers in a wooden crate of salt so they would cure. Beth followed her instruction carefully. Sarah across the yard, helping Leslie and Barbs with a canning project.

"So, once this is done, and the crate is full, then what?"

Mary Anne wiped her greasy hands on her apron and smiled.

"We then move these crates into the cold cellar where the bacon will cure for weeks," she replied. She grabbed another slab of meat that Enis set in front of her on the table.

"And the canning? What portions of meat do you use for that?"

"Well, you can use any cut or portion, but this time we're using ribs with bone on, we're using loin portions, jowls, cheek, hocks and then we'll pickle the feet. We will smoke the hams and pork butt," she answered. Beth nodded and then grimaced. Pickled pigs feet? She hadn't ever tried them and probably wouldn't in this lifetime.

"We'll help with the canning later. After we're through with the bacon," Mary Anne said.

"So, canning, do we put them in the boiling water? For how long?"

Mary Anne shook her head.

"No. Remember, all meat has to be pressure canned. We have another area set up for that. Here, at our elevation, it's fifteen pounds of pressure for one hour and fifteen minutes. We don't want anyone getting sick on improperly canned foods. One of the kettles over there is to sterilize our jars and lids." She pointed to Leslie and Barbs who were busily dipping jars into the boiling water and pulling them out with tongs then setting them on towels.

Beth shook her head and sighed; so much to remember. So much, she still needed to learn. Mary Anne, seeing the frustration on her face, smiled and nudged her shoulder with her own.

"Don't worry. In time you will get it. You can't learn this all overnight. Besides, I've been writing everything down for you."

Beth smiled into her face. Of course, she did. Mary Anne was the queen of notes. Never had Beth seen her without a notebook attached to her hand. She would miss all of this. This feeling of community and the purposeful activity that came with. She would miss Mary Anne and Barbs, Jill and Leslie, Doc and Karen, all of them. She'd grown close to these people, they felt like family to her.

Seeing the shadow of sadness on Beth's face, Mary Anne raised an eyebrow in question. "Why so, glum?"

"Just thinking," Beth murmured then turned her face to Mary Anne's, "you know I love it here, right?"

Mary Anne nodded.

"And if I could stay, I would, right?"

Mary Anne nodded. Heaviness pressed

on her heart. She knew that Beth and Brian, Sarah and Jessie, would be leaving soon. She had pleaded with them to stay but understood that Brian needed to find out if his parents were still alive.

"I know. And maybe one day you and Brian will come back here to stay for good. I will miss you, girl. I hate the idea of you leaving, of Sarah and Brian and Jessie leaving…you don't know how much I wish I could make you stay, but I understand why you have to go." Mary Anne sighed, choking back a tear. Her throat tightened. The sun had grown hot overhead, and she wiped a bead of sweat from her brow. The summer heat had moved in early this year, and she made a mental note to ask those who helped with the garden to give it some extra water today. They couldn't afford to have the young spring plants burn in this heat.

"I just don't want you to think I'm abandoning you or don't appreciate all that you've done for me," Beth whispered. Tears filled her eyes.

"I don't think that. I wouldn't think that. You gotta follow your man, honey, that I do understand, believe me," Mary Anne said, then smiled. And she meant every word. Memories of this same conversation flooded her mind. Memories of when she and Roger first decided they would move from her hometown in Kansas, leaving her parents and family, to start their life here in the North East. The heartbreaking decision of leaving one life behind while she began another life with her husband.

∞

Brian wiped a hand across his sweaty brow. Rusty looked at him and laughed, "Getting old there, boyo?"

Brian grinned in response and lifted the bulky, iron contraption with the help of Spike and Cain, across the ditch on the edge of the boundary fence. This heavy behemoth was the brainchild of Stinky, an old war vet that although well past his fighting days still came up with some great ideas. He took old iron beams that Roger had picked up from God knows where, way back when, and used a torch to cut them into four-foot lengths. Then, he welded legs to them, creating a sawhorse type contraption. On the flat surface of this iron sawhorse he then took iron railroad spikes, again gathered from somewhere in one of Roger's junk piles, and welded them, point up, to create dangerous and lethal barriers. The only problem he could see was the weight of these contraptions. Each one that Stinky made had to be moved to the ditches that ran the entire perimeter of the compound. And each one felt like it broke Brian's back. They had been at it since dawn, and he needed a break. His arms twitched with fatigue and muscle stress, and his neck screamed with the sting of sunburn.

"Okay, that's enough. I need water; lots of it." Brian muttered. He set the last iron contraption into place. He dusted his dirty hands off on his jeans and peeled out of his sweat-soaked shirt, using it for a towel to wipe his neck and face.

"Yeah, I bet lunch is about ready," Rusty replied tiredly. Little Stephen jumped down from his perch on the hay wagon, and Peckerhead, beside him, let out an indignant squawk. He rushed a jug of water to Brian. Smiling down at the boy, he took it and tipped it up to his mouth. What was up with that freakin' rooster? The damn thing had followed Mitch back to the compound where it had promptly befriended Stephen. And Stephen had befriended it too, treating it as a puppy that tagged along everywhere the boy went.

Brian shook his head and laughed. "Thanks, kiddo,"

He handed the jug back. Stephen's eyes shone with adoration when he looked up at Brian. He'd been Brian's shadow since his rescue and had now become his little sidekick.

"We go to eat now?" Stephen asked. Brian nodded and hoisted the boy onto his shoulders, causing him to squeal with laughter. He didn't know what this boy had gone through, but whatever had happened to him set his mind back a bit. Although he looked to be about ten or eleven, his mannerisms and maturity level equaled that of a five or six-year-old. Brian didn't mind though. He smiled, lifting the boy to his shoulders. He heard Stephen laugh as he carried the boy on his shoulders toward the community kitchen for lunch.

After he got a plate for the boy, he fixed one for himself and sat at the table with Cain, Rusty, and Spike. He thought about how close Stephen had grown to him over the past week. The boy attached himself to Brian for love, protection, and comfort. All which he had plenty of to give. But what about when he left? How would that affect Stephen? Right now, he lived with Leslie and two other little girls that were rescued. Mary Anne had assigned each of the refugee's homes at the compound. Barbs lived with Jamie and Terri, Mel lived with Jaden and Chelsie. Lastly, Karen lived with Ben.

Brian knew Leslie adored little Stephen; in fact, everyone adored the little boy. She worked with him every day on his speech, taking care of him like he was one of her own. Brian thought to talk with her later. He hoped his leaving wouldn't set the boy back even further. But hell, he couldn't take him with them. Not out on the trail.

The afternoon ran long and hot. Brian worked with Beth on upping her self-defense with hand to hand combat. He'd been working with her and Sarah, along with training others at the compound. He came at her with his knife in hand, and she quickly sidestepped him and nailed him with a well-placed kick to his back. He twirled and brought his leg under hers, sweeping her legs out and landing her in the dirt hard. He heard the grunt of pain and she glared up at him.

"What the heck, Bri!" she hissed. He stood over her and glared down at her.

"Never mind the bitching. I told you, you can't beat me with brute force. You've got to be quicker, Beth! Use your balance, outmaneuver! Do you think the enemy is going to stop just because you are hurt? Or bitching?"

With a hiss, she stood up and spread her legs, checking her balance and glared at him.

He moved in again, this time swinging his knife low while ramming his shoulder into her midsection. He heard the air whoosh out of her, and he pulled his weight at the last minute. She tumbled and came up off the ground, furious. With a well-placed kick, she nailed him in the stomach then followed up with a hard punch that made him see stars. He backed away and dodged her next strike. He could tell though, that she wasn't giving him her best. She played around, not taking his training seriously. Grinding his teeth, he glared at her.

"That's better, Beth, but not good enough," he hissed. She moved in again, this time feinting to the left, and he countered her move with a quick backhand to her face. She hissed. Blood trickled from the corner of her mouth. Feigning defeat, she bent over and scooped up a hand full of sand throwing it into his face. Blinded, he struggled to see her through weeping eyes while she rained blows onto him.

"You drew blood, you bastard!" she yelled. She angrily pummeled him with her fists. He threw his hands up over his head. Moving in, he grabbed her and pinned her arms to her sides while she struggled furiously. He flung her onto the ground where she landed with a thud then lunged on top of her.

He grabbed both of her arms with one hand and pinned them above her head. He grimaced when he felt her struggle wildly beneath him. He moved one hand to her throat and applied just enough pressure to scare her. His stomach lurched queasily when he saw the terror in her eyes. He hated himself for what he did. He hated that this was the only way he could make her see how dangerous the enemy could be. He'd noticed over the past weeks, that no matter how much he pressed upon her the danger that surrounded them, she hadn't taken it seriously. Even with Roger's death, she had still carried that air of naiveté. She still roamed the compound without carrying her weapon. She still walked around like nothing bad could ever happen. Other than showing her, other than this right here, he didn't know how to wake her up to the dangers they all faced. He looked deep into her eyes, and his heart broke. He growled into her ear.

"Now what? What will you do, Beth?"

He felt her go limp beneath him, and his blood boiled with anger. He'd be damned if he let her give up! Through gritted teeth, he smiled coldly at her and hissed.

"Fight! Remember the man that attacked you on the trail? You fight, Beth, you fight with everything you got because he wouldn't have stopped for your tears. He wouldn't have stopped for your screams! He would have hurt you, Beth, in ways you couldn't imagine!"

He saw tears spring up in her eyes. She bucked her hips, trying to throw him off. He saw the hatred on her face, and it nearly crushed him. He bent his face close to her, and he saw the tiny glint that sparked in her eyes. She slammed her head up and into his face. His nose gushed blood, and his eyes watered. He leaned back and felt her take the opportunity as she exploded with fury from under him, knocking him away from her. She twisted and bucked, kicked and shimmied. He watched her roll to her feet, and she launched a kick at his face. He ducked, catching her leg and spinning it out from under her. He heard her grunt in pain when she hit the ground with a thud. He watched in surprise as she launched herself onto his back, climbing him like a tree, and he hissed in surprise when she wrapped an arm around his throat from behind and laid her blade against his throat. He felt her body shaking like a live wire. She sobbed into his ear.

"I hate you—you bastard!" He felt her climb down off his back, and he turned. Her face crumpled with hatred and horror at what he'd just done to her. He looked at her, his eyes filled with sadness.

"I hate me too, Beth."

Turning, he brushed off his pants with a shaking hand. Disgust, in himself, roiled in his gut. He began to walk away when he heard her hiss softly behind him.

"You don't get to draw blood, Brian."

"I do, and I will, if that's what it takes to wake you up. Do you think your enemy is gonna care if they draw blood?" he asked softly. His eyes pleaded for understanding. He watched tears course down her face as she looked at him. His heart broke. "Beth, I'm sorry I drew blood. I hate that we have to do this."

He stood silently and waited, his hands hanging at his side. Emotions flitted across her face as she processed what he'd just done to her—anger, hatred, and fear. Holding his breath, he watched her walk away.

∞

Mitch watched Brian and Beth circle each other. His face darkened with fury when he saw Brian throw the woman onto the ground. In his opinion, he was too rough with her. He understood that the man had to teach her how to defend herself, but his roughness made Mitch want to kick his ass. Turning, he walked away before he could do something he'd probably regret later.

He strode angrily across the compound. He saw Spike coming from the community kitchen and made his way toward him with a scowl on his face.

"You are crazy to have that man training the women in hand to hand," he snapped. He stopped in front of Spike. Spike shot him a confused look.

"Just what in the hell are you talking about?" he asked. He lifted the cup of coffee he carried to his mouth and took a sip.

"That, Brian! He's too rough! I just watched him beating the hell out of that woman, Beth."

Spike shook his head and smirked. He'd felt the tension between Brian and Mitch and knew it would come to a head sooner or later.

"Do you know who he is? Who he really is?" Mitch asked, his face red with anger.

Spike sighed. He knew Mitch would figure it out. As a fellow law enforcement officer, there was no way he wouldn't have heard of Brian the Butcher.

"I know exactly who he is. I also know that I would want that man to have my back if the shit went south. Do you know who he is?

Who he really is? What his history is? Because I do. I know he would lay down his life for any of us here at the compound. I've seen him go against Bobby and his men despite the odds to save Sarah. Man, you don't know as much as you think you know," Spike replied angrily. Mitch glared at him and shook his head.

"I know more than you think, boy," he muttered. "I know what my eyes see, and I see a killer. I see a man who takes pleasure in being rough with the women he's training. I see a cocky, overconfident bully who's gonna get someone hurt unless he's brought to heel," he growled. Spike felt his face flush with anger. He didn't know this man well, only the stories his grandfather had shared with him about their friendship.

"He is rough! He has to be! Don't you get it, man? These people," he replied, waving his hand around the compound, "they are untrained, weak and soft! Roger, God love him, was too easy on this community. When it came right down to it, he let these people off the hook, believing this compound could never fall. Well, guess what? It can fall; it will fall unless we start getting tough. So, if Brian is rough in his training, there is a reason. He sees the weakness here. And he cares enough to want to help these people defend themselves against those that would love nothing better than to harm them."

Mitch scowled. Although what Spike said

made sense, he just couldn't shake the uneasiness he felt about Brian.

"I hear ya. But don't trust Brian too much. There's something about him, something I can't quite put my finger on, but it's there. My gut tells me this man ain't all that you believe him to be. Aside from his reputation, something ain't right with him," he said. Turning, he walked away, leaving Spike staring at his retreating back.

∞

Sarah stood with her shoulders back and peered through the scope. Rusty gave her a nod, and she pulled the trigger. A resounding bang filled her ears, and she watched the tin can that sat on the wooden fence, jump, and tumble.

"Great shot! Damn, girl! You are getting good!" Rusty said, then laughed. He walked the distance and picked up the can. Her bullet had hit it dead center. He'd been training with her for a week, teaching her how to scope in her target, how to clean the rifle and handgun, how to reload quickly, how to shoot from both standing, sitting and lying positions. She grew more confident with each session and more accurate. At the compound, they'd split up the duties; with him, at the shooting range training; Brian, with the hand to hand combat training; and Spike, teaching seek and cover, perimeter patrol and sniper training from the treetop nests. Since their confrontation with Bobby's gang, they had all upped their game as far as preparing to defend the compound. Leslie, Mel, Barbs, and Karen had all joined in the group activities as well as several other women that they had rescued. Rusty couldn't keep their names straight to save his life, but he could tell you which ones could shoot the eye out of a pigeon, and Sarah happened to be one of the women who could do that.

Glancing at the angle of the sun, he nodded to Sarah. "Good enough for today, kiddo. I've got a meeting to attend so clean up the rifle and police your brass," Rusty instructed.

He turned and made his way to Mary Anne's house. They needed to work on the rotating guard duty list, and she wanted his input on who to assign for this week's rotation. Since Roger's death, he'd been called to take on more and more of the chores that Roger had once taken care of. Assigning guards for weekly duty was one of those chores. He didn't mind. Mary Anne had enough on her plate, dealing with running the everyday operations of the compound. It would make him more than happy if he could ease some of the workload for her.

∞

Darkness found Beth and Brian bent over a map spread out on the small kitchen table. The soft glow from an oil lamp cast shadows into the corners. She was still a bit angry with him, but she also saw the lesson for what it was. He'd reminded her time and time again over the past week to carry her weapon with her, and she'd carelessly ignored him. Yes, perhaps she was a bit naïve, as he had accused her of being, but she hated the thought of always living in fear, always having to watch her surroundings for the bad men, as he called them. She wanted to be able to live life, happy and carefree like she used to before the event; not always being reminded by him of the dangers that surrounded them. She wasn't as naïve as he thought her to be. She knew these were dangerous times; she just chose not to focus on that danger every minute of every day. Shaking her head, she sighed and brought her attention back to the map in front of her.

The Appalachian Trail, a deep line in purple, zig-zagged across squiggly elevation lines. From Connecticut to Tennessee, it didn't look all that far on the map; but they both knew better. Mary Anne had discussed with them their journey. She would provide them with horses and supplies. She'd sent out a radio call to all her friends along the route who all agreed to help. Through hours of discussion and coordination, they finalized the plans. In specific towns along the way, a friend in their HAM radio network would meet with the group, resupply their food and medicine, and provide fresh horses. They would also offer rest spots where Brian, Sarah, Beth, and Jessie would be able to stay a day or two to get off the trail. Brian shook his head in astonishment at how quickly Mary Anne had pulled it all together.

"The second week of June?" Beth suggested. Brian nodded.

"Will your hip be up to it by then?"

Beth smiled. It would be. She felt better and better with each passing day. Her hip only bothered her when she became overtired after pushing herself too hard on one project or another.

"I'll have plenty of Tylenol in my backpack."

He nodded, but worry shadowed his expression. Out there, on the trail, they would be pushing hard each day. Yes, this time they would be riding horses instead of walking, but there would still be some challenging terrain to cross, some long days of sitting in the saddle. And time was not on their side. Leaving mid-June for a trip that was just shy of one thousand miles would land them in Tennessee in late October. That was, if they didn't run into any problems along the way. A knock on the door startled them both, and Brian got up to answer it.

"Hey?" Spike said. Brian smiled and greeted his friend with a nod.

"Can we talk?"

"Sure, come into the kitchen," Brian said.

Spike followed him into the tiny kitchen and nodded a greeting to Beth. Brian sat back down on his chair and looked at Spike.

"What's up?"

"Well, I wanted to talk to you both about going with you to Tennessee," he replied. He wrung his hands nervously. Brian shot a look at Beth.

"What? Why?" Beth asked. She couldn't believe he would want to leave Mary Anne and the compound.

"I need a fresh start. I can't bear to stay here. With my wife and children gone, well, I feel I want to head out and start over," he replied, his eyes filling with sadness.

Beth nodded. Oh, how she understood. She felt the same when she'd lost her husband— the need for a fresh start, somewhere away from the ghosts of the memories.

Brian clapped a firm hand on Spike's shoulder and looked into his eyes.

"Of course, you can come with us. Man, I'd be more than happy if you did. But have you talked to Mary Anne about this? I mean, you're all she's got left for family."

Spike nodded. He did talk to his grandmother. Although she hadn't been happy about it, she understood his need to go away for a while. And he assured her that it wouldn't be for good, just for a while until he could pull his head together. He hadn't taken the time to grieve his family or his grandfather properly. He hadn't taken the time to process it all. By traveling with Brian and Beth, Sarah and Jessie, he would allow himself that time.

"Then absolutely, you can come with us," Beth said. Getting up, she walked over and hugged him. Their little group of three just became four plus a dog.

Chapter Twenty-Four

Just before dawn Mary Anne heard the radio squawk. Darkness filtered through the house, casting shadows in every corner. Dressed in her bathrobe, she made her way to the basement carrying an oil lamp that cast a soft glow over the stairs. Picking up the mike and sitting in Roger's chair, she keyed in her call sign. Immediately Naomi Stilter spoke back to her.

"Hey. How are you?"

"I'm still kicking like an old worn-out mule," Mary Anne replied.

"Well, ya got some trouble coming your way. Big time trouble." Naomi replied. Mary Anne's heart sank.

"Fill me in."

For the next twenty minutes, she listened while Naomi filled her in on what was happening a hundred or so miles south of the compound. A branch of the Alliance had broken away from the main force and was hell-bent headed toward her community; an army of what looked to be a few hundred. They somehow got wind of the battle between the compound and one of their own, Bobby's gang.

"So how do you know all this?" Mary Anne asked.

"Because I've had spies watching them

since April. They've been reporting back to us about their progress and plans," she explained. With a heavy sigh, Mary Anne leaned back in the chair and processed what Naomi was telling her. They didn't have enough manpower to hold back an army of two hundred.

"I'm sending help to you folk. My guys should be at your door in a few days. We've got to stop this group from moving any further into our territory," Naomi continued. "We can't lose the North East to a bunch of gang-banging thugs!"

"Roger that!" Mary Anne replied. She would have to call an emergency meeting. Rusty would need to know about this, and they would all need to start preparing. Wearily she signed off and leaned back in the chair. She closed her eyes.

"Damn it, Roger! Why'd you go and have to get yourself killed?" she whispered into the silence.

News of an early morning meeting rousted Beth, Sarah, and Brian from their beds and they sleepily stumbled to the community kitchen where Spike, Cain, Rusty, Mitch, and Mary Anne sat, talking quietly and downing coffee. Once several more members of the community arrived, including Stinky, Mary Anne stood and filled them in on what Naomi told her.

"So, this is where we're at." Her hands

twisted nervously in front of her. Her face was pinched with an expression of stress, and worry brought a grimace to her mouth.

"Naomi is sending us about one hundred and fifty fighting men and women to help. We can't let this Alliance group move further into our territory," she finished. Brian's eyes narrowed in anger. He shuddered when thought of more fighting headed their way. He swore softly under his breath and felt Beth's warm hand slide into his. He looked at her and saw the fear in her eyes.

"Then we'd better start getting ourselves ready for this." Rusty chimed in, angrily pushing up from his chair. Others in the group nodded in agreement. Stinky grinned and stood.

"I've got a few more nasty surprises in the works back in the work shed." Turning to Conner, he motioned for him to follow.

"I need you to come with me, boy, and give me a hand." Turning on his heel, he quickly made his way to the work shed. Yes, nasty surprises indeed.

Once the meeting was over, everyone scattered and began their tasks of shoring up their defenses. The group had decided that rather than four men patrolling the perimeter, they would add four more to each shift. Brian and Spike sat and poured over a hand-drawn map of the compound, paying particular attention to what might be considered weak areas. They also brought the group of guards together to discuss the hourly patrols of the perimeter, upping that to every twenty minutes. Hand signals, a series of whistles, clicks on the walkies were established for more effective communication. Brian was satisfied with the outcome. Their perimeter and patrol would be tighter than a noose. It would be almost impossible for anyone to sneak through and attack without someone seeing them.

Beth watched the compound explode into controlled and organized chaos. Even the children were pitching in and helping. Stinky had them digging deep holes along the perimeter while he and Connor Malcolme stayed busy in the work shed. The man proved to be a proverbial weapons genius. With a cutting torch he carved long, thin rod-shaped bits of metal from old cars and trucks which Roger had kept out behind the barn. He took the rusty, old junks and put them to good use. For some reason, Roger had seen the importance of keeping them. And it was a good thing he did. After Stinky had amassed two dozen or so of these sharp rusted rods, he brought them to the holes the children dug. Placing four into each hole, he pushed them down into the dirt, standing them point side up, creating punji stakes that would rip a man's leg wide open and puncture up through even the toughest of boot soles. If they didn't bleed to death by stepping onto one of these rusted barbs, then the infection from the rust would surely kill them later. Beth shook her head, Stinky was right; this would be a very nasty surprise.

Mary Anne called the women all together and discussed emergency operations with them. They decided that if or when the attack came, they would move all the children into the basement of the main house to protect them. She looked, seeing their scared faces. She also saw the grim determination. There wasn't a woman at the compound who couldn't handle a gun, a knife, or a baseball bat—if it came right down to it. After finishing up with the women, she headed over to the infirmary to talk with Doc.

Mel greeted her at the door and ushered her in. Jill, Leslie, Barbs, and Karen were all there as well.

"We heard. We've already coordinated with a few of the guys to board up the windows, move in sandbags, and make us braces for the doors. We're putting together trauma kits in case we need them. I'm hoping we won't." Doc said. He waved his arm to a dozen canvas satchels lined up on a table. Bottles, bandages, splints all scattered around the table ready to be put into the satchels along with a variety of other supplies.

"Do we know how long we've got to prepare?" Leslie asked.

Mary Anne shook her head. "No. But

Naomi said they are traveling fast," she replied. How fast was the question of the day? Leslie shook her head. Would the madness ever stop, she wondered? Would they all ever be free of the violence and the constant fear?

Mary Anne watched the sun sink low over the mountains and breathed a sigh of relief. The hectic day had battered her spirits, and she slid on a pair of sneakers and let herself out of the back door. She walked tiredly up the long grassy hill to where Roger lay. Sitting beside the wooden cross with his named carved into it, she rested her head against it.

"Damn you, old man," she sighed softly. "I miss you."

Memories floated softly, and she sank into them.

"I don't know if I can do this, honey. I don't think I know how," Mary Anne cried softly. Tears rolled unchecked down over her cheeks as she listened to the spring peepers singing and the crickets chirping. She watched field mice tunnel through the grass a few feet away and a heard a hawk overhead whistle its lonely cry.

"I know, I'm being a girl again." She tried to laugh but a hitch of pain caught in her throat. Roger always scolded her when she turned on the tears. He had always lovingly teased her about being such a girly girl.

"I am a girl though Rog….and one who's

scared to death!" she scolded back. She tasted the memory. "I'm scared that you are not here to help me, to tell me everything will be okay. I'm scared that I will fail these people!" she murmured. Closing her eyes, she sank into the silence. From her heart, she listened while Roger softly spoke to her. It would be okay. She would be the strong woman he knew her to be. She could only fail if she stopped trying.

Sighing deeply, she pushed herself up off the ground and walked back down the hill. Tomorrow would bring tomorrow's problems. She would let today's problems rest.

∞

Brian crawled into bed beside Beth in the wee hours of dawn. He wrapped an arm around her waist and pulled her into him. Exhausted, he closed his eyes. The coming days worried him. If the Alliance attacked before Naomi's men arrived, they would be in big trouble. The compound did not have enough trained fighters to hold them back long. He nuzzled his face into Beth's hair and sighed. He would do what he needed to—to protect her and Sarah. Even if it meant throwing them on horses and sending them running if things went wrong. He would stay until the very end, no matter which way the battle unfolded; but they didn't have to. He knew Beth would fight him on this decision, but it didn't matter. He would make her promise him that she would run if it came down to defeat. With a sigh, he drifted off into a restless sleep.

Chapter Twenty-Five

For the next two days, everyone stayed busy. The daily work still needed to be tended to, along with the extra jobs of increased patrolling and preparing for the Alliance attack. The staff manning the treetop nests switched out every few hours keeping their eyes on the horizon for any movement. Mary Anne stayed in frequent contact with all the group leaders, bringing them things they requested and jotting down notes. Nightly, the community kitchen stayed open, brewing up coffee and making up sandwiches and snacks for the men and women on patrol.

On the third afternoon, late in the day, little Stephen burst through the doors of the community kitchen, sobbing hysterically. He crawled into a corner and stuck his thumb in his mouth. Mary Anne rushed over and knelt in front of him.

"Stephen? Honey? What's wrong?" she murmured. He stared up at her with terrified eyes. She turned and looked at Leslie, who worked at the counter, making sandwiches.

"Stephen," Leslie murmured, "Honey, tell us what's wrong so we can fix it," she coaxed. Stephen shook his head and stuttered.

"Pppppecker…Ccccain"

Mary Anne shook her head in confusion.

His little face reddened, and he tried again.

"Bbbbbri," he stuttered through his tears.

Leslie shot out the door and ran toward Beth's house. Knocking hard, she waited. Beth opened the door.

"I need Brian! Right now!"

Brian stepped out with a confused look on his face.

"It's Stephen. I don't know what's wrong, but he's terrified and hysterical," she explained. All three took off running for the community kitchen. Brian spied Stephen tucked into a corner, sucking on his thumb with tears running from his eyes. In two long strides, he knelt before the boy and pulled him into his arms.

"Okay, buddy, tell me." Little Stephen looked into his eyes and sighed.

"Pppeckerhead...Cccain, bad men!" he sobbed. Brian hugged him tight and felt a coil of fear roll in his stomach. Handing the child to Beth, he ran out the door and saddled up his horse. Cain was on watch on the southern perimeter. Riding like Hell's demons were after him, he came upon the rooster lying on its side. It was panting heavily, and one wing looked limp and broken. White feathers were scattered everywhere telling Brian the damn bird put up a fight. He pulled the walkie from his belt and clicked the mike.

"Darian...where the hell are you?" he snapped while his eyes scanned the area. Darian,

Jonie, Cain, Lisa, and Mark were the shifts patrol.

A squawk from the mike brought his attention back at hand.

"On the north face why?"

"Where is Cain patrolling?" he asked, ignoring the question.

"Near the stone wall, on the southern perimeter."

Brian swore. He looked directly at the stone wall. At the base of it lay Cain's rifle and a small pool of blood. "He's missing. I'm heading out to find him. You alert Rusty that we've had an intruder," he barked into the radio. "And come get this blasted rooster. Bring it to the doc. He's injured."

"Copy that Brian," Darian replied.

Brian climbed back into the saddle and jumped over the stone wall. He began tracking whoever took Cain.

∞

Beth felt her heart plummet as Darian informed them of what happened. Someone had breached their defenses and took Cain. Brian took off after them hell-bent on following. Mary Anne growled. She motioned for Leslie to take Stephen from her arms.

"Shit!" Panic hit her as she ran out the door. She quickly found Rusty with ten other men. They were saddling their horses intent on setting out to follow Brian. Mary Anne stopped them.

"No. We need to let Brian do this on his own. He knows what he's doing." They all looked at her in confusion. It was one of those times that she wished Roger was standing beside her.

"This is a ploy. Don't you see it? They took Cain hoping we would send out a group to find him. If we do, you can bet they are watching and waiting. They will attack the moment you all leave."

Rusty nodded. He'd been so hell-bent on giving chase that he hadn't given a thought to the motive behind the attack on Cain. It was an obvious diversion.

"Guys, grab your guns. I think this shit is gonna get real, very soon. Get everyone ready," he barked. Shit, he wished the men from Naomi's compound would get here soon.

∞

Brian found the trail quickly enough, and he followed it for an hour before deciding to turn around. Something nagged at his gut. Whoever took Cain moved fast. Turning his horse around, he headed back to the compound. This stank of a trap.

∞

Beth sat on the porch and stared off into the darkness. She held a 12-gauge shotgun across her lap. Everyone was on high alert, tense and edgy. Brian had made it back and was set off, out on patrol with several others. Her stomach churned with worry over Cain. Who had taken him? Was he still alive? She glanced up when Sarah opened the door and stepped out carrying her rifle.

"And where do you think you're going?" Beth asked. Sarah smiled, but Beth could see the shadow of sadness in it.

"Beth, I've got to help. I can't sit here doing nothing," Sarah replied softly. "I'm a good marksman. I've been training with Rusty for weeks. They are gonna need me out there in this fight."

Beth nodded. She knew arguing with the girl would do her no good.

"You promise me, if the shooting starts, you keep your head down!" Beth hissed.

Sarah laughed softly and nodded. "I promise."

The first shot rang out just before midnight. The attack began, and the community was on its own. Beth grabbed her rifle and ran toward Mary Anne's house. The children would be brought there for safety.

"Oh, Brian," she whispered. A wave of terror washed over her, and she ran for the main house. He and Sarah were out there, in the dark, in the middle of the fighting.

Chapter Twenty-Six

Naomi rode lead with one hundred and fifty men and women behind her. The rise in the road gave her a view of the compound spread out before her. Hearing a barrage of gunfire, she turned in her saddle.

"Clint, take your group and go at them from the left, Barker, your group to the right!" she yelled. She pulled her rifle from its scabbard. "Remember, boys and girls; we are from New Hampshire, the Live Free or Die State! And we sure as shit don't take prisoners! Now go!"

Kicking her horse, Matilda, into a run, she aimed right for the heart of the beast. And her men and women, one hundred and fifty strong, backed her up. She'd be damned if she would let the compound fall to a bunch of city gang bangers! Not on her watch! Not today! Clicking the button on her handheld, she waited.

"Go!" a voice on the other end yelled.

Smiling, Naomi shouted to let them know she was coming in fast and hard. "Knocking on the door, boys."

"Copy that and welcome to the fight," the voice replied.

Chapter Twenty Seven

Beth looked into Mary Anne's eyes. She saw the fear reflecting back at her. Even the thick walls of the cellar couldn't drown out the cries, the screams, and the sound of gunfire. She worried about Sarah even as the children clung to her legs, terrified and crying. Sarah was out there in all that fighting, and it made her stomach churn with nausea, just thinking about it. Looking down, she laid a soft, gentle hand on little Stephen's head.

"It's okay, son. The noise is scary, I know."

Stephen gazed up at her with his thumb buried deep in his mouth. Whimpers of fear shook his body and tears rolled down his chubby cheeks. Beth shot a helpless look at Mary Anne.

"You've got to take him. I've got to get to the infirmary. Doc is gonna need all the help he can get," she murmured. Indecisiveness tore at her. Stay here with Mary Anne, Leslie, and Barbs to protect the children or shoot out across the compound to help with the wounded. Mary Anne looked at her and nodded.

"You go. We got this." She bent and pulled Stephen into her arms. Tammi, Pru, and Jamie clung to each other on the overstuffed sofa that sat against the far wall. Ben and Chelsie sat on the floor next to Leslie while Terri and Jaden sat close to Barbs. There was a total of twenty children, hiding in the cellar — children whose names Beth didn't know. The walls of the basement were thick stone. No bullets would penetrate. And with only one way in, the enemy would have to get past the women first. Each woman held a rifle at the ready.

"Stay low and in the shadows," Mary Anne warned Beth. She turned and gave one last glance at the group. Her stomach rolled with anxiety. Was she crazy? Down here, it was safe but up there, out in the open, not so much. Drawing a deep breath to quell her fear, she nodded and bounded up the stairs two by two.

She shot out into the yard at a fast run, staying to the shadows next to the buildings. Screams erupted in the distance and her heart skipped a beat with the horror of it all. Those were her friends out there. Those were the people of this community fighting and dying to protect it. A sob tore from her throat, and her hip screamed with burning pain.

A thwack on the building next to her sent her diving for the ground and a bullet slammed into the wood of the building next to her. Crawling on her hands and knees, she felt the sting of pebbles and dirt biting into her skin. She threw herself through the door of the infirmary where her eyes were met with at least a dozen wounded, lying on the floors, sitting on the chairs, and leaning against the walls. Doc and Jill were moving quickly in the chaos preparing those for surgery who needed it, while the medics, Grace, and Eli, were shouting back and forth to each other as they bandaged wounds and provided triage. Max, Tillie, and Evan, the other three medics, were out on the battlefield, dodging bullets as they dragged the wounded back to the infirmary. The odor of blood, of vomit, hit her nostrils in a wave, and she swallowed hard. They were getting massacred.

"Tell me what you need!" Beth shouted as she waded into the chaos. Grace turned and looked at her, helplessly, with tears in her eyes.

"Right now? A miracle!" she sobbed. Her face contorted with stress and sorrow as she covered the young boy she'd been working on with a sheet. Nodding to Eli, they hoisted his body and took him to the room that had once been Beth's. Now it served as the morgue. Beth bent to the nearest man and began to assess his wounds.

He gazed at her through fevered pain and sighed. "How bad?"

She smiled at him. "You'll live."

The bullet had entered the man's thigh, piercing clean through. Grabbing a four by four and padding it with a thick Kotex feminine napkin, she taped it against the wound to stem the flow of blood.

"What's your name?" she asked. She

pulled a syringe from the nearest trauma bag and gave him a shot for pain.

"Erik Jenson. My wife and I live in the third cottage down behind the barn," he murmured. There were so many at the compound she still didn't know.

"Your wife? Where is she?"

He nodded his head toward the compound. "Out there. Fighting." Beth's heart fell.

"How bad is it?" she asked.

Erik sighed. "Bad. We're getting creamed."

Standing up, Beth shook her head. Sarah was out there. Her girl, out there in this madness. Suddenly an explosion rocked just outside the building, and she screamed in fear. She saw Jill cringe as dust blew in through the boarded-up windows.

"What in the hell was that?" Beth yelled.

"A bomb, dynamite, grenade? Damned if I know! They've got explosives. They've been launching them at us left and right." Erik said softly.

Fear knotted in her stomach. Explosives? No wonder they were getting creamed! How in the hell were they gonna stand against an enemy that was better armed than them? For the first time, Beth feared that they couldn't. That they would lose this battle against the Alliance and fall. What then? What if they couldn't hold them back? What would happen to the children? To them all?

The banging of the back door and the sound of gunfire sent her diving to the floor. Screams from the operating room sent chills down her spine and spun her mind into a frenzy. She scanned the room for a weapon. Grabbing a gun from the nearest wounded man, she rolled and came up firing at the three men who stormed the triage room. From beside her, she heard Erik firing his weapon. She screamed when she saw Jill spin from a bullet that had hit her, and she fell to the floor. Grace, beside her, screamed when a bullet slammed into her shoulder.

A blow to her face from the butt of a rifle knocked her back. A set of strong hands grabbed her. Struggling, her eyes widened in terror, as a fist plowed into her face. She didn't even have the chance to throw her hands up to block it. Sparkles danced before her eyes and she staggered to catch her breath as another blow landed on her. Shouts, screams, and moans filled her ears.

∞

The radio squawked, and Spike ducked behind a tree. He slid it out of the leather case.

"Go!" he snapped. Bullets slammed into the ground beside him, and he moved further behind the tree for cover.

"The compound has been breached! I

repeat! The compound has been breached!"

Swearing, he looked behind him into the vast night. The dim light from the solar sticks shown over the center of the compound where he saw men running toward the infirmary, toward the main house, and toward the community kitchen, trying to set up a defense. Hitting the button on the radio, he barked out orders.

"Team Three, fall back to the center. Team One, hit that infirmary now!" Team three responded with an affirmative. Team one stayed silent.

"Team One, respond!" he shouted. Again silence.

"Team Four, to the infirmary!" he barked and breathed a sigh of relief when he heard Stinky's voice reply.

"On it!"

Sweating, he pulled up his rifle and aimed at a group of attackers clustered behind the stone wall. Squeezing the trigger repeatedly, he fired off a volley of shots. He smiled coldly when he saw several of them fall. A scream erupted to the right of him, and he turned to see a man pulling his leg up from one of the punji pits. The man howled in agony and he fell to the ground writhing in pain. Spike leveled his weapon and fired again, blowing the man's head off and ending his screams.

∞

Rusty crouched on the northern perimeter of the compound and shuddered at the sight of the bodies littering the ground. Team One, his team, had all but been annihilated. Bodies lay scattered on the ground like fall leaves blown from the trees. Everywhere he looked, he saw bodies. Pain drove into his head and he ran toward the stone wall. They needed to drive the enemy back. Fighting for breath and cursing every cigarette he'd ever smoked; he dove behind a large rock and into a cluster of men. He never saw the bullet that slammed into his face, blowing it apart.

∞

Naomi Stilter knelt on the ground behind a row of thorn hedges. On either side of her were ten of her best sharpshooters. Dropping her hand, they opened fire, mowing down anyone in front of them that moved. She smiled bitterly when screams erupted, and men fell like pins in a bowling alley. Calvin, her second in command, turned his head and grinned at her.

"Let's blow these bastards away," he growled. The compound was taking a hammering, and now it was their turn to even out the odds. If they didn't stop the Alliance here, then all of the North East would be in danger. She and her crew were not about to let that happen. Even if it meant following the enemy to the gates of Hell, should they turn tail and run.

Chapter Twenty Eight

Beth

A shout drew her eyes to the back of the triage room.

"Grab them and let's get the hell out of here!"

She felt her hair being wrenched when her attacker pulled her to her feet. She brought her fist up and connected with her assailant's throat and grimaced when she heard him gasp and cough. Panic frenzied her mind and she turned and tried to run away. The scent of blood and sulfur filled her nose and clogged her throat.

"You're gonna pay for that, bitch!" he growled. He twisted her arm up behind her back. She felt her shoulder pop, and a scream of agony tore from her throat. She bent forward and vomited on the floor. Then darkness hit the edges of her eyes. She struggled to stay conscious. Her face was planted on the metal table and pain rocked through her. Her vision filled with shadows, her ears filled with the sound of screams and gunshots. Tears ran down her face. She fought the urge to give up and let this man kill her.

"You don't get to draw blood," she had said to Brian. And he'd been right when he replied that the enemy wouldn't hesitate to draw blood. Her mind snapped. The reality of what

Brian had tried to tell her hit home. Her vision blurred. She heard his words ringing in her ears. They were drawing blood! They were slaughtering everyone! Sucking in a deep breath, she heard Brian's voice deep in her mind. She fought off the darkness that wanted to grab her and drag her down deep.

"Fight, baby, fight with all you've got in you or you will die right here."

With a roar of anguish, she gritted her teeth against the pain and pushed herself up from the table. She threw herself backward, head-butting her attacker, while her good hand grabbed the only weapon she could find; the scalpel Doc had been using. Twirling, she reached out with her arm, now slick with blood and struck quickly with the blade and feeling it sink into her attacker's arm. He howled. She slashed and stabbed, her eyes and ears blinded and deafened by rage, her body now numb to the blows he landed on her as he tried to fight her off. An all-encompassing rage drove her to stab him again and again until he lay on the floor, blood pooling around him, and even then, she didn't stop. Howls screamed from her as her fear poured out, and animal instinct took over. Finally, spent and sobbing, she stopped and collapsed beside him.

Looking around through a haze of pain with her cheek lying in a pool of blood, she saw the damage. Doc lay face-up on the floor with half of his face blown apart. Jill and Grace were both wounded. Erik sat in the corner, leaning against the wall, with a bullet in his chest. The three attackers, nothing but crumpled heaps while their bodies bled out onto the floor. She crawled on her hands and knees to Erik.

"Did we get them all?" he hissed. His eyes held the glassy look of a dying man.

"We did. You did, soldier," she sobbed. She pressed her hand against the wound on his chest to stem the flow of blood although she knew it wouldn't do any good.

"Good. Good."

Erik smiled and Beth watched his head slump forward. Curling up and hugging her knees, she whimpered and sobbed in agony, fighting to keep her mind from shutting down. The smell of blood filled her nose and clogged her throat. Bodies surrounded her; bodies of the dead. Moans and cries from the wounded tormented her ears. She couldn't do this. She didn't have anything left, nothing. Her heart ached with hollow pain.

"You don't get to draw blood," she moaned. But they did. They did, and how naïve she had been.

∞

Brian's mind filled with cold numbness. He threw himself into the battle. He saw Sarah a few hundred yards away running toward the compound, and his heart skipped a beat.

Screams tore at his ears, and a smoky haze from the Molotov cocktails filled the air, choking him. Bullets spit up dirt around her as shots were fired from the dark woods. Turning, he sprayed the woods with gunfire. Sprinting, he followed Sarah. From the left, he saw a shadow moving fast and hard toward her. Brian screamed, praying she heard him above the sound of gunfire and explosions. He watched, as the man launched himself onto to her, and he pumped his legs harder gasping for air; keeping his eyes on her. He saw the glint of a knife blade as the man brought it down. With a roar, he launched himself the last few feet landing on top of the man and knocking him from Sarah.

He sprung to his feet and drew his knife. The man faced him with a vicious grin and chuckled.

"Too bad mister. I already killed her," he hissed. Brian felt his mind snap and he tore into the man with the savagery of the killer he'd once been. His knife sang as it stabbed and sliced, hacked and tore. His arms and hands grew slick with the other man's blood. A shout from Sarah brought him back from the brink of this fevered madness that had taken him.

"Brian, stop! He's dead!"

Panting, he looked at her through fevered eyes. She struggled to get up from the ground. Her face was flayed open from temple to cheek. The man hadn't killed her. Brian had seen that he'd been aiming for her throat, but instead, his knife had sliced open her face. He drew a deep breath to calm the shaking in his body.

"Oh my God, Sarah, I thought he'd killed you," he murmured. He pulled her into his arms.

She gave him a weak smile. "Ummm, I'm feeling a bit woozy here? Could you help me back to the infirmary?"

Brian quickly scooped her up into his arms and ran with her across the compound, listening to the battle explode around them.

Chapter Twenty-Nine

Spike swore and punched the wall, his knuckles splitting and pain rocking up his arm. Tears filled his eyes. Frustration and pain clouded his vision. They won, driving the enemy back, but not without significant losses. His eyes set on Mary Anne who bent down in front of Beth. He watched her gently pull the distraught woman into her arms and rock her back and forth while her pitiful sobs split the air.

She looked at Spike, and her eyes filled with tears. There were children who were now orphans, clustered at her house, scared, and doing their best to be brave; there were men and women who lay wounded, people turning to her for answers.

"I'm lost. I don't know what to do anymore," Mary Anne cried. They lost too many. First, Roger, now Rusty, and so many others. She walked through dozens of bodies that were laid out in the center of the compound. Friends that had trusted her to keep them safe. Friends who had believed that if they came to the compound, they would be able to live peacefully; away from the violence outside its walls. Oh, they all knew life would be different, much harder, but they were making it. They had hope and now? Now all hope was gone, blown away by those who wanted to destroy what

Roger and she had so lovingly built. Her hope cast itself before her, teasing her, tormenting her. How stupid she'd been to believe that the compound would keep them safer. How foolish she'd been to think that life would thrive here.

Leslie, Tillie, and Max worked on the wounded in another area, and Mary Anne steeled herself against the moans that drifted to her ears through the open door. The violence they were trying to escape from all those months ago was now on their doorstep. Many of the faces of the dead stared up at her with lifeless eyes. Guilt chewed at her gut. Could she have done more to protect her community? Did she miss something vital?

Spike's gut burned with anger and pain, with a sorrow so deep that there were no words or tears. The wounded, who Beth, Jill, and Grace had been working on, had been executed in cold blood. Bodies lay in the corners, leaning up against the white walls of the infirmary, slumped on the floor like discarded husks. He fought the urge to crumple to the floor and howl in anguish…to wrap his arms around his head and wail like a child. He watched as Mel and two other men gently and quickly moved the bodies to stretchers, bringing them to another room. They needed the space to work on the many wounded. Her face looked haggard and worn.

"We'll get through this. I promise," Spike

murmured. His promise sounded empty and hollow.

Brian carried Sarah into the infirmary. He was spent and depleted. Beth stumbled over to him and wrapped her arms around them both. Stinky came a moment later and stopped in shock looking at the scene before him. The floor swam in blood. He thought he'd seen the worst carnage possible in Viet Nam, but this, this was worse than anything he'd ever seen there.

Brian pulled away and walked over to Spike and stood in front of him, seething and shaking in anger. His body felt like a live electric wire and fury tore through him. "They will pay for this!" he growled through clenched teeth. He balled hands into fists.

Spike nodded. Yes, they would pay for sure. They had driven the enemy back, but it had cost them dearly. They'd fought on the defensive, but now they would turn the tables and take the fight to them. They needed to finish this for once and for all. If they didn't, then the Alliance would regroup and attack again. Of that, he was sure.

Naomi

Naomi stood in the center of the compound and shouted orders while the men and women scurried around, tending to the wounded, covering the dead with sheets and taking stock of the damage. Clint, commander of

Team One and Calvin, commander of Team Two, stood beside her with a group of prisoners, guns at the ready — just in case any of them tried to escape. Naomi smiled. Bitterness filled her heart. She'd lost ten of her men and women to the enemy. Far less than the compound had but still too many in her opinion. They would execute the prisoners, eventually, but they would interrogate them first. She glanced at them coldly. She couldn't find pity or even empathy in her heart for these men and women, not after seeing the bloodshed of this battle.

"I'm going to the infirmary. If they move, shoot them," Naomi muttered. Tiredness trickled through her legs as she walked, making her steps stiff. She walked through the door of the infirmary and her gaze set on Mary Anne.

"Tell me what you need my men and me to do," she said. She looked upon the carnage in the room and shook her head.

"I could use some hands in here, preferably medics, if you brought any with you. They killed Doc and two of my medics." Mary Anne croaked, her voice laced with pain. Naomi grimaced and felt a burn at the back of her eyes that she quickly pushed away. The last time she'd seen Mary Anne was two years ago at a gathering of the Truth Seekers. She wondered if her own face showed the aging the way Mary Anne's did.

She wanted to reach over and hug her

friend but held herself back. There would be time enough for that later. Right now, she knew the woman needed support, not hugs. She glanced over at another woman who was leaning heavily on a metal table. She was beaten and bloody, her face twisted in misery and pain. A younger woman stood beside her with a protective arm around her shoulder. Next to Mary Anne stood a tall man with a thin build and ropy muscled arms.

"This is my grandson, Spike," Mary Anne said, and the man stepped forward and shook her hand. "And those two over there? The older one is Beth, the younger one, getting her face stitched up is Sarah."

Naomi nodded.

"I've got medics. I'll send them right in," Naomi replied and turned on her heels. Spike followed her out.

They had driven the enemy back but hadn't been able to annihilate them the way she'd hoped to do. Many got away. And this chewed at her like a rat with a block of cheese. If the enemy decided to launch another attack right away, before they pulled themselves together, then the compound would fall. They needed to go on the offensive, to go after them and finish this. Shaking her head, she quieted her mind so she could think clearly. She motioned for Clint and Calvin to join her and Spike.

"We need to work quickly to clean this up and regroup. I want everyone ready to ride in four hours. We're going hunting, boys," she snapped. Her gaze fell onto the mountains in the distance. The sun began to peek up over, and her eyes narrowed. They were going to bring the fight to the Alliance. All three men nodded. Not a damn one of them wanted this war, but now that it was on their doorstep, they intended to finish what the Alliance started.

Mary Anne sat at a table in the community kitchen with her notebook opened to a blank page. Her cup of coffee grew cold while she stared off into space. The clanking of pots and pans battered her ears while several women began to cook breakfast. The long day caught up with her. She was hungry, exhausted, disillusioned, and heartsick.

Her hand shook as she began writing the names of the dead. When she came to Rusty's name, a sob tore from her throat and tears spilled onto the page. Her best friend, her second in command, Roger's army buddy, dead. She looked up with watery eyes. She felt Beth squeeze her shoulder.

"Maybe you should do this later?" she murmured. Mary Anne shook her head. It wouldn't be any less painful later.

"The meeting is starting," Beth said softly. Mary Anne closed the notebook and got up to join the others. Spike sat at the far end of the long table next to Brian, Naomi next to him, and so many others she didn't know. Stinky sat beside Mitch. There were ten or so of them all together.

"We'll be heading out before dark." Naomi, taking charge, stood and said to the group. "Fifty will stay behind to protect the compound and help bury the dead. The rest of us," she said waving her arm around the table, "will take our teams and spread out, covering every inch of this territory until we find the enemy." It would be a combination of her group and the compounds group, a large enough force to take on the remainder of the Alliance. "We will keep in contact on channel twelve only. If you find the enemy do not engage until the rest of us get there. This is our only shot, people! Don't screw it up!" she barked.

Chapter Thirty

Ryder Gilroy rubbed a tired hand across his face. The man they had taken, Cain, sat tied to a tree. Sucking in a deep breath, he turned to Rocco.

"What in the hell happened out there?" he screamed angrily. They got their asses handed to them by a bunch of ignorant country folk. Him! His men! Jesus Christmas! These men, his group? They were the toughest gang on the streets of New York! They never lost a fight! How in the hell was he going to explain this to his boss at the Alliance?

"I don't know. We had them. We were inside their compound then we got hammered from behind!" Rocco stuttered. And they'd had them. They'd breached their defenses. But then it all went to shit.

"You mean to tell me, with our firepower, our superior fighting force, you all turned tail and ran like a bunch of schoolgirls?" Ryder snarled. Rocco's eyes dropped.

"Get the hell out of my sight before I slit your throat!" Ryder threatened. He watched through narrowed eyes as the man slunk away with his head down. Turning to Maria, his woman, he snarled.

"Get Jensen on the radio. We need back up!" Maria nodded and walked into the tent they shared to do what he ordered. She learned from experience that when he was this angry, it was best to keep her mouth shut and do what he asked.

He paced back and forth, burning off the angry energy that sang through his veins. What a shit show! He'd lost twenty-five percent of his men to those local yokels. Twenty-five percent! His eyes fell onto the camp. Tents sat clustered in every available open spot between the trees. He hated these woods. He was a city boy. Give him tall buildings and crowded streets any day over this backwoods crap. New York, his city, and his territory. A cough from behind him brought his attention back.

"Jenson is sending another fifty men. They'll be here at dawn." Maria said. She moved up close to him and pressed her body into his. He felt his anger drain, and he pulled her into his arms.

"Woman," he murmured. She turned her face up to his and smiled.

"Easy. The men are beaten to shit. Take it easy on them, okay?" she murmured. She knew how to defuse his temper. Space, a bit of time, then her body. She had the routine down well. He glanced down at her and smiled, narrowing his eyes.

"Don't push it, Maria," he warned. She nodded and lifted her mouth to his, kissing him deeply.

"We will win this battle. Then the compound will be yours. Don't worry." she murmured. She nuzzled her face into the curve of his neck. They needed to win. If not, then his life would be short-lived. Jenson had already warned her of that. And if that happened? It gave her chills just thinking about it. Jenson would lay claim to her, and she'd rather die than be his woman.

"Go away from me. I've got some thinking to do." Ryder said. He pushed her away.

Maria sat near the campfire and watched as Ryder moved among the men, speaking with each. Dayton tended to the wounded and his woman, Delia, helped him. Dayton was their only medic, and his hands were full.

She sighed tiredly and rubbed a hand on her throat. It felt worse. It hurt to swallow. Picking up the cup of tea she'd made, she sipped at it slowly; hoping it would ease the razor-sharp pain. Ryder glanced over at her, and she smiled. He was her man. Had always been hers. She'd known him since she was twelve. They'd grown up together. They'd fought together. She was as much a part of his gang as any member.

When the event happened, they'd moved fast and hard—bloody street by street, fighting to assure their territory. But together with their brothers and sisters, they'd done it. They now ruled much of the Upper East Side, from Central

Park to 59th Street, the East River, and 96th Street. They protected their community and expanded their territory. All the stores and businesses, which would have been looted by others, were safe under their watch. They painted their gang sign on every street corner, every building, and every telephone pole. And no one dared challenge them.

Then Jenson and the Alliance came in and offered them a deal. She begged Ryder to refuse it. She didn't like Jenson one bit. His slimy, greasy attitude and his shifting eyes sent her gut reeling with dread. But Ryder wouldn't listen.

Shaking her head, she began to form a plan in the event this whole thing went south. She'd protect her man and herself. If it meant killing Jenson, then so be it. She'd be damned if she would let all she fought for fall into his and the Alliance's hands. Her brothers and sisters would back her up she knew if it came down to it. Setting her cup on the ground, she looked at Alyssa and nodded. The young girl got up and picked it up, carrying it to the bucket of water near their tent to rinse it out. Maria's eyes followed her every move. She despised the hostage, but Ryder wanted her and what Ryder wanted he usually got. If it were up to her, she would slice the girl's throat and be done with it. It didn't matter though; he would tire of his little plaything. When he did, he'd cut her loose where another man in the gang would pick her up as his own. It was a hard life for the young girl, but then again, it was a hard life for everyone.

Chapter Thirty-One

Beth stumbled. Her legs were tired and her hip screamed with pain. She clenched her teeth. The man in front of her, Raymond, stayed perfectly still. She threaded in and out of his skin with the needle. A bullet had carved a six-inch gash in his thigh. Mel stood at another table working on a boy of fifteen who'd taken a knife to his lower back. Beth could hear his soft groans as Mel cleaned and stitched his wound. They'd been working on wounded for hours along with three other medics from Naomi's group. The last time any of them had seen shut eye had been yesterday. It was beginning to affect them.

Beth looked up when another patient came in. A young girl of about sixteen. She had a gash to her forehead.

"Set her up over there," Beth said tiredly. "How many more?"

Sarah shook her head. Her face throbbed from the twenty-two stitches that Mel had sewn into her.

"About ten more, superficial," she replied. Beth nodded. They would be working at least another couple of hours. Her shoulders slumped with fatigue while she finished bandaging Raymond's thigh. She nodded to Sarah to help him out. There was no room left in the infirmary, so they transferred all the non-critical patients to the guardhouse. There were plenty of beds there for them. She motioned to the young girl.

"C'mon over, sweetie, let's take a look," she murmured.

A commotion from outside stopped her, and her breath caught in her throat. She glanced nervously toward the door, her heart thudding with fear. Sarah drew her gun and positioned herself for trouble. Beth motioned for the girl to climb under the table. She reached for her gun. Tensely she waited, holding her breath.

The door flew open with a kick and Spike dragged another wounded man in. Everyone was on edge, jumpy.

A few hours later, Sarah sighed loudly when she entered the room. "This is the last one," She guided the man in, helping him to sit on the edge of Beth's table. His had a broken arm. Beth sighed and looked at him.

"I'm going to set this. It's gonna hurt like hell. I'm giving you a shot of morphine for the pain, but you'll still feel it a bit," she said. She slipped the needle into his arm.

The man grimaced and nodded his head. His green eyes carried the same shadow of shock as most of the rest of them. Beth's heart gave a tug of pity. They were all in shock. They were all exhausted, just moving numbly from one thing to another. She knew that those outside who were able, were helping with burying the dead, cleaning up the damage caused by the pipe bombs and Molotov cocktails that had been launched at the compound, cooking up food for the community, and whatever else needed doing.

"Do what you need to," he croaked gruffly. He'd been in pain for so long a little bit more didn't much matter. He sighed in defeat. His mind replayed the events of the past twelve hours. He'd lost many friends in this battle, and his heart ached heavily with sadness.

"I'll try to do it quickly," she said. She grabbed his lower arm and gave a yank. Sarah winced as she watched his face drain of color and moved behind him in case he passed out. She watched Beth move quickly, putting two splints in place then wrapping them with an ace wrap. She didn't have the materials for casting him properly, so this would have to do. Would his bones heal straight? She didn't know.

She watched the morphine begin to take hold and his eyes become glassy. Nodding to Sarah, they helped him off the table.

"Make sure you take him directly to his bed. With the morphine loaded in, we don't want him trying to walk around. Shit, knowing our luck he'd fall and break his other arm," Beth muttered. Sarah nodded and led the man out the door.

They moved the man to a storage room which Beth and Sarah had cleaned out. An I.V.

fed into one of his veins and Beth watched it drip slowly, feeding him fluids to compensate for the blood he'd lost. He needed a transfusion but not knowing his blood type, it wasn't worth the risk, in her opinion. Sarah laid a warm hand on Beth's shoulder.

"I'll stay with him. Why don't you grab a bite to eat then take a shower? You are exhausted, Beth," she urged. Beth nodded. She didn't want to leave his side, but fatigue hammered at her, and her eyes felt itchy with grit.

"Did you check on Jessie? Let her out and feed her?" she asked. Sarah smiled.

"Yes, Jessie's fine. Now go. Take care of you," she said softly.

The shower, followed by a cup of hot coffee, did wonders for her fatigue. She needed a good solid eight hours of sleep, but the work ahead of her made that nearly impossible. She saw that Mary Anne had pulled together the community, those who were either not involved in the battle or involved in the care of the wounded and had set them to work. There were meals that needed preparing, animals and gardens to be taken care of, laundry to be washed and hung to dry. A group of men set to work filling sandbags and another group was digging fox holes. The mood throughout the compound was one of heavy sadness and disbelief. So many had died, so many were wounded. The battle had shattered the hearts of them all.

Spying Mary Anne sitting at a table outside the community kitchen, Beth walked over and sat down beside her. Her graying hair spilled out of the haphazard bun atop her head as she bent over the notebook in front of her. Gazing at her face, Beth thought she'd aged so much overnight. Faint lines creased the corners of her eyes, and her shoulders slumped with fatigue. Her shirt was filthy with dirt, blood, and God knew what else.

"Hey?"

Mary Anne looked up at her and smiled. Beth could see the sadness of her smile, and it hurt her heart. This woman, who always had a kind word, always uplifted everyone, looked beat down to her socks, defeated and racked with misery.

"Hey, how are you?" Mary Anne asked. Beth grimaced. Her shoulder screamed with an ache so deep it almost made her want to cry. Her face hurt from the battering she'd taken from the attackers in the infirmary, her heart ached with sadness. Other than that, she was thankful to be alive.

"Well, I could bitch and moan, but frankly, it won't help. So, I'm instead running on pure anger," she replied bitterly.

Mary Anne nodded.

"I hear ya. This?" She waved a hand

toward the compound, "Our community took a beating. We all took a beating. I don't know if we'll survive another one. We've got to do better, be better than what we were last night," she said, her face wrinkling with frustration. "But I don't know what to do to make it better, to make us better. Roger would have had an answer, he would have come up with a plan, but I can't. I've been racking my brain, but I don't have a soldier's heart or knowledge," she groaned. "I don't know how to plan defense, how to strategize a battle. And the men that did have that knowledge? They are now dead," she said, speaking of Roger and Rusty. They were the soldiers. They were the ones who'd strategized and planned in the event of an attack. They were the ones who came up with the training for the men and women in the community.

Beth shook her head and sighed.

"We've got Naomi and her men we can rely on for help, we've got Brian, we've got Stinky, Spike, Mitch and we'll get Cain back. That old codger, Stinky, knows more about war than any of us." Beth replied, encouraging Mary Anne not to give up hope. "We've still got good soldiers. Yes, we lost many last night, and we are down, but we are not out!" she continued. "You need to rely on all of them, let them take the lead in this. Otherwise, you will drive yourself crazy."

"I know, I'm just having a moment," Mary Anne replied, then sighed. "I need sleep. We all need sleep. But…there is just so much to do."

"You're right. Everyone is exhausted. We are running on coffee and adrenaline. It doesn't make for clear thinking." Beth replied. "Why don't you go get some rest? I'll take a gander over to the infirmary, see how things are going there, then check in on Leslie and Barbs. I'm sure they got the children all settled by now. Stinky can handle directing the repairs to the fences, and men are working on shoring up more foxholes and filling sandbags. Spike is working with the guards and laying out tonight's work schedule, and I know Mitch is working with a group to bury the dead." Beth assured her.

Mary Anne nodded. She needed to get a few hours rest before tackling anything more. Her brain swam in a fog of fatigue, and her body screamed for rest. Pushing herself up from the table, she looked at Beth gratefully.

"You're right. I need to step away from this before I drive myself crazy. A few hours' sleep and I'll be better able to tackle these problems." Giving Beth a quick hug, she walked slowly to the main house. She'd done what she could and it had to be good enough for now.

Chapter Thirty-Two

Beth sat by the bed and watched Brian sleep. Her body ached to crawl in beside him, curl up against his chest, and snuggle into the warmth she knew he'd give her. She loved this man. And it surprised her. She hadn't thought she'd love again after the death of her husband but here she was, stupidly, crazily in love.

Jessie curled up by her feet, and she absently let her fingers drift into the soft fur by her ears, patting her lightly. In a few hours, he would be leaving to go and fight again. Her heart cried with the pain of so many deaths of those she'd grown close to. Tiptoeing, she made her way into the living room and sat on the couch.

She looked up when Sarah quietly entered the room. Beth noticed she had showered and was dressed in clean jeans and a pale green tee shirt. Two handguns hung from her side, and a rifle slung over her shoulder. On her back she carried a light, canvas backpack.

"And where do you think you're going?" Beth whispered. She didn't want to wake Brian.

"The troops are getting ready to leave in a few hours. I'm going too." Sarah replied. The look in her eyes, the steel glint of determination, told Beth there was no use in arguing. She sighed sadly.

"You don't have to. You can stay here. We need help here too," Beth whispered. Her voice broke with despair.

Sarah shook her head. She was a soldier now. Life forced her to become one. This life, the Alliance, the Bobby's of the world, they all forced her to fight.

"Beth, you know I can't. They need me out there. I need to be out there," she replied softly. Nodding, Beth wiped a tear from her eye with the back of her hand.

"I wish it were different. I wish you could be just a normal girl with normal girl worries," she cried softly. But nothing about this new life was normal.

"I'll be careful. I'm on Spike's team. We're a good group. Strong," Sarah replied, reassuring her.

"You make sure you come back to me in one piece, girl," Beth growled. She stood and hugged her tight. She didn't want to let her go, but she knew she couldn't stop her.

"I will try, I promise," Sarah murmured. Turning, she walked out to join the group. Sunset was only a few hours away, and they had planned for an early evening attack. Just after dark, when the enemy wouldn't see them coming.

Spike saddled up his horse and watched while his group did the same. He was battle-weary and dreaded the thought of more fighting on this night. Sarah moved up beside him and grinned impishly.

"C'mon old man, we got some bad guys that need an ass-kicking," she teased. He scowled then grinned at her.

"You know, Brian will kick my ass if you get hurt, right?"

Sarah laughed softly. Brian had wanted her on his team, but she'd refused. She knew his attention would be on protecting her rather than on concentrating on the battle. And that was a risk she just wasn't willing to take. He hadn't liked the idea of her choosing Spike's team, but she didn't care. If he got hurt because of her, she'd never be able to forgive herself.

"Better you than me. Brian scares me," she joked. Then she climbed up into the saddle. With a light kick, she sent her horse into a slow canter. Spike shook his head and followed. The girl had some guts. Last night she'd fought as well as any of them. She hadn't backed down, even when the enemy breached the compound. Instead, she climbed down from her nest in the trees and dove into the firefight on the ground. Brian should be proud of her. Pissed yes, but proud.

He thought of the battle plan that Naomi, himself, and her two commanders had laid out. There were four groups of them heading out. They knew where the Alliance had holed up; Naomi sent out scouts earlier to locate their camp. They planned to split off and go at them from all four sides. His group and Clint's group would initiate the first wave of attack, with Naomi and Calvin coming in from behind. Brian and Mitch would breach the camp and rescue Cain. Stinky and another of Naomi's men were assigned to stay at the compound with about forty men, just in case some of the Alliance slipped past them and headed in that direction. On paper their plan sounded good; but, Spike knew, even the best-laid plans often went to shit.

The sun had just set when they crept up on the camp. Naomi's group was in position, and two clicks to the radio alerted him that they were ready. He drew his knife from his side and silently made his way through the brush. Grabbing one of the guards, he wrapped his fingers in the man's hair, drew his head back and sliced his throat before he could shout a warning. A few yards away, he saw Clint doing the same thing with another guard. Both men fell to the ground quietly. On the other side of the camp opposite them, Spike knew Naomi's men were performing the same task. Taking out the guards.

Turning, Spike motioned for his men who were a hundred or so yards back into the thick woods, to move in closer. Sarah, much to his dismay, took the lead and she ran quietly to a tree, climbing it like a monkey. She perched herself on a branch and raised her rifle.

∞

Brian shot Mitch a glance and nodded. From the shadows, they crept forward. They saw Cain roped to a tree, with one man standing guard. The boy looked beat to shit as his head slumped to his chest. Shots rang out around them. Brian crept up behind the man while Mitch made his way to the back of the tree. With one swift movement, he lodged his knife into the back of the man's neck, severing his spinal cord. Pulling it out, he turned to see another man standing behind Mitch with his gun aimed at the back of Mitch's head. Mitch lifted his eyes just as Brian let loose of his knife and sent it soaring toward him. An expression of surprise crossed his face. He threw himself to the ground and drew his gun. Coming up on one knee, he aimed at Brian.

"You missed!" he hissed. His finger rested on the trigger. Brian grinned and lifted his chin to the area behind Mitch.

"No, I never miss." he drawled. Mitch turned his head and saw the man lying behind him with Brian's knife buried deep in his chest. Shaking his head, he quickly grabbed Brian's knife and bent cutting away the rest of the ropes that held Cain. Raising his eyes to Brian, he grimaced. He'd almost made a big mistake.

"Here, help me get him up."

Brian walked over and dragged Cain to his feet. He wrapped one arm under a shoulder while Mitch did the same and side-by-side, they dragged him into the woods and out of the line of fire.

Ryder

The first shot rang out, and Ryder screamed for his men to take cover. He dove behind a large boulder. He saw Maria dive behind a tree pulling the hostage with her. Pulling his gun, he scanned the woods, peering into the fading light, looking for something to shoot. How did they get past his guards? How did they find them?

Glancing up he saw the girl up in the tree firing down on the camp and swearing loudly he raised his rifle, aiming for her. With a snap of his finger against the trigger, he fired and watched her tumble from the limb of the tree. Another shot ricocheted off the boulder he stood behind, and he ducked quickly. Screams erupted around him, and his men scrambled for cover while firing blindly into the woods. He glanced over and saw Maria crawling toward the girl to finish her off.

"Maria! No!" he yelled watching the bullets fly around and near her. Rage fired through his veins and he stood and provided cover fire for his woman. The first bullet struck him in the leg, the second, in his shoulder, spinning him like a marionette before he fell.

Sarah

Sarah hissed as a white-hot fire shot through her leg. Dragging it, she crawled behind the tree. Tearing the sleeve from her jacket, she wadded it up and pressed it to the wound to staunch the flow of blood. Glancing up, she saw Spike running toward her and then fall when a bullet slammed his leg out from under him. To her left, she saw the woman, knife in her teeth, making her way toward her. Her heart skipped a beat and fear choked the breath from her. She struggled to stand, and her leg buckled, sending her face-first into the dirt. A heavy weight slammed into her, and she rolled, kicking out her good leg as she pushed the woman off her.

"Bitch! I'm gonna cut you up!" the woman growled. She lunged at her with the knife and an expression of pure hatred in her eyes. Sarah rolled again and sent a sharp kick to the woman's knee. She heard a scream of rage as the woman jumped for her and saw the glint of the knife blade as it slashed toward her face. She rolled her head to keep from eating the blade of the knife. With a heave she rolled away again, reaching for the knife on her belt. A loud explosion from behind sent the woman crashing to the ground as Spike unloaded his shotgun into her back. Breathing heavily, she sat up. Her eyes set on Spike a few feet away and she nodded grimly.

The battle roared around them and screams filled the air. The night's silence was shattered with the sound of gunfire. Sarah leaned against the tree, aiming, firing, aiming, and firing. Her arms ached from the weight of the gun, from the recoil with each press of the trigger. She watched as Clint and the others moved in and located one after another of the enemy, destroying the threat. She felt her body weakening, her strength dwindling, while she bled freely onto the ground. With a sigh, she closed her eyes and laid the rifle across her lap. Her head spun dizzily, and she fought it off. Wave after wave crashed over her. She was tired. Just plain tired. She drifted and floated as the noise around her dulled to a soft roar.

∞

Ryder crawled to Maria and howled in agony. He lay beside her broken body. Spike stood over him and grimaced in hatred. He looked down into the other man's eyes and aimed his gun. He saw pure agony staring back at him. He pulled the trigger.

∞

Beth sat on the porch with a rifle laid across her lap. The night closed in around her like a soft wave. Sighing, she closed her eyes and leaned her head back. She couldn't sleep, knowing Brian and Sarah, Spike and others from the compound were out there somewhere in the night facing the enemy and God knows what else. Worriedly, she chewed at her lower lip. What were they going through right now? Her stomach curled with fear. Lost in her thoughts, she failed to see the shadow until it was too late. A sharp blow to her head sent her reeling and darkness closed over her. Barbs stood over her slumped body and smiled, hatred burning in her eyes. If they had just minded their own business, if they had just left Bobby and the town alone. But no, they'd had to come in and ruin it all. Memories of her brother brought tears to her eyes. Ernie hadn't deserved what this bitch's man had done to him. Well, they would pay. They would pay dearly.

She motioned to the two men standing in the shadows. "Grab this bitch and let's get the hell out of here!"

"Why don't we just kill her? I just wanna get out'a here," Jessie whined. With a hiss, she turned on him.

"No, I've got plans for this one," Barbs hissed through her clenched teeth. "This bitch is gonna suffer!"

Chapter Thirty-Three

There wouldn't be any sounding of horns, nor the sad singing of the Battle Hymn of the Republic. There was only blood, death, and sorrow. This was a new world, and its wars would be fought at home. No more watching through the television, from the comfort of the living room, as rockets fired into the night on foreign soil. Every person was now a soldier; the young, the old, and everyone in between. God have mercy on us all.

About the Author:

N.A. Broadley lives in New Hampshire, on the homestead where she stays prepared. She lives a simple life, surrounded by family and friends.

Writing has always been a passion, and she's grateful for the time and opportunity to engage in activities that allow her the pleasure of following that passion.

Join her in The Written Apocalypse and Women of The Apocalypse, two great Facebook groups for more exciting books and releases from many great authors. A place to chat, swap stories, and keep up on the latest and the greatest.

https://www.facebook.com/groups/writtenapocalypse/

https://www.facebook.com/groups/WomenoftheApocalypse/

Thank you for reading, if you enjoyed this book please consider offering a review.